ISBN 9781734721508 (ebook)
ISBN 9781734721515 (print-pbk)

Cover design by Natasha Snow Designs
Editing by Heather Demetrios and Veronica Jorden

Interior Format

finding EDWARD

A Novel By

SUZANNE MCKENNA LINK

Also By
Suzanne McKenna Link

Saving Toby (Save Me Series Book 1)

Keeping Claudia (Save Me Series Book 2)

Dedicated to Angela, daughter extraordinaire ~
Our adventures in world travel began in Italy,
experiencing "La dolce vita," on a trip I will never forget.
May the wonders of the world be forever yours.

*The world is a book, and those who
do not travel read only a page.*
~ Saint Augustine of Hippo

Chapter 1

THE BINDING OF *TWENTIETH-CENTURY AMERICAN Art* creaked slightly as I pulled the cover open and lifted it to my nose. I closed my eyes and let the scent of the colorful lacquered pages curl in the back of my throat, reminding me of the day I'd bought the book.

"Eddie, you weirdo, stop sniffing books and get moving." Ray came out of the house with another plastic bag of my stuff to load into the back of my pickup truck.

I closed the book and dropped my head, already missing my usual Sunday morning routine. There'd be no lying around today until I moved my things out of the house.

"Hey, Malik!" I called out and waved to our easy-going neighbor across the street.

"Eddie, Ray, good luck on the move. Keep in touch." Malik waved back before driving away.

"I didn't know that guy knew our names." Ray watched the exchange.

"He's only been our neighbor for, like, three years." I returned my art book to the box with the others. "Haven't you ever talked to him?"

"No. Chatting up people is your thing, not mine. You're just like Mom," my brother said.

"Am not." I spun around to enlighten him as to why, but Ray had turned his back.

His attention moved to my beat-up silver truck and the six overstuffed trash bags and boxes that filled the truck's bed.

"All you have are clothes?"

"And books." I nodded, proud of that fact.

Ray grunted. "You're such a girl."

"Clothes maketh the man," I said, letting my brother's comment roll off of me.

On the verge of thirty, Ray still wore different combinations of the same T-shirts and jeans, day in and day out. Easy wear at a cheap price; his life's uniform, the same stuff he wore to the construction sites where we worked.

What did the entirety of my personal effects, bunched into thrifty luggage, say about me to others? It showed my appreciation for clothes. *A deep appreciation.*

It also said I had a lot of books—probably too many for a guy so into his clothes.

I followed Ray back inside the house. Our rental, a small unassuming house on the north side of our Long Island town, was where Ray and I had lived most of our lives. Our mother moved out a few years ago to live with her boyfriend, Mike. She'd packed her things and handed Ray and me the keys. The bills, too. It was an adjustment, but it worked out okay. We split the monthly cost and the chores, though Ray kept better track of the 'to-do' list than I did. I managed our social life, rounding up friends for poker nights and Ultimate Fighter viewing parties.

Today, though, Ray was moving on. My brother popped the big question to his longtime girlfriend, Amy. The two of them wanted their own place to start the next page of their story—without Ray's little brother cohabitating with them. I couldn't comfortably afford the rent and take care of an entire house on my own, so it was moving day, for all of us.

Inside the kitchen, the pale-brown cabinet doors hung open, their gaping mouths exposing shelf after empty shelf, all layered with years of grunge. On the battered, round kitchen table, a surface spoiled by careless boys and more recently, busy adult men, lay one of Grams' letters, this one written to Ray.

The letters punctuated Grams' recent passing a few months ago.

I braced my hands on the table and read the letter again, my breathing measured, hoping to cool the burn behind my eyes. My callused fingertip scraped the smooth paper as I traced my grandmother's perfect script. At a legal meeting to settle Grams' estate—the sale of her small house and property—we were informed she'd written three letters, one to each of us: Ray, our mother, and me.

A lingering voice from the beyond.

We'd all been awaiting the arrival of our personal letter. Ray got his first. The typewritten correspondence from Grams' lawyer came enclosed with her letter to Ray. It outlined the steps my brother had to take to get his share of the inheritance. Grams wanted him married. When he met those terms, he'd get the down payment to buy a house.

"I'll finally be able to buy a house," he'd said when we first learned.

"Grams putting on the pressure from the grave," I'd teased.

"Nobody's forcing us to get married." There had been an edge of defensiveness in his tone. "Amy and I wouldn't do it if we didn't want to."

That was a month ago. Ray and Amy were now engaged. With the inheritance imminent, the two of them were preparing to buy a small house in Center Moriches, a Long Island town, farther east of where we lived. They were planning a wedding for the following summer.

I leaned against the counter and looked at Ray. My brother had gotten his act together. He'd lost that painful childhood stutter that made him the butt of jokes and an easy target for bullies in school. Because he was four years older, Ray never liked being shorter and thinner than me. Height couldn't be changed, but after years of manual labor, he'd put on some weight, and his once scrawny chest and arms had thickened. My brother wore his hard-won confidence like a dimpled coat of hardened marine varnish. No one messed with him anymore.

Toby Faye, his best friend, had helped him survive those years. Toby gave him a job when he'd really needed one. In fact, he'd given both of us jobs. Ray worked hard at everything he did, including his job and winning Amy over. The efforts were paying off. He'd moved up the ranks at work and won the woman. Kind, sweet Amy had seen something in my brother no one else saw. The new house wasn't much to look at, but still, Ray was about to be a homeowner. I never saw that coming. Guys like us were renters, not property owners. I was happy for him, happy for them both.

Me, I was still just another guy on the crew. No plans on my horizon.

"Wonder what my letter will say." I scratched the back of my head.

"Mom said she got her letter yesterday." Ray turned away and began packing dishes into a box.

"Funny, she didn't mention it to me." I grabbed a roll of packing tape on the counter and began to close and seal a few of the boxes of kitchenware.

"She was weirdly closemouthed about it." Ray pushed another box at me.

Our mother, a serial oversharer, had no qualms about texting her boys at any hour. Day or night, she messaged us about unimportant things. Photos of her manicured nails, the dog playing with a new squeaky toy, a question about an actor or entertainer that she could easily Google herself. Not telling me about the letter seemed odd.

"Why would that be?" I asked. "I won't have any problem doing whatever Grams wants me to."

"You say that now." My brother pegged me with a wicked grin. "What if she asks you to try something new, something that scares you? You'll have to do it, otherwise you won't get a dime."

"Whatever. I just hope the change of address doesn't screw up the delivery of my letter." My hands shook as I finished taping another box and pushed it aside. Stressing over the letter made little sense. I didn't have a reason to worry. I didn't have a girlfriend, and now, not even a home. What could Grams ask of me?

Dishes clinked as Ray kept packing.

"If it gets forwarded to me, I'll let you know," he said.

I left the kitchen and went down the narrow hallway toward the bedrooms. In the first bedroom, Amy packed, singing along to Rihanna. The room across from their room was mine. My childhood room looked smaller without all my crap. I smiled, thinking about how many coats of paint it would take the landlord to cover the deep-velvet purple walls and the many characters I'd painted on them.

On center stage, a life-sized Conan the Barbarian dominated the room. The behemoth held a menacing sword over his head, ready for a throw-down. Over the one window that looked out on the small yard, a lean, muscular Spiderman swung in from the corner to join the scene. Low, under the window, the iconic Mario hopped a spotted mushroom. His brother, Luigi, toddled behind him.

Next to the door, I'd painted a trippy mosaic of colors, years in the making. I'd added new colors after each birthday and holiday when I had money from my grandparents to buy new tubes of paint. I remembered those times as a teenager, standing before the rack of paints in the craft store, the assortment of colors like candy. Reds, greens, blues in every tint and shade of the color wheel. Cadmium red, burnt umber, raw sienna, hooker's green, yellow oxide. Even the non-colors, white and black, had many shades.

I remembered how my palms itched because I'd wanted them all. But I'd always had to settle for only one or two.

I took out my phone, snapped a few shots of my walls for posterity, and grabbed the last bag. A trash bag of dried up dreams filled with old tubes of paint, brittle paintbrushes, sketchbooks with yellowed pages, and several near-finished canvases. Bulky with squared edges that threatened to poke through the plastic, the bag was heavier than all the others. I dropped it off at the curb for waste pickup.

Bayport, the next town over, was my new zip code. Toby and Claudia had offered me a fixed-up basement apartment in their big blue Dutch colonial. I would now call my boss and his wife landlord. I liked the area. Every house had trees, green lawns, and edged driveways instead of dirt and broken-down cars like my old neighborhood.

Claudia's sleek, all-electric blue Tesla glistened in the double-wide driveway. After the birth of their second kid, the family had gone green. The basement apartment's entrance was on the side of the house. I parked my truck and crossed the black asphalt, warm from the late summer sun. I balanced a box of books under one arm and grabbed two trash bags of clothes from the back of the truck. Just as I reached the gate, Claudia called from the front door.

"Hey, come in this way. It'll be easier," she said.

I changed route and climbed the set of wide wooden steps to the front porch. The box of books under my arm slipped, making a sonic boom as it hit the ground. The contents spilled out. With a grunt of annoyance, I dropped the bags of clothes and crouched down to re-box the books.

"Hang on, let me give you a hand." Claudia squatted, belly between her knees, scooped up a few hardcovers and shuffled through the titles. "Lots and lots of books about art."

"I got them." I took the titles from her. "I might not come from the right side of the tracks, but I'm not about to let you help me move my shit in your condition."

"My condition?" She stood, hands rested on hips. "I'm pregnant, not incapacitated."

"Doesn't matter." I shook my head. "Toby would kick my butt into next week if I let you so much as lift a finger."

Claudia rolled her eyes but resigned to step back and hold the door for me instead. I passed her and headed toward the back of the house, stopping before I reached the basement steps. In the big, bright family room, colorful images flashed across the large screen television. With toys scattered around their little feet, Claudia and Toby's two daughters were dancing and singing along to a cheesy, saccharine tune coming from the TV.

Grinning, I stopped to watch them.

"Can I join this party?"

They met my question with two ear-piercing screeches.

"Uncle Eddie's here!" Five-year-old Julianne, fair like her father, jumped up and wrapped herself around my right leg.

"Weddi's here!" Two seconds behind her, Beatrix, almost three, whose darker-toned skin and hair favored her mother's Mediterranean heritage, curled her chubby short arms around my left leg.

My heart ballooned in my chest. The girls, blue-eyed, freckled and adorable, were miniature angels made in the images of two of my favorite people.

"Girls, Uncle Eddie is busy." Claudia leaned a hip against the back of the couch. "Maybe later, if you ask nicely, he can come back and read you a bedtime story."

"Oh, quit it. They're fine." I set my stuff on the floor and dropped onto the family's large sectional couch. "I always have time for my favorite girls."

Beatrix handed me a tiny pink plastic hairbrush and a Barbie doll with a pouf of tangled, frizzy hair. I smiled and attempted to tame the ratty mess while Claudia carried on a stream of mostly one-side conversation from behind me. Beatrix curled into my side. Her older sister sat next to me, opened a kiddie book and read aloud.

This was a great house with the coolest family. I appreciated that Toby and Claudia insisted the girls call me uncle, but they weren't related to me. After our mother, though, the four of them were the closest thing to family that Ray and I had.

Claudia lowered herself into an overstuffed upholstered chair across from the couch.

"I guess I'll have to acquire a taste for obnoxiously upbeat music." I motioned to the television.

"Stick around here long enough, it grows on you. You'll find yourself singing along." Claudia smiled at her girls. "Then, you'll join the dance party. I suggest you don't fight it. It's inevitable."

"I'm down with that. You know I like to boogie," I said. "In fact, I'm itching for a night of dancing. You got a pretty neighbor or anyone I can take out?"

"Oh no, I'm done playing matchmaker." She shook her head. "You didn't like anyone I fixed you up with in the past. You're too picky."

"Because they didn't meet my criteria."

"And that is?"

"They have to be like you. You are the perfect woman."

"Having you around the house will do wonders for my ego." She laughed, as I knew she would. "It's a good thing Toby and I are secure in our relationship."

"Yeah, he totally doesn't view me as a threat otherwise he wouldn't let me move in here with you. And since you're taken, I need a girl who's got her sh—" I caught myself and lifted a hand to stroke the dark brown ringlets on the back of Beatrix's little head. "I'd like a girl—no, a woman—with a certain level of maturity. I want to get busy making a few rug rats of my own, so I need a woman who's got her act together."

"*Righttttt.*" Claudia dragged the word out, holding back a smile. "Because you've got *your act* together."

My face warmed with her assessment. A mere day-laborer working under her husband's leadership, and now, her family's basement tenant—I didn't have bragging rights.

Their life, a house, marriage and kids, was reaching.

"That's about to change." I gave Barbie back to Beatrix and stood to retrieve my stuff. "I'm expecting a sizeable influx of cash from the sale of my grandmother's house."

"What will you do with the money?" She draped her hands across the lump of her abdomen.

I readjusted the box under my arm and looked around.

Toby's upbringing, while not the same as mine, had crossovers. We'd both faced hardships earlier in life. No dad in the picture to usher us through those formidable years; money was always in limited supply.

I'd witnessed Toby turn a pathetic existence into gold, through his work and investments. Together with Claudia, they'd built an epic life.

I could do that, too.

His trajectory would be my blueprint. I'd simply do what he did. Grams' money would speed up the process.

"I'll buy some investment property. Plant myself and create stability," I said.

"A loose plan, but at least it's something." Claudia gave me an approving nod. "Oh, speaking of which, you got a Fed-Ex delivery earlier. I signed for it and left it on the counter downstairs."

A cold sensation crept down my spine. Grams' letter had found me.

"Better get my stuff unloaded before it gets dark. Catch up with you later." With a wave, I retreated.

A set of carpeted steps at the back of the den led to the door of my new subterranean dwelling. The apartment had one primary room divided into two areas by a raised counter. On one side, a narrow galley kitchen, on the other, a double bed, a TV, and a second-hand love seat. I slid the box of books onto the counter where a large flat mail envelope lay addressed to me.

I ignored it while I unloaded my stuff from the truck. Ignored it while I tucked my outrageous amount of clothes into the small chest of drawers and lined up my shoes in an even smaller closet. Ignored it as I organized my toiletries in the tiny bathroom.

With nothing left pressing for my attention, I picked up the letter.

Feeling too confined in the apartment, I used my exterior entry to go outside. I popped up the cement steps two at a time, dropped onto one of the family's lounge chairs on the back deck and tore open the mailer. It contained a cover letter and a plain white legal-sized envelope.

The letter, from the law offices of Richard J. Morris, was the exact duplicate of the one I'd seen at Ray's. A few lines of legal jargon on the pristine, weighted paper informed me that inside the enclosed envelope was a personal letter written to me, part of the will and testament of Anita Marion Davies, now deceased.

I pressed the envelope to my chest and closed my eyes against the sun. Grams had loved both Ray and me, but she and I? We had a special bond.

My grandmother had started my art book collection.

In my first year of high school, when my grades took a nose-dive, my grandmother stepped in. My mother's mother took me to a bookstore, stuck a crisp twenty-dollar note in my hand, and told me to pick something out. I could keep the change she promised, further vowing a repeat performance the following month, with a few small conditions: that I read the book I picked, and then tell her about it.

That day, I'd chosen *Twentieth-Century American Art* because of Andy Warhol's iconic painting of Marilyn Monroe on the cover. Besides, the ratio of glossy pages of art seemed higher than the pages of text.

I was still late to school every morning, but never late for our book discussions.

Over the last year, her health had begun to fail. She grew weaker as the months slid by. I visited often; saw the decline. I'd sat with her in those final days, holding her cool wrinkled hands, so small and frail between my much larger ones. I thanked her for helping me get through my school years, for buying me art books, and for always being that one person who listened when I needed to talk.

She slipped out of this world with me at her side.

I'd never seen a person die before. Every morning I opened my eyes since, I thought about her, thought about the last smile she'd given me. The ache sat in my chest until I pushed it from my mind and made myself get up.

This letter, this last letter, written to me, frightened me for reasons I couldn't express. Part of it, I knew, was because it would be the absolute final words I'd hear from her. The other part had to do with the substance of our conversations. I'd told Grams stuff I'd told no one about—my dreams, my fears. I'd been honest with her, more honest than I'd been with anyone. Ever.

Unable to sit, I pushed to my feet. I paced the width of the deck twice before I opened the envelope.

My Dearest Eddie,

As I write this letter, the last words you'll have from me, my heart is full of love and memories of our time together. When you were small, I loved buying you books and finger paints, seeing that sparkle in your eye as you leafed through the pages or drew me another masterpiece for my refrigerator door. You had a natural eagerness to learn, to absorb. On a recent visit, I noticed your eyes still light up when you talk about new projects. You're creative. You always have been.

Over the last year, through our weekly talks, you expressed some of your greatest setbacks and disappointments. One of those disappointments was how you wasted your high school years not applying yourself, because maybe then, you would have gotten into art school and be doing what you once dreamed about.

You grew up without a male role model, and a mother who had herself spurned school. You had no encouragement to excel. By no fault of your own, you landed where most would have expected.

You also spoke candidly about having a father who abandoned your family. How his refusal to know you left you questioning what you'd done wrong.

Your words pained me, Eddie, because this is not your story.

As a widow on a pension, I only have my house to leave my one daughter and two grandsons. I hired Mr. Morris, an estate planner, to set up a disbursement account to handle the proceeds from the sale of my house. The money will be divided among the three of you: Ray, you, and your mother.

As I think about the legacy I leave behind, I've decided it must be about more than money. To get your inheritance, I request that each of you meet one requirement; something I believe whole-heartedly will make you see life through another set of eyes. Ray needed an incentive to make an honest woman out of that lovely young lady. I gave him one. Yours and your mother's requirements are tied together. When she fulfills what I ask of her, you will understand why.

I want you to go to Positano, Italy. I made arrangements to cover your airfare and hotel stay. When you return home, you will receive tuition money for the school of your choice. Whether it is a technical program or art school is up to you. Mr. Morris will take care of the details when the time comes.

To understand why, I have made your mother's requirement to share a truth with you, a secret I have kept for her.

I wish I had more time on Earth to see you through this. I promise to whisper in your ear, to remind you to have faith, to be brave and carry on, that you will find the right path, the one that fulfills you.

If I didn't tell you then, I'll say it now—let your past regrets go. Go forward with intent. You can change your future just by taking a step in a new direction.

Always in my heart,
Grandma
P.S. Please take Mary to Italy with you.

I blinked several times and lowered the letter.

Positano, Italy? I didn't know where that was or why Grams decided I needed to go. In all our talks, I had never mentioned that I wanted to go to Italy.

Mom had a secret—one Grams had required her to share with me.

Required.

Somehow, my mother's requirement would explain mine. Such a cryptic letter. I had a premonition that my oversharing with Grams was about to bite me in the ass. I bit my lip until it bled, punishing myself for bringing Grams down with my disappointments.

The next step meant checking in with my mother. I texted her to make sure she was home before heading over.

For the past six years, Mom shared a simple, one-story house with her boyfriend in Holbrook, ten minutes north of my new digs. Mike was a motorhead with a Harley, an enormous truck and an even bigger attitude. We weren't buddies, but that was okay. He'd stuck around, unlike our quote, unquote Dad, Tom Rudack, whose whereabouts were currently unknown.

Mom answered the door wearing her usual jeans, leather vest and boots, rocking the aged-biker-chick look. She left me to let myself in, saying nothing as I closed the door behind me. She stood, arms crossed, as I pulled the letter from my back pocket.

"I got Grams' letter. She said you're supposed to tell me something."

I might've overlooked her slight, wilting hesitation had it not been for the long-winded sigh that followed.

"Sit." She gestured to the couch. "I'll grab us something to drink."

Mom disappeared into the kitchen. The letter shook in my hand. A growing hunch told me that whatever my mother's truth was, it would affect our relationship. I sat down on the well-worn blue microfiber couch, next to Whiskey, Mike's pit bull mix, curled up, asleep. I absently reached over to pet her, attempting to rein in my runaway worries.

My mother came out with two shot glasses and a bottle of bourbon. She poured some liquor in each glass and put one in front of me on the coffee table. She downed hers before taking a seat on the couch next to me.

My throat grew dry at the thought of bourbon curling around the knot in my stomach.

"For some strange reason, Grams wants me to go to Italy. She said you had a secret to share, something that could explain why."

My mother fidgeted silently, hands in her lap. I braced myself.

"Tom Rudack is *not* your father."

I held my breath for a long moment, staring at the boring beige rug under my feet. I didn't know what I expected her to say, but it wasn't *that*. I wrangled my bottom lip between my teeth and winced from the bruising I'd given it earlier.

"Stop biting your lip." She slapped my arm.

I released my lip and lifted my gaze to her face. "Are you saying the man you were married to is not Ray's and my father?"

Chin lifted with an air of defiance I didn't quite understand, she watched me, her brown eyes partially hidden behind long bangs, unnaturally dark for her age.

"He's Ray's father. Not yours."

I let out a noisy breath and shook my head. "Then who... who is my father?"

"He's a man from the garden center where I used to work. An Italian who came here on a work visa. He worked a year and went back to Italy."

My real father was *Italian?*

"He didn't know anyone," Mom rambled on, a rise in her voice. "I was just being nice, at first, but I was lonely. After Ray was born, some nights Tom didn't bother coming home. He'd sleep off his hangover with some tramp he'd met in a bar. He wasn't much of a father to Ray."

"He was around when I was little. I remember him." The glass of bourbon called to me. My stomach no less riotous, but oh, how I wanted it.

"I never told Tom about the affair." She lowered her eyes. "Grandma said from Day One I should've never married him. I couldn't have her gloating. I tried to make it work."

"How can you be sure he isn't my father? Did you do a paternity test?"

"No, honey bear. I just know." She put a hand on my leg, and her eyes met mine. "I see him in you, in the darker tone in your skin and hair, your lean build."

Annoyed, I pushed her hand away. "Well, who is he? Did I ever meet him?"

"His name was Giovanni Lo Duca. He left the country before I realized I was pregnant. This was before we could go online and find someone as we can now." She glanced down at her hands, twisting her fingers together. "I never got to tell him about you."

"He doesn't even know about me? Un-freaking-real." I stared hard at her. "What am I supposed to do with this information? Does Grams expect me to go to Italy to *find* him?"

"I think so." My mother shrugged. "I looked him up on the computer a few years ago. He lives in Positano, on the Amalfi Coast. At least I think it was him. You kids are so much better with that online stuff."

Now, I reached for the bourbon—the bottle, not the glass. Mom went silent as I twisted the cap off and raised it to my mouth. The sharp smell made me wince—I preferred beer to hard liquor but forced myself to take a big gulp. I capped the bottle and stood, digging into my jeans' pocket for my truck keys.

"Where are you going?" My mother followed me to the door.

"Suddenly you care?" I snapped.

"Honey bear—" She reached for my arm.

"Don't." I ripped my arm away from her.

She lost her balance and fell backward into the door. I opened my mouth to apologize when the door handle turned. I grabbed her arm and yanked her out of the way.

The door swung open. Mom's boyfriend, Mike, appeared on the other side of it.

"What the fuck is going on?" His large frame filled the doorway, his bare muscled arms damp with perspiration. "What d'you do to your mother?"

"Nothing," I said.

His eyes combed my mother's face, wet with tears, her eyes red and makeup-ringed. His bottom lip disappeared, curling inwards.

"Don't look like nothing, Eddie. You mouthing off to her?"

"What do you care, Mike?" Venom filled my mouth, inducing my rattlesnake strike. "You're just another guy in a *long* list of guys that my mother slept with."

Mike was fast for a big guy; I'll give him that. I never saw his fist before it struck me solidly, right in the middle of my face. The force of it sent me backward, but somehow I managed to hold on to the bottle of bourbon. With a hand on my nose, I stood on wobbly legs and pushed past the two of them. Mom yelled—at me, at him—who knows. I didn't stick around to find out.

Chapter 2

I GRIPPED MY TRUCK'S STEERING WHEEL and stomped on the gas pedal, headed home to ice my throbbing face. The engine responded with a shudder, taking its sweet time to build to a speed that matched my mood.

Outside of my new digs, I threw the truck into park and reached over to the passenger seat for the bottle I'd pinched from my mother.

She owed it to me.

I slunk through the shadows of the moonlit yard and fumbled with the catch on the gate until it opened. The pain in my head increased with each step down to the basement. I opened the door with my new key but left the lights off, afraid the brightness would make my head hurt worse.

Overhead, the floor creaked with moving footsteps, the faint murmurs of talking, and the television in the background—Toby, Claudia, and their kids. But the only company I wanted was that shiny bottle of bourbon. My mother's shocking confession meant my good-for-nothing dad, Tom Rudack, wasn't my dad. Being Tom's son never got me anything, but I'd carried that asshole's last name all of my 26 years. Somehow, having a stranger for a father seemed worse than having a deadbeat dad. A trapdoor had opened beneath my feet and everything I knew about myself was tumbling, free-falling through it.

I braced myself and took a big gulp. The bite of the bourbon's intense earthy flavor struck the back of my throat with a blaze of heat. It made me gag a bit, but that didn't stop me from drinking more. It didn't take long for me to see the benefits of drinking the hard stuff. It was more merciful than beer, so much faster at dulling the thoughts that spun like a sadistic carousel in my head.

I took another pull from the bottle and had a sudden urge to lie down. I snatched up my grandmother's letter and bumped my way through my new, one-room living space. Unaccustomed to the layout, especially in the dark, the left toe of my sneaker caught the leg of the bed. In my alcohol-induced fog, I fell gracelessly, catching my chin on the low table before I hit the carpeted cement floor. The pile of books I had on the table toppled, fanning out around me. Pain exploded throughout my face and ripped a loud swear from my mouth.

The door at the top of the steps squeaked and light poured down into my dungeon darkness. I sat in a ring of books, dizzy. The hand I swiped under my chin came away wet.

"Dude, you down there?" Toby called down the steps.

"Yes." I tried to get up. Pain leaped up to my face, sending a white, blinding haze over my sight. "Holy shitsters."

Something was very wrong.

"You all right? Claudia said she heard something crash."

"I fell, and I... um, I think I might need some help."

Toby switched on the light and his footsteps fell in a steady beat down the stairs.

"What the fuck happened?" Offering me a hand, my friend pulled me to my feet.

"Took a header on the table." I moved my jaw, testing it out.

Toby handed me a bunch of paper towels to wipe the blood off my face. I tucked the letter in my back pocket and followed him upstairs. The girls were in the family room watching an animated movie, their little heads leaning against Claudia's sizeable baby belly.

"Oh goodness, Uncle Eddie!" Julianne shouted, comically slapping her hands to the sides of her face. "What happened to you?"

"Oh, goodneff un-Weddie! Wha-appened you?" Beatrix parroted her big sister. Both of the girls' big blue eyes targeted me.

"I'm fine. Don't you worry about Uncle Eddie." I winked at them.

"Julianne, I need you to watch Beatrix while Mommy and

Daddy talk to Uncle Eddie." Claudia hoisted herself off the couch and waddled toward me. After she tugged me into the kitchen, she flipped on the bright overhead lights and gently probed my chin with her fingertips.

"Oww." I flinched. "That hurts."

"Looks like your chin will need a few stitches. Why is your nose swollen, too?" She shook her head. "That must have been some spectacular fall for you to hit both areas of your face at one time."

"Oh, the nose happened earlier. Got punched."

"You need to get an X-ray. It could be broken." Claudia pressed her lips together, her eyes catching Toby's. "I'll make a couple of ice packs, one for your nose, one for your chin, and then Toby can take you to the emergency room."

The door yawned open. A young woman with a lab coat over indigo-colored scrubs came into the hospital exam room.

"Hello, I'm Doctor Barnes." She shook both of our hands, her eyes and smile lingered in Toby's direction before she turned her attention to me. "No surprise. Your X-ray shows a broken nose. It will heal by itself with little discomfort. You'll have discoloration and bruising around the eyes for a couple of weeks until it heals. I'll send in a PA to put a few stitches in your chin. Keep it clean and go easy for a couple of weeks."

She made a few notes on my chart and, after one last peek at Toby, almost walked into the door. With a girlish giggle, she left the room.

Not seeming to notice the doctor's behavior, Toby put his hands on his hips and stared at the wall. I armored myself with stylish threads and haircuts, but Toby kept it simple. Like Ray, he was mostly a jeans and t-shirt guy. Despite the simplicity, he had a presence in any room.

I did okay with girls, especially with those five years and under, but I'd give my left arm to have a mature woman react to me like that.

"A broken nose and stitches. Boy, when you do it, you do it up good." Toby shook his head and crossed his arms. "Who's this guy that punched you? Do I need to give him a tune-up?"

"No." My face warmed. A tempting thought. I'd seen him mess up a few guys back in the day, but what an ass I'd look like if I sent Toby to fight my battles. "It was Mike."

"Whoa, that's awkward." His brows knitted together. "Did you slug him back?"

"You know that's not my style." I shrugged. The analgesic they had given me was taking the edge off the pain. "I'm more of a lover than a fighter."

"Yeah, yeah." He tried to hold back a grin. "What did your mom say when this went down?"

I picked up the pen the doctor left behind and began doodling in the margins of my medical paperwork. "Well, I imagine she felt bad."

"How come she didn't take you to the hospital?" He pressed.

I stared down at the series of intersecting lines and concentric circles I'd drawn, considering my answer when the door banged open.

"Hello!" The physician's assistant, a Hispanic guy in hospital scrubs, entered the room. He set a steel medical cart next to my chair. Atop the cart lay a tray of surgical supplies: a curved needle for the sutures, gauze, and a long, scary needle. He talked while he numbed my chin with a series of quick injections. I trained my eyes on his shirt, trying not to think about what he was doing. His scrubs were blue, a deeper shade than the doctor's scrubs. Cobalt, I decided.

"By the way, I need a couple of weeks off," I said, my lips and tongue growing thicker and more sluggish with each passing second.

"Weeks? Not possible. It's the end of the season. The beach houses need to be closed up and winterized," he said.

"I got several weeks of unused vacation time. I need two weeks to take care of some stuff."

"What stuff?" he asked, but the physician's assistant lifted my chin to begin the stitches.

"I have to travel to get the money my grandmoffa leff me,"

I tried to respond. "I'll haff a pocket full of 'old, hard cash to inffest when I gef back. I want in on the next inffestment house."

Out of the corner of my eye, Toby paced the length of the exam room, scratching the back of his head. "If you need the time, you have to take it immediately. It's the only time we can afford to be a man down. Ray and I will need you back the first week of October to wrap up the rental season. And, if you're serious about investing, I have my eye on some property."

Toby and I got back to the house late. He headed inside. I sat outside on their front stoop looking over my calendar app.

The beginning of September was a peaceful time over on Fire Island, but my least favorite time of the year. The place emptied out. Vacationers on Fire Island kept things interesting. Toby needed me back by the earlier part of October, which was fair. Empty rentals allowed the crew to be more productive with repairs and improvements. For me, though, the narrow timeline meant I would only have four weeks to plan a trip to Italy, go find my father, and come back.

I sighed, staring up at the sky. Was it possible? Did I even want to find this Giovanni Lo Duca guy?

Behind me, the storm door whined on its hinges.

"Hey," Claudia called out to me. "Get your butt in here."

I climbed the steps. "I didn't wake you, did I?"

"No, I was up." She waited until I came through the door to shut and lock it behind me. "The little guy is active tonight. Here, feel this."

She pressed my hand to the side of her stomach. Through the cotton of her T-shirt dress and the tightened skin of her belly, a flutter of motion brushed my fingertips.

"He's dancing in there," I said. This was the third pregnancy I'd seen her go through, and what a woman's body could do, never failed to amaze me.

"Wish he weren't dancing on my bladder." Unfazed she glanced up at me. "How're you doing?"

"You have a few minutes to talk?"

"Sure. I'll make us tea." Claudia led the way into the large homey kitchen and turned on the light.

A pleasant trace of lemon cleaner hit my nose. She plugged in the electric teapot, flipped the switch, and set up two mugs with tea bags. I settled onto a wooden stool at the countertop. One of the best things about moving into Toby and Claudia's basement apartment was having Claudia there to help me figure things out.

"Are you okay? Toby told me Mike hit you."

"I'm fine." I pressed my eyes shut, squeezing away the smack of emotions brought on by her concern. "Mike got in the middle of an argument between my mother and me."

"Seems so unlike Mike. What were you arguing about?" She poured hot water into the mugs and placed one in front of me.

"What my grandmother wrote in her letter." I pulled Grams' letter from my pocket and laid the crinkled pages on the countertop between us. "Turns out, my mother kept a pretty hefty secret from me."

After Claudia finished reading the letter, I filled her in on the bomb my mother dropped on me.

"Wow. Are you okay?" She reached across the counter to touch my forearm.

"On the surface, I'm still me." I scrubbed an impatient hand over my cheek. My knuckles brushed against the bandage on my chin. "But it sort of changes things."

"How could it not?" She glanced back down at the letter and pointed at my grandmother's postscript note. "Who's this Mary?"

"The Virgin Mary." I chuckled, instantly regretting it as a zing of pain raced up my jaw. "My grandmother gave me a plastic statue when I was younger. She believed it kept me safe."

"Looks like you and Mary are going to Italy," she said, sounding resolute. "And when you get back, you'll pick out an art school."

"Not doing the school thing. Grams probably remembered me yapping about being an artist as a kid." I waved a hand. That ship sailed long ago. "I'm using that money to buy a rental property with Toby."

"Okay, so you get an all-expenses-paid trip to Italy and when you get back, money. What's the downside to this?" she asked.

"The biological father thing. It doesn't say I'm required to search for him, but do you think I should?"

"Sounds as if that was your grandmother's intention." She placed a hand on the letter.

"I don't know this man. He isn't even aware that I exist." I glanced down at my mug of tea. "Say I find him, and that's a big 'if,' what happens then? The guy lives in Italy. He probably has a family."

Along with two spongy discarded tea bags on a dish, a beat of silence sat between us.

"I can't say what will happen. Maybe the trip will spur a relationship with this man? At the very least, you'll get a trip to Europe. Toby and I flew to Italy for two weeks on our honeymoon. It's magnificent." She rested her chin on her hand, a look of contentment softened her face. "I loved every moment."

Her expression buoyed me.

"If I'm going, I need to get to moving on this right away. The boss man needs me back by October. Think you can help me plan the trip?"

She covered my hand with hers. "Are you kidding? Of course."

With Toby agreeing to let me take the two weeks off, I used my grandmother's allocated funds to book an Airbnb vacation house and a flight to Italy. On the evening of my departure two weeks later, Claudia drove me to the airport for the 10 p.m. flight. I threw my body-sized duffle bag into the back seat of her Tesla, in between the two child safety seats. I got into the passenger seat beside her, stowed my backpack on the floor by my feet, and buckled on my seatbelt. But before Claudia would put the car into drive, she made me go through a checklist with her: ticket, passport, Euros, emergency contact info.

Only after she verified I had everything I needed did she hand me a folded piece of red construction paper with a crayon drawing of a stick-figure horse, or dog, and a multitude of colorful stickers. "This is from Julianne and Beatrix. They're going to miss Uncle Eddie and his famous babysitting-art parties."

"I'll miss them, too." The girls and I had spent a lot of time together in the last two weeks. I carefully folded the paper and slid it into a pocket in my backpack.

Claudia insisted on parking the car and accompanying me inside JFK's international terminal. Probably because I looked like a guy about ready to go to the electric chair instead of a trip to Europe.

She stood beside me as I moved through the Alitalia ticket counter check-in procedure. Once my duffle bag was tagged and carried off on a conveyor belt, she took my arm and started toward the security line. Despite her pregnancy, Claudia easily kept stride with me. We stopped at the entrance, an official-looking roped-off area. A few feet within, a uniformed security agent walked a vested German shepherd among the people on line.

I had nothing to hide, but the sight of the drug-sniffing dog was sobering. Security here was serious.

"This is so exciting. Think of all the wonderful things you're going to see," she said. "I'm certainly happy you asked me to drive you, but considering the situation, I'm surprised your mother didn't offer to see you off."

The mention of her was a kick to the gut. It must've shown in my face.

"Eddie?" Claudia grabbed my arm.

"I haven't talked to her since she lobbed that bomb on me." I shrugged, avoiding Claudia's searching eyes. "Keeping the identity of my father from me is unforgiveable. I'm pissed."

"I get it. Your anger is understandable." She nodded. "But you should give her a call anyway. You're traveling far away. She's your mom. Being a mom myself, I can say without a doubt, she'll want to know you arrived safely."

I looked over her shoulder and blew out slowly.

"I guess you're right. It's the farthest I've ever been from home." I tugged my backpack up higher on my shoulder and glanced around, the muscles in my chest suddenly tight. All around us, people were moving, pulling suitcases, hauling backpacks and luggage. Everyone everywhere, moving, moving, moving.

I bent forward, leaning my hands on my thighs. "I don't know if I can do this."

"It's not uncommon to be nervous before an international flight," she said, leaning down to peek at my face. "You flew to Mexico a few years back, with some friends. Everything went fine, right?"

"I got my passport. Then we canceled the trip." I shook my head. "This is my first time on a plane."

"Ever?" Her voice rose with surprise. "You must have been to Florida."

"Yeah." I sucked in a breath. "We always drove."

"Oh, well flying is easy." She reached over to pat my back. "Chew a piece of gum on takeoff, watch a movie or two, take a nap. Before you know it, you'll be landing. You'll do great."

"This is so screwed up. Me, flying for the first time in my life to find a man I've never met, looking like this." I slowly pulled up to my full height and pointed to my messed-up face. "Sporting two black eyes and a scarred chin."

"Stop that." She put her hands on my shoulders and looked me square in the eyes. "Your body will heal. I know you're nervous, but even if you don't succeed in finding him, think of this as an opportunity for adventure."

"Yeah, right," I mumbled. The bruising had faded, but the sallow rings under my eyes still caught people's stares.

She twisted me roughly to get at my backpack and yanked two books from the front zippered section.

"These books say you need to go." She shook them at me, fanned to expose the covers.

"How so?"

"*The House of Medici* and *The Art of the Italian Renaissance* are not exactly casual reading. It tells me you're inquisitive, and even though you spent most of your life hiding it from everyone, you're extremely intelligent."

"You give me too much credit. Remember, I'm the guy who barely graduated high school."

"Because you were bored, Eddie, not stupid." She narrowed her eyes in thought. "I have a strong hunch that someone, somewhere, a teacher or someone you looked up to, made you feel you were less than you are. No one realized you had checked out.

With your mom, Ray and your friends, it's easier for you to fit in than stand out."

"You missed your calling, Dr. Freud. You should've been a psychologist." I rolled my eyes and laughed.

"But I'm not wrong, am I?" she asked.

Unable to meet her gaze, I shrugged without comment and adjusted the strap on my shoulder. Other than my grandmother, Claudia was the only other person who really saw me.

Not even my own mother did.

"You love learning about art. You draw pictures for the girls, and you paint, too."

"Used to paint." I took the books back from her.

"Florence is the birthplace of the Italian Renaissance." She watched as I returned the books to my backpack. "You have the opportunity to see world-famous, historic art, live, and in-person. How does it get better than that?"

"Yeah." Releasing a slow breath, I gazed upward at the high vaulted ceiling of the terminal, my mind racing with the possibilities. "It would be cool to see Florence."

"And now you can." Smiling, she leaned to kiss my cheek. "Take a deep breath and go! Have an adventure."

Her encouragement choked me up.

"Thanks." I pulled out my passport and gate pass, but stopped to motion to her belly. "You gonna have that kid before I get back?"

"With any luck, Lucas will be here to welcome you home. Now go." Claudia pushed me toward the procession of travelers in line for security and called out, "Don't forget to message me when you arrive. Ciao!"

I waved back, glanced around one last time, and then, with a death grip on my ID and boarding pass, I headed into the fray.

Two hours later, I was securely seated-belted in, could see the nearest emergency exit, and learned my seat cushion doubled as a flotation device. A litany of instructions came over the PA system. I listened to every word in all three languages. If the plane went down, I was armed and aware of what I needed to do to survive.

My stomach spun as the Airbus accelerated down the runway, but the enormous metal bird took to the air with surprising grace. We rose into the clouds with a slight shimmy and then, rising above them, the plane settled, and so did my stomach.

"Folks, this is Captain Wilkes speaking…" On the overhead speaker, the pilot made a brief speech, introducing himself and his co-pilot, and welcoming us aboard.

An airline pilot sounded like a respectable line of work. And with great perks. Fly planes. Visit exotic locations. Date beautiful flight attendants.

I toyed with the idea.

"Who're you kidding?" I muttered with a shake of my head. Bettering my future meant buying a rental property, not an unrealistic job change.

"Rudack, Edward?" A female flight attendant stopped at my row.

There was comfort in knowing I was a Rudack in name only. Not a drop of Tom Rudack's blood in my veins. But Edward, I was stuck with. A pretentious name if ever there was one. However, on this polished woman's lips, it sounded damn fine. Regal, even. But no one called me Edward. Not even my mother, who'd stuck me with the name. I was Eddie. Just Eddie.

But Eddie would never find himself on a plane headed to a foreign land. I raised my hand.

"I'm Edward."

The Alitalia employee confirmed my meal selections on her computer tablet. From behind my sunglasses, I checked her out. She was a nice-looking older woman with an air of confidence, and with the ebony hair and olive skin, probably Italian. I wouldn't mind breaking my current dry spell with her.

I gave her my most charming smile. Her return smile, though, was entirely professional. She was not about to meet me in the restroom for initiation into the mile-high club. Meal confirmed she moved on.

Whatever. I was too keyed up to enjoy a good, meaningless hump.

I twisted one way, and then the other, trying to sleep. When

I'd made the online reservation, the website boasted of comfortable seating in the economy section. The leather seat reclined mere inches, and before I realized the insufficiency of armrests, the woman in the seat next to mine took ownership of the one between us. The comfort-marketing jargon seemed deceptive and made me wonder if the airline needed to embellish stuff like that to fill the plane. No one was coming off this trip thinking these seats were comfortable enough to sleep in.

"Your first time to Italy, Edward?" the woman next to me asked. It was the first time she'd talked to me since I had sat down next to her in the middle section.

"Yes." I sat up and smiled at her. "First time out of the states, in fact. How about you?"

"It's my third time. I'm meeting an old friend in Rome." She was older than my mother. Her body rounder and softer than my mother's coffee-diet stick-figure. "Vacation?"

"Yes and no. Here to see the sights, but also to find someone. I recently learned I have family in Italy."

"How exciting. Where?"

"In the southern region. If I'm not too busy, I might try to look him up. I don't know." I knew far too little about the man. "We'll see."

I took my sunglasses off to rub my tired eyes.

"Oh, my." She raised a hand to her mouth. "What happened to you?"

I'd forgotten about my matching set of blackened eyes. I almost put my shades back on, but the cat was out of the bag.

"My mother's boyfriend punched me," I huffed. "I guess Mike felt like he had the right to take me down because she and I were doing one of our rounds. I never met my father, which is why I'm—"

My face reddened. Oversharing with a stranger. No, I would not behave like my mother.

I shook my head. "Just your typical family drama. I'll spare you."

"Your eyes don't look so bad." The woman smiled kindly and patted my arm. "You will love Italy. I'd suggest trying to sleep for a few hours. This way you'll be rested, ready to explore."

"Thanks." I nodded and slipped my sunglasses back on.

Claudia's pep talk had worn off. Nothing about this felt fun or exciting.

Chapter 3

THE PLANE LANDED AT LEONARDO da Vinci International Airport, Rome. It was late morning. A distinct zip of excitement rose sharply in my chest. I lost track of the older woman who had been sitting beside me, and as I stepped out of the plane into a sea of people speaking a language I didn't understand, a sudden panic eclipsed that feeling.

I thought myself knowledgeable. I'd been to countless places, but only within the pages of the many books I read. This was different. An actual trip. My maiden voyage, the first time away from my small hometown by myself. This was a world away from my weekly grind. My normal routine started each Monday, with me already pining for the weekend like a get-out-of-jail-free card. The time to hang out with buddies, drink a lot of beer, and hopefully, find a honey to dance with. Sundays, I holed up with a book to offset the noise and alcohol. Rinse and repeat. Operating on weekend warrior mode had its perks. It was easy. I knew people. They knew me.

Here, I knew no one.

I followed the masses exiting the plane, all of us bleary-eyed, fuzzy-headed sheep, slogged our way to customs, passports at the ready. With Italian phrases locked on my cell phone screen, I prepared to answer discriminating questions about my visit.

"Hello. *Buongiorno.*" The bored uniformed guard held out his hand for my passport.

I expected him to look foreign, but other than thickly his accented English, he appeared no more Italian than some guys back in New York. Comparing my face with my ID photo, the agent's attention caught on my blackened eyes. He said nothing though. Apparently satisfied, he stamped my passport and handed it back. Dismissed, I moved forward, into the busy foot traffic of the arrivals wing. The sight of the large airport, bright and modern, shook me awake.

I stepped aside to let other travelers pass, shrugged the backpack off my shoulder, and reached inside to find Mary. I took the small statue of the robed Madonna out and holding her in my hand, inhaled deeply.

Grams wanted me to come. I had to leave Eddie and his comfortable routine behind me. Steadied, I tucked Mary away and refocused. Overhead, I spied the sign for the luggage claim area and got on a down escalator. In those few steps, somehow the air felt different, frenetic, alive with possibilities. A tickle of anticipation to explore rose within me.

Edward had things to see, people to meet, great foods to eat—a whole new world to discover.

Outside, the air held the day's heat, balmy and still, except for quick bursts created by airport traffic. Vehicles cruised by briskly, a chaotic buzz of motion.

"*Signore*, a ride? *Prego*." A middle-aged man motioned to a four-door vehicle parked at the curb. "Where are you going?"

I pulled out my cell. The man waited patiently.

S*tazione Ferroviaria* had a string of rolling r's and robust vowels my tongue was not capable of. I made a sincere effort but butchered the attempt at saying the train station.

"Ah, *sì*, the station. Come, prego." The man took my duffle bag and opened the door.

I'd spoken my first Italian words *in Italy*. In the backseat of the car, I sat tall, proud of the minor victory. The taxi driver careened through busy Roman streets. Pride slipped away, overtaken by the roll of my stomach. He glanced over his shoulder every few seconds, cheerfully conversing with me in simple English, cataloging a list of places I should see during my visit.

He'd give New York City cabdrivers a run for their money. I watched the road, a death grip on the door pull, and tried to respond to him. Several long minutes later, we stopped out in front of the station. My shoulders sagged with relief.

"Tickets there." The driver pointed to a sign that read, *biglietti*.

"Thank you." I counted out Euro coins to pay the fare. With a nod, I added, "*Grazie*."

The unmistakable outline of the Roman Colosseum rose over the roof of the station, punctuating the skyline of Rome. The movie, *Gladiator*, came to mind, and I felt an intense need to see the famed historic amphitheater. I had to travel several hours south to get to Positano, but hopefully, before I left Italy, I'd have time to see the famous sights of Rome and its trove of ancient secrets. As I carried my bags into the station, I promised myself, above all, I would see Florence and Renaissance art with my own eyes.

Out of the windows of the high-speed train, on my way to Salerno, the metropolitan city faded away, making way for smaller towns and villages scattered across the southwestern coast of the Italian boot. I slept a bit before reaching the next destination. In Salerno's Piazza della Concordia, the main square, I bought an apple from a roadside vendor before boarding a bus for the Amalfi Coast. From the road, the view of the area was as exciting as it was dizzying. A panorama of asymmetrical mountaintops met the sky and rolled headlong down to the water, providing the bluest blues I'd ever set eyes on. Sun-bleached pastel houses, in gold, peach, white, and red, stacked high like a seawall. Precariously perched, they appeared ready to tumble into the sea at any moment. I imagined the people who lived in such a vertically challenged geography would be mentally tenacious and squat, physical powerhouses.

The bus driver expertly handled the twisty road through the scenic mountainous coastline, swerving around hairpin turns. Each bend singled out the visitors. We were the ones who gasped and held on to our seats.

The sky hadn't yet dimmed when the bus pulled into Positano. Though evening had descended, the temperature was still summery warm. With my backpack on my shoulders and my oversized duffle bag in hand, I walked to Piazza del Duomo. It was like stepping back in time. Multi-storied terra-cotta buildings rose over my head, except to the south, where a beach of dark pebbled sand melted into sapphire waters. Wide, endless stone steps, leading up to a Byzantine-era church, dominated the piazza.

I felt like a randomly placed pushpin on a wall map. Despite the road-weary fatigue crawling through my brain, one thought persisted: I needed money.

I found an Italian ATM, a *Bancomat*, and withdrew a few hundred Euros. With it, I bought myself a bottle of water and found a bench. I sat to rehydrate and acclimate to my new surroundings.

Italians strolled the cobblestone streets, owning their stylish clothes; the men, sockless, in narrow-legged cuffed pants and sophisticated dress shoes. I looked down at my store-bought ripped jeans and expensive high-top sneakers and decided Edward required a more mature look.

A men's boutique a short walk away caught my eye. I spent most of my recently acquired Euros on three button-up shirts, two pairs of pants and one pair of sweet, black Italian leather shoes. Before I left, I got directions to my Laetitia Airbnb rental from the friendly shop owner, a slim man with a thick, black mustache. He assured me the mountainside apartment was an easy walk, only minutes from town.

On the stone walk outside the store, I took out a map and tried to orient myself. I'd booked the reservation online. The photos promised a spacious room with a king-sized bed and a romantic view of the hill area. I would have that giant bed to myself. On the plus side, with no one to distract me, I would have more time to do what Grams asked of me, to look for Giovanni Lo Duca.

After learning about my biological father, and before the trip, I spent days trying to find out where he might be. Positano wasn't that big, only about four thousand people, but hours of chasing down endless rabbit holes garnered disconnected bits of information—nothing uniquely helpful in locating the man. I held little hope of finding him.

The road wound upwards. With my body arched forward, I navigated several sets of steps up a hill. Sweat pooled under my arms and across my forehead. It wasn't nearly as close as the shopkeeper had made it sound. I trekked along a narrow lane, the muscles in my arms ached from carrying my duffle bag. Its weight grew heavier with each step. The angle of the sun had the light hitting my eyes. I stopped aside a fenced-in grassy area to catch my breath. A few yards away, a woman on a horse trotted in my direction.

The horse, tan with a black mane, was handsome, but as horse and rider drew nearer, it was clear the woman was even more striking. Long, glossy ebony hair framed a perfect, symmetrical face. So flawless, I could easily imagine her high-stepping down a runway at a New York City fashion scene.

"Ciao." The woman, sitting erect in the saddle, posture impeccable, looked down at me and smiled.

Her concentrated deep brown-eyed gaze and kind smile made my tongue thick and my reply slow.

"Ciao," I finally returned. Remembering my destination, I held up the map. "*Laetitia?*"

"*Lungo la strada.*" She pointed down the road. "*Brucio.*"

Although I didn't understand the exact meaning, I nodded. Her response made it obvious I was headed in the right direction. Remembering the apple I'd purchased earlier, I took it out of my backpack and held it up for the woman to see.

"*Sì.*" She nodded.

I held the apple out over the fence. The horse sniffed it, took it from my hand, and finished it in a few loud crunching bites.

"*Nome?*" I used one of the few Italian words I could remember to ask the horse's name.

"Alba." She stroked the horse's neck affectionately.

"Ciao, Alba. *Bella*," I said.

"Grazie. *Buona sera.*" She capably nudged the horse's girth with the heels of her riding boots. Horse and rider trotted off into the pasture.

Painted tile placards listed each residential number. At 1531, *Laetitia*, the trees stopped and opened to a clearing. All that was visible, though, was a blackened, burnt mess of what was once a building. I stood there confused by the sight of a set of charred brick steps that led up to a crosshatch of black-rippled wood beams and piles and piles of gray cinder and ash. A hazy, white smoke lingered low over the rubble.

"This is so not good," I said and pulled out my cell. The owner must've notified me. There'd be an email or text message awaiting, with an explanation, an apology and a new address for me to stay.

Except I had no signal.

My palms grew sweaty, and I almost dropped the phone.

I strode a few yards to the left, then the right. No signal. I was out of luck. I silently thanked Claudia for insisting I print the Airbnb reservation and keep it in my wallet. All I needed to do was find a public phone. I dug into my pocket, but my pocket was flat. Empty. I threw my backpack to the ground and knelt to pull everything out.

No wallet. Where the hell had I left it?

My earlier fatigue evaporated. I hustled back down the hillside, heart racing as my feet gobbled up step-after-step of many flights of stairs, to return to the clothing store. The store's yellow awning had been retracted. The window, dark. The store, closed.

With a sinking feeling, I returned to the piazza and slumped down on a bench.

I had no business being in Italy, clueless, alone, and now hotelless and penniless. I wanted nothing more than to tuck my tail between my legs and go home. How they would laugh and shake their heads because Eddie had done exactly as they expected.

Loser.

The sun was taking its time setting, but it was late. The street and beach crowd had thinned out. I pulled my book from my backpack, but a moment later, I shoved it away. My arms and legs were heavy, my brain fried and lethargic from all the traveling. I couldn't concentrate. Couldn't move. I pushed my duffle bag to one end of the bench and rested my head on it. Under my shirt, my passport dug into my chest. I wrapped my hand firmly around it and closed my eyes.

Chapter 4

I AWOKE WITH THE MORNING SUN in my eye, my muscles stiff, and a crick in my neck. My empty stomach rumbled.

My hunger pangs were hard to ignore, but nothing was open yet. Inside my backpack, I found a packet of nuts from the flight and devoured them. With the straps of my gear over my shoulder, I strolled the narrow empty walkways, fascinated by the colorful stonework and architecture. At a juncture in the alleys, a Romanesque face carved from clay spouted water from its mouth into a clay basin. I leaned in to sip the water. Clean and cool, I drank my fill.

With nothing but time to kill, I headed to the beach. The walkway down was covered in flowers that grew from thick stems that climbed the cement walls of the trestle, creating a canopy of bright purple-pink blooms over my head.

I dropped my bags on the dark volcanic beach sand and took off my sneakers to wade in the early morning surf. Pewter-colored pebbles clattered rhythmically along the water's edge. The cold Tyrrhenian Sea invigorated my tired feet. Several yards out in the water, a line of anchored boats bobbed in the waves. Behind me, the church bell rang, making me glance back at the town. Tall, slender, Dr. Seuss-looking trees lined the paved walkway that preceded the beach. Brightly painted houses built into the craggy mountainside formed the backdrop of the scene. My eyes climbed the stacked terraces, to the buildings and the many balconies with flowers and palm trees. Above them, in a picturesque pale blue sky, fluffy snow-white clouds lazily floated south.

Day two in hell.

The morning eased on, the temperature rose. Traffic on the main road picked up. The chatter of fresh beachgoers and storekeepers carried through the air. I kept a watchful eye on the front of the men's store I'd been in yesterday until I saw him, the same thin, well-dressed, mustached man from yesterday, at the shop door.

Grabbing my stuff, I sprinted barefoot off the beach and across the cobblestone walk.

"Hey, hey!" I rushed to the man.

He stepped back, eyes widened.

"I was in your store yesterday." Panting, I shook the shopping bag at him. "I must've left my wallet on the counter."

"No, no signore." He shook his head. "I have no wallet."

I pushed past him to check out the store myself. It wasn't there. Suddenly I remembered the Bancomat. I must've left it there. A wallet near an ATM? Easy pickings. It definitely would be gone. I looked anyway.

No luck. I returned to the store and handed the man the bag, the receipt still inside.

"I need to return these."

"Signore, these shoes, such fine Italian leather. Look at them." He held out the stylish black shoes that looked as good as they felt on my feet.

I raked my teeth over my bottom lip. I needed money.

"You will not find ones such as these for a better price!" He turned the pair side to side, pointing out the fine, handcrafted details.

They really were great shoes. If I kept them, I'd still get back most of the Euros.

"Okay," I blurted. "I'll keep them."

"Very good." He nodded, a pleased but respectful smile on his face. He reached into the bag to pull out the clothes I wanted to return.

"*Signore*, these pants, and this shirt, the fabric is magnificent. Come, feel the fine texture." He slipped the materials into my hand.

They were smooth, soft—better than any clothing I'd ever owned.

As a salesman, this guy knew his stuff. I kept the shoes. And one outfit.

With a few hundred Euro in my pocket, I stopped to get a pastry and coffee, an Americano as they called it. Hunger temporarily staved off, I walked through the more populated areas to see about a place to stay. Maybe I had enough cash for a night or two at a cheap hotel. And a couple of simple meals. It definitely wouldn't last me two weeks. I needed to get in touch with the Airbnb owner and my bank. ASAP.

I entered an older, unassuming establishment, *Hotel al Limone*. The white exterior plaster had cracks, and in places, the paint had chipped away. I counted on a cool air-conditioned lobby, but the temperature inside the hotel was as warm as the street. I waited behind an older gentleman as he chatted with the desk clerk. The man leaned informally on the counter and rubbed the back of his neck. Though the desk clerk had made eye contact with me when I entered the lobby, neither of the men seemed in a hurry to wrap up their conversation.

The older man took out a cloth handkerchief and wiped his brow. I stood silent with growing impatience, until the man made a gurgling sound, slumped over and crumbled to the floor.

I rushed forward, tossing my bag and backpack aside.

"Sir, are you okay?" I dropped to my knees and put a hand on the man's shoulder. The man grabbed his chest, his sweaty face contoured in pain. "I think he's having a heart attack. Call an ambulance!"

The clerk leaned over the counter and gaped at me before shouting, "*Emergenza! Chiamare il medico!*"

An answering shout came from somewhere behind the counter.

"The doctor is nearby," the hotel clerk said, looking at me. "What is to be done now?"

I'd been in the same situation with Grandpa Davies. Adrenaline surged through my veins. Clear-headed, I recalled what I needed to do. I leaned over the man. Keeping my eyes on his chest, I lowered my cheek over his mouth. I neither saw nor felt breathing. I pulled open the man's shirt to locate his sternum. "What's his name—*nome?*"

"Franz," the clerk hurried to answer. "He is the owner of the restaurant next door."

"Franz, stay with us!" I shouted and started CPR. After a round of two rescue breaths and thirty chest compressions, Franz sputtered. Then he started to breathe on his own.

"Do you know if he takes medication?" I patted the man's shirt pocket. The clerk answered me with a blank expression. "Heart medicine," I added.

"Sì, *cardiologia!*" The clerk hurried from behind the counter. Bending over Franz, he fished into the man's pants pocket and pulled out a small vial of pills. Nitroglycerin.

I reached for the cylinder, but a hand from behind me snatched it away.

"*Scostare!*" A stern young woman flapped her hand, and the clerk backed up.

I stared open-mouthed. It was her—the horse rider from yesterday.

"Scostare signore! "

There was no trace of recognition in her eyes. Looking more than a little annoyed, she pushed hard at my shoulder. I slid back, giving her space. She moved past me, stirring the warm air as she took my spot next to Franz.

"Ciao, Franz. *Sono io, Ivayla.*" She talked to the man like he knew her. While she held his hand, she shook out a few pills and stuck them under the man's tongue. Exactly as I'd been ready to do.

The man seemed to be coming to. She continued to speak to him in Italian, low and soft. Some time had passed since the call for a doctor. I pushed to my feet and watched the man with concerned eyes.

"Is everyone here slow, even in an emergency? Where is the doctor? Is he even coming?"

Holding the man's wrist, the woman glowered up at me. Her espresso eyes, steely cold, pinned me in place.

"*I am* the doctor," she said in perfect English.

Heat swarmed my face. "I didn't know."

"*Ragazzo bello ma maleducato,*" she said with clipped impatience. I didn't have a clue what she'd said, but the cutting tone did not sound like praise.

A siren wailed out in front of the hotel. I held the door open. Two medics rushed past me with a gurney. The young doctor began issuing orders to get the victim into the ambulance. I stood back in awe as she orchestrated the scene with authoritative confidence that could only come with practice. Maybe she wasn't as young as I'd first thought.

I chased Franz's gurney out to the ambulance, hoping to talk to her. She climbed in behind her patient without a backward glance. The doors slammed shut, and the emergency vehicle roared away.

Once the ambulance siren receded, I went back to the front desk.

"I am Berto. I am at your service, signore." The concierge, a tall reed of a man with an immense nose, finally acknowledged me as a guest.

"Do you think Franz will be okay?" I asked.

"He is in competent hands." He nodded.

"That doctor, how did she get to the hotel so fast?" I asked.

"Doctor Lo Duca is a local."

"Lo Duca?" I leaned in. "Really?"

"Sì, a dreary name. Not so impressive as the families of Neapolitan, where I grow up." He rambled on about how life in the north was superior.

I didn't hear much past the fact that the beautiful doctor's name matched my biological father's. I needed to find her.

"So," I ambled. "I don't have a reservation. My hotel burnt down, and I don't have anywhere to stay. Do you have a room available?"

"Yes. Of course," Berto said.

"Great. How much?" My bones were brittle with fatigue, but still, I waited to hear the price.

"For you, *niente*." He waved a hand at me. "You save Franz. Tonight, you are our guest."

I almost fell to my knees in gratitude. Up one flight of stairs, I unlocked the door to a small but clean hotel room. It had a window overlooking the main road, and, disappointingly, no air conditioning. I cranked open the window as far as it went. Within minutes, a bee came in to keep me company, a solitary one, buzzing speedily around the room. The bathroom was only marginally larger than the one on the airplane. A toilet on one side faced a bidet on another, and a miniature porcelain sink, slightly askew, jutted out of a wall under a narrow window. The shower stall had different colored tiles as if added at a later date.

Sweaty with road dirt, I peeled off my clothes and stepped under the spray of the shower. With little room to turn around, I banged my elbows on the walls, but the water pressure and temperature were perfect. For a few minutes, I bowed my head and let the water massage away the tension.

Putting on fresh clothes, I released Mary from the T-shirt I'd rolled her in. I thought it almost funny that my grandmother asked me to take the six-inch tall statue of the Virgin Mary, but not unexpected. I'd been told that as a toddler, whenever we visited my grandparents' house, they would often find me talking to the Madonna statue in their garden. For my fifth birthday, Grams had given me a small, portable replica of it. My very own to keep next to my bed whenever I felt the need to talk to someone.

Except for the times when I'd been younger and gone to sleepovers at friends, or older and spent the night with a girlfriend, the now faded plastic statue was the last thing I saw before I closed my eyes and the first thing I saw when I opened them. My family wasn't religious at all. Mom never took us to church, but Mary somehow always made me feel safe. Maybe it reminded me of being at my grandparents' house. Even though I'd never told my grandmother how the statue comforted me, it seemed obvious she'd known.

I set Mary on the bedside table.

Despite the lack of air conditioning, the hotel had Wi-Fi and once connected, my phone chimed with dozens of incoming texts, mostly from a worried Claudia. And my mother, too. First, I alerted my bank and credit card companies I'd lost my wallet and put a hold on my credit line. With access to my email once again, I found a frantic message from the Airbnb owner about the fire and my reservation. They wired a full refund.

But without an ATM card, I had no access to the money.

I remembered Claudia's parting words at the airport and sent a quick text to my mother letting her know I'd arrived safely. Obligation fulfilled, I sat down to message Claudia.

Me: Hey, made it. Hate it. Lost my wallet and rental is a smoldering heap of ash. Slept on a bench last night.

Claudia: What happened? Are you okay?

Me: I'm fine. Got a head start on my tan. But that's not all. A local guy dropped in front of me. Did CPR on him until the doctor arrived.

Claudia: OMG!

Me: I think he's OK. But get this, the doctor's name is Lo Duca!

Claudia: Any relation?

Me: Don't know. Plan to follow up tomorrow. Look, bought these amazing shoes. Real Italian leather!

I snapped a shot of my new black shoes.

Claudia: Those are hideous!

Me: Says you. They're all the rage here. I have no cash, but at least I'm stylish.

Claudia: I'll wire you $$. Where should I send it?

Claudia would offer. She'd been kind to me since the day we met. The thought, however, of Toby and Ray hearing about this made me pause. They'd be bailing me out again. Was it worth the humiliation? It was a lousy situation, but not unbearable. If the credit card company couldn't deliver a new card by tomorrow, I'd talk with Berto. Maybe I could do some work in exchange for another night's stay.

Me: No. Hotel owner loves me for saving guy's life. Letting me stay for free. Will hit up credit card co for cash if needed. How are you?

Claudia: Still pregnant. Please let me know if you need anything. Seriously, anything.

Me: Anything? Leave Toby, come to Italy with me. I'll raise the baby as my own.

Claudia: Can't. Those shoes are too ugly. But I love you. Be safe. Keep in touch.

Smiling, I fell onto the bed without pulling back the covers. My feet hung over the edge, the mattress too short for me—or any normal-sized human. It wasn't the best hotel, but it was free. I thought about the woman doctor, a Lo Duca, my first lead. Maybe she was a cousin. Tomorrow I'd go to the medical center to find her. I was too tired to do anything else but sleep.

Chapter 5

JET LAG HIT ME HARD, and I slept the rest of the day, but the next morning, I awoke feeling like a new man. When I checked my emails, I found one from the credit card company. They made provisions to deliver a new card to me immediately, right at the hotel. I put on my new clothes and shoes. The plus of having Italian blood, I never sunburned. A few hours in the sun the day before had baked my skin amber. With my new shoes and clothes, I could pass as a local.

At least, until I opened my mouth.

"Good morning, my friend!" Berto grinned widely as I stepped up to the front desk.

"Morning, Berto," I returned, smiling too. "How are you? No, wait — *Buongiorno. Come va?*"

I'd practiced the few Italian phrases before I'd left the room.

"Ah, very good, signor Rudack!"

"Call me Edward, please," I said, liking my bold, well-traveled alter ego more and more. "Have you heard anything about your friend?"

"*Grazie Dio!* Franz improves, much thanks to you." He smiled. "You appear much rested. I trust you slept well?"

"It was fine, thank you." I lowered my eyes. "You said they took Franz to the medical center. How do I get there?"

"Are you ill?"

"No, I want to talk to the woman doctor."

"Ah, *signorina* Ivayla. She is lovely," Berto said with a knowing smile.

"Yes, yes she is quite beautiful." I returned the smile and

resisted correcting him. If it made him happy to think he was matchmaking instead of making a connection between possible relatives, I'd let him have it. What did I care?

"It is up the hill," he said and took out a map to show me the directions.

"Thank you." I hesitated. "Um, by the way, Berto, I had some terrible things happen when I first arrived. One of them is, I lost my wallet."

Berto scrunched up his face as if he smelled something sour.

I told him the story of the burned down rental villa and my lost wallet, assuring him a new credit card was on its way.

"You stay, signor Rudack. We discuss payment another time."

"Thank you. Grazie, so much," I gushed, amazed by his absolute trust in me.

"Grazie *mille*," he said. "That is how we say it."

"Grazie *mille*," I repeated.

Franz Schmidt. That was the unfortunate man's name; a German transplant who'd had the heart attack in the lobby. After a cappuccino and a quick bite to eat, I followed the directions Berto had given me to the medical center where the ambulance had taken Franz. It was the only one in the area, and apparently, Dr. Ivayla Lo Duca worked there, too.

I had no idea if Dr. Lo Duca worked that day, but at the very least I might find out how Franz was doing. And if I poked about, someone might tell me a little about the doctor and her family.

When I mentioned her name to the hospital receptionist, she pointed to a window overlooking a sunny piazza. From the sea of scrubs and white lab coats, apparently, the piazza was a popular place for the hospital staff to take coffee breaks.

I spotted her at once, sitting at a bistro table off to the side. She wore a white coat, and hair twisted in a tight bun. Compared to the woman I'd met riding a horse, today she looked highly professional and much less accessible. An older man with pale skin and brown graying hair sat across the table from her. Like her and many others, he wore a white lab coat.

At a café at the edge of the piazza, I ordered a cappuccino, and the cup in hand approached the table.

"Buongiorno, Dr. Lo Duca, may I speak with you?"

Her eyes darted up, and she stiffened with recognition.

I decided then not to use my botched Italian. This woman would not think it cute. Especially since her ability to speak English almost exceeded my own.

"I think you got the wrong impression of me yesterday," I hurried to explain.

"No, I believe I got an accurate impression." She crossed her arms, defiance darkening her brown eyes.

The man sitting across from her barely restrained a smile, daring me to persist. As small and inconsequential as I felt to this woman, I moved closer to the table.

"I'm sorry if I offended you. It was unintentional. I totally see how sexist it was for me to assume you were a man, and for that, I'm really sorry." Groveling sucked, but I forced myself to meet her eyes.

"My dear, the poor fellow has humbled himself. You must forgive him." The man chuckled and reached across the table to pat her hand. His accent held the distinct flair of the southern states back home. "This here's my fellow compatriot. A Yankee if my ears don't deceive me."

"Yes." I nodded and looked at her.

Her expression hadn't changed. She wasn't about to help me find my father.

"We've heard a man at the hotel saved signor Schmidt. Are you that man?" he asked. The nametag attached to his coat lapel read Dott. Monroe. I assumed translated it meant Dr. Monroe.

"I wouldn't say saved. I just performed CPR until Dr. Lo Duca came," I said. "Do you know how he's doing?"

"He's resting comfortably."

"That's good. I hope he makes a full recovery." With nothing more to say, I nodded at them and turned away.

"Wait."

A hand caught my arm and stopped me. I looked down to find Dr. Lo Duca's long fingers wrapped around my wrist. Warmth flooded my face.

"Please, forgive my rudeness. Franz is like family. I am thankful you intervened until I could arrive." Her brown-eyed gaze held mine unwaveringly.

"Sure, I was happy to help." I held still under her inspection.

She gripped my wrist tighter, commanding my attention. "There is something about you that is familiar to me. I am not sure why."

"I saw you riding the other day. I gave your horse, Alba, an apple."

"That was you?"

"I was looking for—"

"Laetitia. Yes, yes. I remember now." She released me. "That place burned down two days ago. I told you, *brucio*, but now I see you are not fluent in Italian."

"I don't speak *any* Italian." I shuffled my feet, embarrassed. "But, that's why I was at the hotel when Franz collapsed."

"I see." She studied me. "You look different."

"Do I?" I stood a little taller, pleased at how the new clothes transformed me.

"Your eyes, the bruises, they are less noticeable today." She drew a circle in the air in the direction of my eyes.

She remembered my blackened eyes.

"Oh." I released my deflated breath. "I got a lot of sun yesterday. Guess it helped."

"Sun and fresh air are the medicine I most prescribe." Her lips shifted into a soft smile. It transformed her face and, if possible, made her even more beautiful.

Monroe pushed out a chair. "Stay a moment and finish your cappuccino. You haven't even told us your name."

"Ed—" I paused, catching myself, and held out my hand. "Edward, from New York, as my accent betrays me. Long Island to be exact."

"Dr. Ralph Monroe, neurologist." The man gripped my hand first. "Born and raised in the great state of Georgia."

"Nice to meet you," I said.

"And I am Ivayla Lo Duca." She took my hand and gave it a firm shake. "Doctor of medicine in the great country of Italy. Compania, to be exact."

I sat down and crossed a foot over my knee, tapping my fingers on my thigh.

"What brings you to the Amalfi coast? Sightseeing?" Monroe leaned back and aimed his blue-eyed gaze at me.

"Sightseeing? I wish," I said with a sigh, and they both looked at me. "I'm here to find a man I've never met. I hardly know where to begin."

"Sounds like quite a task, son," he said with a grin.

"Yeah, a tall order. To add to that complication, I know nothing about the man, other than his name." I glanced at the beautiful woman. "His last name happens to be Lo Duca, the same as yours."

Dr. Lo Duca's eyes narrowed a fraction, but she held my gaze without blinking.

"What is the nature of your business with this man?" Her voice went cool once again.

I considered the situation from her side of it: a stranger, a foreigner no less, asking for information on a possible relative. Who could blame her for being defensive? Hell, if our positions were flipped, I'd have my guard up too.

"He's a distant family relative. My grandmother asked me to look him up." I hoped the somewhat improvised answer would reassure her I had no ulterior motives.

Her indifferent expression fell away, and she treated me to the warm sound of her laughter.

"Oh, but to find a Lo Duca is so very easy! Almost as easy as you've found me." She gestured beyond us to the cobblestone square. "Stop any person in this piazza! If they aren't one, they know one. What is the first name of this signor Lo Duca that you seek?"

"Giovanni." I leaned forward, hopeful. "Do you know him?"

"Giovanni?" Her cheeks rose with mirth before Monroe's laughter joined hers. "*Allora*, Edward from New York, that won't help much. Giovanni is a common name."

"Son, here, that name's about as common as a Michael or a John is in the states," Monroe added.

My face warmed. "If it's that common, then Dr. Lo Duca must have relatives named Giovanni, a brother, cousin or uncle?"

"Does Paolo have any Giovannis in his family tree?" Monroe asked her.

"We are not close to that side of the family, but I am certain I have no American relatives." A moment after she said that, her lips parted almost unwillingly with a gentle smile. "Tell me, what else do you know about your Giovanni Lo Duca?"

"I don't have many details about him, other than he is from this area and traveled to the states in the early 1990s. I would guess he's about my mother's age, fiftyish."

The glance the two of them exchanged didn't boost my confidence.

"I'm not sure why my grandmother thought this might be possible." With a sigh, I stood. "I won't take up more of your time."

"Papà says anything is possible, but only if you are committed to it," she said.

"That's not bad considering the nonsense that often comes out of Mario's mouth," Monroe said with a roll of his eyes. Then he checked his watch and pushed out his chair. "We need to get back to the hospital. Come, Ivayla."

"Yes, he is right. I must go." Dr. Lo Duca stood but hung back. She pulled a pen and a small notepad from her lab pocket, dashed out a note, and shoved it into my hand. "Here is my mobile number. I will help if I can. Ciao, ciao!"

I killed a few hours walking around Positano, exploring its endless narrow walkways that twisted and veered uphill, stopping often to take in the view. In Via Pasitea, I stumbled across a streetside wine and cheese shop that doubled as a grocery and deli. Inside, the aroma of cooked foods and fresh meats had me salivating. I purchased a sandwich, a bottle of water, and fruit for later. Outside, I grabbed a seat at one of the tables in the narrow, bricked area along the front of the store. It had been nearly two days since I'd had a real meal. The meatball and eggplant parmigiana sandwich, a combination I'd never had before, came recommended by another customer. I practically cried at the first bite. A host of flavors—tomato, sweet basil, and garlic—serenaded my tongue. Tempted to wolf it down, I had to force myself to take my time and savor every morsel.

I took a chance and sent Dr. Lo Duca a text between bites of my meal. A few minutes later, she replied, agreeing to meet me around five o'clock, after work, and then she sent me an address.

I sat back, belly full, watching people stroll by. Day three was turning out not to be so hellish.

The address Dr. Lo Duca gave me was to an art shop called *Opere d'arte del Duco.* Artwork by the Duke. While I waited for her to arrive, I browsed the art inside. Painting after painting of large canvas oils depicted the beautiful mountainscapes of Amalfi, so realistic one could almost feel the sun's warmth as surely as the painter must have when his brush stroked the canvas.

Envy sprouted, rousing a dormant desire to draw. It had been a long time, too long since I'd picked up a graphite pencil or a stick of charcoal. I didn't think to bring a sketchbook with me. A few years back, you wouldn't have found me without one.

"You like?" A soft voice startled me out of my musing. The young Italian doctor was dressed down, in jeans and a sweatshirt, her hair in one long braid. She looked more like a cute college co-ed than the staunchly professional woman I'd met at the hospital.

"Oh, hello Dr. Lo Duca." I swallowed back a sudden case of nerves and smiled. "Yes, this artist, he's remarkably good."

"You may call me Ivayla," she said and reached out a finger as if to stroke the painted terrain of brightly stacked houses.

On reflex, I caught her hand.

"Artwork shouldn't be touched." I drew her hand away from the painting. "The oils in our skin can ruin it."

Her hand was delicate but strong, with long, capable fingers. I liked the feel of it in mine and held it longer than necessary. I looked up and saw her studying me as if trying to gauge if I was for real.

"Sorry." I released her hand, my face heating under her scrutiny. "Automatic reaction."

"No, of course, you are right. I am often tempted, but I do not touch." She twirled the gold bracelet on her wrist. "I agree, the artist is remarkable. I often bring visitors here to see his work. The Duke really captures the feel of Amalfi. He is a celebrated local artist. His artwork is loved by all of Positano."

"Duke doesn't sound Italian."

"His real name is Paolo Lo Duca. And Lo Duca literally means 'the duke' in English."

"Lo Duca?" A flash of hope flared.

"Sì, but assuredly the painter is not part of the family you seek." She shook her head, swiftly putting the kibosh on any hope of me having a famous painter relative. "Paolo's been in Amalfi a very long time, and sadly, is quite a hermit. He leaves the house mainly to paint." She sighed and motioned to the piazza. "Would you like caffè, Edward from New York? I am in need of a lift."

We strolled across the cobblestone street. At the café window, Ivayla placed our order in Italian. I quickly threw down some Euros. It was the least I could do. She smiled her appreciation, and we took our steaming miniature cups to a long counter against the building wall. Ivayla took one little sip, drinking hers straight. No sugar or extra creamer. I wanted to add sugar but was painfully aware it would probably be like waving a red flag, revealing that I was nothing more than a tourist.

"This is my first espresso," I said.

"Your first?" Her eyes went wide.

"Um, yeah," I said, embarrassed.

"You cannot come all the way here and not experience what is around you. That is criminal, Edward from New York." With an air of teasing, she lifted her cup. "Part of the experience of drinking espresso is the scent. Take a deep inhale. Let the aroma enlighten the senses. Then, you sip. Two or three sips, while the crema is still on top. Quick, but not so quick."

I did as instructed. It was both bitter and weirdly satisfying.

"Well done." She rewarded me with a charming grin before taking a paper from her pocketbook. She put it in front of me and pointed at the lines of printed text. "On my break, I put together a list of residents in the area. You see, the ones here, higher on the list? They are close by, within the city. As the list goes down, the further distance they are."

The page listed many Lo Duca families with addresses and phone numbers.

"You did this for me?" I peered at the list, then up at her.

She nodded and twirled a hand. "It is a public listing. I thought it might help your search."

"Thank you very much."

"Allora. It was easy. No problem."

"Allora," I repeated. "What does that mean?"

"It's a verbal pause, much like when Americans say *so...* or *well...*"

"Allora." I smiled, enjoying the exoticness of a new word in my mouth. "Another word to add to my growing repertoire of Italian. So, tell me Doctor Lo Duca, what kind of medicine do you practice?"

"*Medicina d'emergenza*—emergency medicine."

"Oh, I didn't know that was a thing. You like it?"

"Yes. The first line of care, it moves fast," she said. "I must think quick. Always."

She appeared highly intelligent. It was easy to imagine her confidently making split-second life or death decisions.

"Your English is surprisingly good," I said.

"I did a U.S. residency after graduating from the Italian English MD program at Milan University." She played with the edge of the paper between us.

"Where did you study?"

"Minnesota, four years. It was very cold there." She wrapped her arms around herself, feigning a shudder. "But my English greatly improved, and that is where I met *Il mio fidanzato*, Ralph."

"Fidanzato-rolf? Sounds like some kind of Italian sausage."

She threw her head back and laughed. Having impressed me as a smart, levelheaded woman, the easy, uninhibited laughter was unexpected. It made the insides of my chest feel funny like my lungs were performing a high-flying trapeze act.

"You are amusing, Edward from New York. Fidanzato is what you would call a boyfriend. And Ralph is Dr. Monroe, my American companion you met this morning," she said.

"Dr. Monroe is your boyfriend?" I raised a brow. "Really?"

She fixed me with a stare. "Yes, why do you ask *really* like that?"

Ivayla Lo Duca was too young and far too beautiful for the ancient dude I'd met that morning.

"No reason," I said, trying to reassure her with my smile. I wasn't willing to lose what little footing I'd gained with her. We returned our empty cups and stepped away from the coffee stand.

"I guess, first thing tomorrow, I'll look these people up and start making calls. My Italian is, well, horrible. What do you think my odds are that any of these people speak English? Would you help me rehearse what to say in Italian?"

"No need. I will make the calls for you," she said.

"Thank you, but I can't ask that of you. It's too much."

"I insist." She straightened her shoulders; a gesture I understood meant she was not to be defied. "I have a late shift. I will be home early. You will come to my father's house. I will make the calls from there. It is the very least I can do after you helped save Franz's life."

"You don't have to repay me for that. Anyone would have jumped in."

"Franz is dear to me. His son, Otto, is my aunt's boyfriend. Our whole family is especially thankful that you were there."

"Well, then I am especially glad I was there." I smiled. "How he is?"

"He is doing well. Thank you for asking." She tipped her head to the right as if caught in thought. "You are a very nice man, Edward from New York. I already told Papà and Babbo about you and your quest. They are fascinated to know more and have asked to meet you."

"Papà and who?"

"Babbo, my other father," she said.

"Your *other* father?" I asked with a laugh.

"Yes, I have two," she answered.

"They're together, a couple?" I asked, embarrassed that I hadn't first considered a gay couple.

"Yes, Babbo and Papà are married." She nodded.

This woman had two fathers. I had none. How was that fair?

I returned to the hotel after my meeting with Ivayla and sent Claudia a text.

Me: Found the lady doctor! Not a relative, but offered to help.

Claudia: Nice! What did the police say about your wallet?

Me: Didn't report it. It's long gone. Out a hundred bucks. But have my passport. Eleven days until I come home.

Claudia: That bad, huh?

Me: Things are looking up. Ate amazing sandwich. And lady doctor is hot!

Claudia: Ooh, vacation romance?

Me: Ha! Not likely.

Claudia: She didn't like the shoes either?

Me: No! She's dating a prehistoric doctor dude from Georgia. My shoes are awesome.

I snapped a photo of them on my feet and sent it.

Claudia: Please, no more pix of them. You scared Julianne and Bea! Gotta go. We all send hugs xx

Chapter 6

"SIGNOR RUDACK!"

Berto called me from the concierge desk the next morning, waving a thick envelope over his head. My replacement charge card had arrived. I didn't waste time calling to reactivate my account.

I stopped at the nearest bancomat, tense as I slipped the plastic card into the slot. The transaction went through without a hitch. Relief flooded over me. Card and Euros in my pocket, I returned to the men's shop and bought myself another wallet. I promised the store owner, Riccardo—my new friend—I'd be back. I left the store smiling, energized and ready to roll.

The day marked my fourth in Italy. My mother me sent a text with details about Giovanni she thought would be helpful. I walked to get some breakfast thinking about my progress in finding my father. I had connected with a Lo Duca family. Today I would meet them, and hopefully, find an association.

At a local shop, I bought a croissant and cappuccino. I ate my breakfast enjoying the noise and sounds of the shop keepers greeting their customers. Their speech had a musical cadence. I even recognized some of the words. I stopped to make another purchase, a bottle of wine recommended by the store owner, to give to Ivayla's fathers. The address Ivayla had given me meant a fifteen-minute trip straight up the mountainside. Most of the houses here were wider, sprawling across multi-tiered properties. It spoke of affluence. Ivayla and her family were rolling in the dough.

The fortress-like house several stories high, sat insulated from the road by a stately stone wall. Hardy ivy encroached upon a metal marquee set above an imposing pair of dark-stained entry doors. It read: Villa Campanella. I couldn't make out much beyond the massive doors, other than the house was white concrete with vivid emerald green-shuttered windows.

At the doorstep, a skinny gray cat curled around my shins, meowing for attention. I bent down and scratched it on the shoulders. It arched its back with approval. To the right of the doors, I spied an old-fashioned twist doorbell. A turn of the key emitted a loud, sharp buzzer over my head, followed by feet tip-tapping down a set of steps. One of the burnished wooden doors swung open with a breezy whoosh revealing Ivayla, smiling.

"Ciao!" She scooped the cat into her arms and kissed the top of its head. "I see Romeo is making friends with our Edward from New York."

I followed her up a narrow stairway of dark polished wood. Her ivory dress moved with her, swishing gently across the back of her tan thighs. The top of the stairs opened to a covered, terracotta-floored terrace. Ivayla deposited the cat onto one of the several turquoise cushioned patio chairs.

Ceiling fans with giant leaf-like blades circled overhead, creating a cooling breeze. Past an ornate black metal railing, lay an unobstructed, grand, panoramic view of the sea. The gentle rumble of the water could be heard off in the distance.

I whistled, long and slow. "Sweet. I bet you never tire of that view."

"Often a problem." A man's voice answered.

I swiveled to find its owner, a man sitting in the shade at a table off to the side, a cloudy ring of cigarette smoke wreathed his head.

"When you no remind yourself, you forget value," he said, his English heavy with the regional accent.

I stared, not knowing how to or if I should respond.

"Babbo." Ivayla went to him, her voice soft. "This is Edward. He is from New York, the one I told you and Papà about."

Babbo leaned back in his chair. Wavy blue-black hair, long in the front, swept carelessly over one eye. In the gentle breeze, the white linen of his pants and a tunic billowed on his lean frame. Ivayla had his wavy full, blue-black hair.

"Ed... Edward." I stepped closer and held out my hand.

His eyes dipped to my hand, but he made no motion to take it. He studied me for a long moment and then snubbed out his cigarette. A kaleidoscope of colors stained his hands, from long lean fingers to bony wrists. Was it ink, markers, paint? I couldn't be sure.

"*Buona giornata.*" With a nod, he shook my hand. "I am Paolo Lo Duca."

I clamped onto his hand and swallowed.

"Paolo Lo Duca... the artist?"

"Sì. I paint a small bit," he said.

A small bit? Was the guy kidding? No wonder Ivayla had dismissed any family connection between the artist and me. The man was *her* father.

"I saw several of your paintings at the gallery store in town. Your work is amazing, the level of detail, incredible." I shook his hand again before casting Ivayla a look of betrayal. "Ivayla didn't tell me you were her father."

"As I wish," he said, offering no explanation.

A flash of yellow burst through the door behind us. A round-bellied older man in a canary yellow shirt came bustling into the room carrying a large plate piled high with olives, meats, and cheeses. He appeared similar in age to Paolo but with salt and pepper hair and a bushy mustache.

"Ah, there he is!" His joyful smile pushed up full, round cheeks, just like Ivayla's. He deposited the plates on the table and trounced on me. I found myself wrapped in a full-body hug. "I am Mario. Prego! Welcome to our home!"

When he let go, I handed him the wine and readjusted my shirt collar. "Thank you, sir."

"Sit, *mangia*. Ivayla, get glasses." Mario kept a hand on my shoulder. "Allora, we open your wine."

Mario handed the wine off to Paolo, and when Ivayla returned with short table glasses, he began filling them.

"*Edoardo*, we are happy for your visit. You save dear Franz.

Now, we take care of you." Mario pulled a chair out for me, and his meaty hand thumped my back. "What would you like to do while you are here, hmmm? Take a ferry ride to our lovely island of Capri? Stroll through *Piazza Tasso*?"

I accepted a glass of red wine from Paolo. "I really came to see if I could find families nearby with the Lo Duca name."

"Ah, sì. Ivayla has told us you wish to find this man, Giovanni Lo Duca. A relative?" Mario asked.

"Yes. He came to visit my family in New York twenty-seven years ago. We lost contact with him, and we've all wondered what became of him," I said.

Paolo picked at the cheeses and meats from the plate of oily antipasto, appearing uninterested in my tale. Mario, though, leaned in, hand under his chin and listened attentively to my every word.

"Paolo, *amore mio*, this sound familiar to you?" Mario asked.

Paolo grunted in such a way, it conveyed he didn't. Neither his husband nor daughter batted an eye at the grumbling non-verbal reply.

He reached forward for another slice of salami and said, "Send him to Luigi. He is a researcher."

"I think an investigator, yes, Babbo?" Ivayla added with a smile.

"*Molto bene*." Mario clapped his hands together, his volume matched his personality. "Dear Luigi Delatorre, a finder of persons! You speak to him. He help you."

I liked Mario and found myself smiling. The more he sliced and diced the English language, the more I couldn't wait to hear the next thing he'd say.

"Signor Delatorre lives up the hill." Ivayla swung a hand in an upward motion. "I will take you to meet him."

"That'd be terrific." I nodded with enthusiasm.

"What work you do back in the States?" Mario asked.

"I work in construction, fixing up and maintaining rental properties," I said. "In the winter, our company does snow removal."

"This work, you enjoy?" The question came from Paolo. He sat back in his chair studying me from under his heavy-lidded eyes.

"Not exactly. Pays the bills," I said, with a short, nervous chuckle.

"Where you stay, Edoardo?" Mario asked.

I told them the name of the hotel. Ivayla shook her head.

"That is the terrible place Berto Vinchetti owns," Ivayla told Mario.

"It's not the Ritz, but after losing my wallet—"

"*Che brutte notizie!*" Mario gasped. "Terrible!"

"Berto has been kind," I pushed back.

"That no acceptable." Her father tsked-tsked. "That place Berto call a hotel, it is not desirable. It is not to be helped. He is Neapolitan. Edoardo, bring your things here. You save Franz. I insist you come, be guest here."

I pulled back, speechless.

"I have work to do." Paolo shoved away from the table and left without haste.

I leaned forward, lowering my voice. "The hotel is okay. I'd rather not cause any problems."

"You come. I insist." Mario flapped a hand. "Give no mind to Paolo."

Give no mind to the renowned artist? In his home? An impossible request.

"Are you sure?" I *really* wanted to stay, but not if it pissed off Il Duco.

"You may trust that it is no imposition," Ivayla said. "Our house has many rooms, and Papà is fond of entertaining."

"*Sì*, and now, it is *troppo silenzioso*. Too quiet." Mario shook his head. "*È così*. It is what it is."

"Well, that would be great. Thank you both." The wine and food had me feeling warm and full, and for the first time since arriving in Italy, I felt relaxed.

Mario lifted his wineglass in a toast. "You welcome, Edoardo."

"His name is Edward, Papà," Ivayla chided gently.

"No, look at him! He is an Edoardo." Mario waved expressive hands toward me. "And Edoardo belongs here."

"I don't mind, Ivayla." A grin spanned my face. "It makes me feel more Italian, like I fit in."

Ivayla smiled. "See, Papà, he is nice, just like I said."

"You didn't seem to think that when we first crossed paths," I said. "You called me something, *ragazzo mal dukie?*"

The most becoming shade of pink warmed her cheeks.

"I called you *ragazzo bello ma maleducato.*"

Mario's laugh bounced off the walls. "My daughter thought you a rude, pretty boy."

I arched a brow. "A rare moment of impatience, but in light of how I acted, I get the rude part, but a pretty boy? Now that hurts."

"Yes, allora, look at you. Your hair cut so stylish and facial hair trimmed just so, your muscles." She waved a hand at me.

I warmed under her praise but feigning insult; I pulled back, hand to chest. "So, you're saying I look good, but somehow that's offensive?"

"Handsome men of Italy enjoy a mirror," Mario said.

"So much so, they are often distracted by their admiration to themselves," she added.

"You no have mirror." Mario jabbed a finger in my direction. "Ivayla like what she see!"

I bit back a smile.

"Papà, please," Ivayla pleaded his silence in a gentle, hushed tone. "Come, Edward, I shall take you to meet signor Delatorre and begin our search."

I didn't miss the way she referred to the search as ours. Knowing I'd have her help reignited my spirit for the search. I thanked Mario for his hospitality and followed Ivayla down to the street level of the villa. Parked in a covered area sat an assortment of colorful rides, two compact cars, one bright orange, the other green, and a lemon-drop yellow Vespa. Though shiny and new, not one of the small vehicles boasted of the family's financial stature.

Ivayla handed me a white helmet and tugged on a bright yellow one of her own. Slipping a leg astride the scooter, she plugged in the key, squeezed the left handle, and started the engine. It caught and buzzed to life.

I held the helmet in my hand and stared.

"We're taking that?"

"Yes. It is the best way to get around," she said.

The motorbike, like the many that cruised the local streets, had a long black seat, two small wheels and two ear-like mirrors on either end of the handlebars. No protection to offer its riders.

"I don't know," I said. "I'm kind of attached to my arms and legs."

She laughed and patted the seat.

"Have no fear, Edward from New York. I am a terrific driver."

"Well, you are an ER doctor." I swung a leg over the bike, settling on the seat behind her. "If I lose a limb, at least you'll be right there to sew it back on."

Ivayla's driving was terrifically terrifying.

She drove like she was racing in the Indy 500, as did every other person on the road, motorbikes, cars, and trucks alike. My stomach rolled at every corner she raced around, and I had to hold my breath as she navigated the narrow space between cars coming and going. There were several moments I was sure we'd crash, but then I'd open my eyes to live on for the next dizzying moment. The sun warmed my arms and her raven hair blew back to curl around my head. I decided to keep my eyes closed and just hold on tight.

After a time, we veered off the major road and headed uphill to where large farmhouses dotted vast properties. As we climbed, I grew more hopeful thinking this Luigi guy must be an outstanding detective to live in such an exclusive location within a densely populated area.

Ivayla turned into a long winding driveway of dirt and rock and we made a slow ascension to the yellow house at the top of the terraced land. It was large, but old, with the kind of character that made me want to explore the inside.

Ivayla took off her helmet, shook out her hair and shouted, "Signor Delatorre!"

"*Signorina* Ivayla! Ciao! Prego!" A short, portly man came rushing from the shadow of a nearby tree, a big smile on his face. Panting, he hugged Ivayla and kissed her face. "It is most wonderful to see you." He took my hand and shook it with vigor. "Mario has just phoned. You need to find someone! I am at your service."

He bent at the waist, a formal bow. Ivayla and I grinned at each other.

"Prego, sit and tell me about the man you wish to find." He motioned for us to join him in the side yard.

A wooden table sat under the canopy of an enormous tree. The garden dining area flowed seamlessly with the outdoors, almost as if the furniture had magically sprouted from the ground. Delatorre's English, heavily accented but passable, boosted my already growing confidence in the man.

The shade of the tree brought welcome relief from the scorching sun. Ivayla and I chose two adjacent cushioned chairs opposite Luigi. I referred to my cell for the information my mother had given me.

"Giovanni Lo Duca was in New York in the early 1990s, on a work visa," I read aloud. "He was employed at a garden center, a place called Island Garden House. He met a woman named Diane, who also worked at the garden center."

"I see, and this woman, she is Lo Duca's relative?" Luigi uncovered a basket with crusty bread and a dish with an assortment of green and black olives and pushed them across the table at us. Ivayla took a small sampling from each plate.

"No. She's my relative. Lo Duca and she had a relationship. They were intimate." I glanced at Ivayla to see her response to a part of the story I hadn't told her.

"Allora." She nodded, seemingly unaffected by the additional details. "You are saying this Giovanni and your relative had a sexual relationship, yes?"

"Um, yes." They didn't know the woman in question was my mother, but it still made my face redden with embarrassment. I speared a few olives with my fork and popped one in my mouth. The pleasantly salty and bitter flavor made my mouth water. A piece of crusty bread dipped in oil was the perfect accompaniment.

"This *rapporto sessuale,* did it produce children?" Luigi inquired.

"Yes. One," I said, keeping my expression neutral. "It's my understanding that Lo Duca was eager to return to Italy and didn't stick around for the birth of the kid. Diane estimates Lo Duca was in his early twenties at the time, which would make him about fifty years old now, give or take a year or two."

"Allora." Our host scratched his chin thoughtfully. "It is possible signor Lo Duca does not wish to be found. No matter. I find him."

Luigi picked up a glass carafe from the table and poured a liberal amount of the deep purple-red liquid into glasses. He handed each of us a glass, raised his, and said something that sounded like *chin-chin.*

"*Cin cin* is an Italian toast to good health." Ivayla winked at me.

Like the others, I raised my full glass of murky, blood-red liquid in salute. By the looks of it, I was certain Luigi had whipped the homemade stuff up in a dusty old cellar somewhere on his property, and likely, with prehistoric-aged equipment. The taste would be a fruitier variation of American moonshine—nasty grape-flavored turpentine. On theory alone, my gut protested. I inhaled; bucking up for the assault on my taste buds, and took a small sip.

It wasn't all that bad. Stilled by my surprise, I watched as a warm breeze ruffled Ivayla's hair and dress. If I'd been home, I probably would have been in my basement apartment on the computer. Instead, I was here in an Italian city sharing wine and olives on a warm sunny evening with a local man and a mature, beautiful woman. Heightened by the foreign sights, sounds, and smells, my senses were becoming acutely discriminating, picking up scents and flavors I hadn't known I was capable of. I felt a deep-found appreciation for it all, even the sharp taste of Luigi Delatorre's wine.

With a subtle tip of my glass, I smiled.

Thank you, Grams.

Luigi suddenly bucked forward, hitting and shaking the table, and cutting off my prayer to Grams. He muttered something under his breath and waved his hand as if he were shooing away a cat. He bucked again, but this time an animal's gravelly baying accompanied the motion.

A white goat appeared under the table and head-butted my leg.

"Oh, hey! Stop that!" I'd never been around farm animals and tried to push the animal away, but the crazy beast stood resolute, having none of it.

Luigi clucked his tongue and made frantic shooing motions. "*Va' via! Va' via!*"

Another goat, black with white spots, joined the white one in butting my knees. I pulled my legs away, but the goats came out from under the table and kept right on hammering at me. I pushed at one of their heads just as it munched on my pant leg. Its hair felt coarse and gritty under my hand.

"Get away! Va' via!" I shouted, but the obnoxious goats didn't seem to understand English *or* Italian.

Ivayla laughed so hard, she had to hold her sides and did nothing to help. Finally, Luigi stood, ran a few steps, hands waving, and chased them away. He came back sweating and panting.

"Are those yours?" I asked, dusting off my pants.

"Sì. Tilly and Maria. They are ... *amichevoli*." He looked to Ivayla for help.

"Friendly. The goats are friendly," she said, and added with a smirk, "Obviously they like you."

Delatorre invited us into his house where he showed us a room filled with surveillance equipment, cameras, and spy gadgets and a small laptop. He rushed to demonstrate how he could take a photograph and record us without even aiming the camera our way.

"It would be my great pleasure to assist you in finding your signor Lo Duca," he said.

"How much do you charge?" I asked.

"Let us not talk about money now. That is no concern," he said. "I will begin the process immediately."

"Great," I said. "How long do you think it will take?"

"It is difficult to say." Delatorre walked us to the door. "A few days, a few weeks, maybe more. I will phone you soon."

Hoping he could locate my father before I had to leave, I gave him my cell number and email address.

We shook hands and left the house. I slid my hands in my

pocket, satisfied I was well on my way to getting my grand-mother's request done.

Helmeted and back on the motorbike, Ivayla and I descended the sloped driveway. More relaxed with Ivayla's driving after the wine, I still held on, my arms locked around her waist.

Off to one side of the property, in a patch of shade created by an enormous tree, a large herd of goats grazed and frolicked. Two broke from the pack and started running towards the bike. One white, the other black and white.

"Oh, crap." I squeezed Ivayla's waist. "I think that's Tilly and Maria, again!"

No sooner had I said that all the other goats got to their feet, and the herd of them, roused and baying, started running after the bike.

"They've got friends, Ivayla. Drive faster. Get us out of here!" I shouted.

"Hold on!" Ivayla yelled. She leaned low to the handlebars, and with a twist of her wrist, we zoomed down the driveway onto the main road, leaving a cloud of dust behind us.

Over my shoulder, the goats had given up the chase and were returning to the shade amongst a cacophony of bleating.

"I just hired a private investigator-slash-goat farmer!" I shook my head, unable to believe how ridiculous that sounded.

The bike engine and traffic were too loud for Ivayla to respond, but I felt her body shaking with laughter. I wished I could hear it.

Chapter 7

IVAYLA PARKED HER VESPA IN the piazza a few doors down the street from Berto's hotel. The dinner crowd was out in force. The walking areas were packed. At a nearby restaurant, she settled at an outdoor table in the shade.

"Go pack. I will relax here, sipping an *aperitivo*." She shooed me off to check out of Berto's hotel.

I hadn't unpacked, so it didn't take much time before I approached the hotel desk, duffle bag and backpack slung over my shoulder.

"I'd like to check out." I handed Berto my new credit card.

Berto accepted the card, his face full of concern. "Signore, you are not happy here? Please, tell me how may I accommodate you?"

"I've been invited to stay with my new friends, Dr. Lo Duca and her family," I said.

"Villa Campanella?" Berto's eyes grew large. "That is the home of Paolo Lo Duca, the famous painter."

"Yes, I've met him and seen his paintings," I said.

"That is not all he is famous for." Berto lowered his voice and leaned in. "There is much talk of his nature. *Caldo*. Be careful, signor Rudack."

I quickly searched 'caldo' on my cell. The word meant hot. Berto believed Paolo had a hot temper. I thanked him for his concern but dismissed it. Paolo hadn't been overly friendly, but weren't most artists known for being temperamental? For actors, writers, and artists, expressing themselves was the nature of their work. The moody presence was all part of the allure. I wasn't afraid. In my brief time with Paolo, the atmospheric virtuosity that surrounded him fascinated me.

Then again, maybe it was regional pride. The people I'd met so far had a great deal of that. Whatever Berto's concern stemmed from, the beautiful woman waiting for me made this too good of an opportunity to pass up.

I left the hotel smiling but stopped several yards from the restaurant. A crowd of people had surrounded Ivayla's table. My heart dropped into my stomach, and I rushed forward, calling her name.

"What the hell's going on?" I pushed through the crowd until her deep mahogany eyes met mine. "Are you all right?"

"Yes, perfectly fine!" She waved a hand at the people. "They are not here for me. They are eager to meet the local hero who saved Franz's life." She stood, put a hand on my shoulder, and turned to face the group. "*Questo è l'uomo.* This is the man. This is Edward Rudack from America."

Cheers and happy greetings accompanied pats on my back. Local shopkeepers, men, and women, came forward to shake my hand. One offered me a sack of baked goods, another, a basket of beautifully ripened fruit. I got invited to visit shops and to dine at restaurants, *sulla casa*—on the house.

They stunned me to speechlessness, but I followed Ivayla's lead and accepted the shopkeepers' gratitude. It didn't stop until I'd shaken everyone's hand and the little bistro table was stock-piled with gifts.

Alone again, I sat down next to Ivayla, still buzzing from the experience.

"Wow, that was both awesome and crazy. People really like Franz," I said.

"My aunt owns that restaurant." She pointed to a darkened storefront down the block. "She is close to these people. They treat each other like family."

On Ivayla's suggestion, we loaded the Vespa's saddlebags with the presents, hung baskets from the handles, and strapped my duffle bag to the seat. I pushed the bike up the hill, Ivayla walking beside me.

The sky canopied the rising town with shifting colors like bleeding watercolor paints, ebbing from blue to orange and pink. Despite the late hour, the temperature was still warm. My shirt grew damp pushing the loaded bike up to the top of the winding, inclined road.

"When I woke up yesterday morning, I had no idea everything would turn around for the better. I had just hoped to talk to you again."

"In only a couple of days you saved a man's life, have been hailed as a local hero, and now," she said as she strolled, staying at my side, "we are friends."

Friends? Oh, that word on the lips of a beautiful woman. Nothing could crush a guy's spirit more.

Still, could a guy get any luckier? Well, he might, if it weren't for a gray-haired doctor dude with a southern accent.

È così, as Mario said. *It is what it is.*

"You know, an old man asked me if I knew his cousin in America." I chuckled softly. "He said his cousin lived in Florida. I almost laughed."

"I hope you didn't."

"I didn't. Only because I realized he was serious." The man wore one of those old-style caps and he'd clutched my hand, the skin around his eyes held deep time-thickened wrinkles. "The best part is, he wasn't the only one to ask me if I knew of an Italian friend or relative who lived in the United States. They think everyone in the States knows everyone else."

"It's a small community. Most of the older generation has never left the area. They've grown up with these people." She stopped at the crest of a hill to let me rest a moment. "Here, everyone knows everyone else. As you've seen from your greeting in the piazza, word gets around quickly. When good fortune comes to one of our neighbors, we all celebrate."

"I can't imagine what that's like. My family has lived in the same house for most of my life, and we hardly know our neighbors."

"I like to travel, meet new people, and explore things I've only read about. But I love coming home." She inhaled, and I watched as her eyes traveled the streets, her gaze trailing over the surroundings familiar to her. "I love it here."

Her shoulders rose, lending conviction to her declaration. I studied her profile outlined by the watercolor sky. Strong brow and nose, softened by prominent cheeks and full lips with an exaggerated bow as if painted, perhaps, by her artist father. Blue-black hair, the same color as Paolo's, falling in luxurious waves down her back.

I couldn't move. Didn't want to move. She might be off limits, but I could look. I wasn't dead. And damn, I wanted to keep looking. Her beauty stirred something deep inside me. I craved a pencil or a piece of charcoal and a sketchbook to capture the moment.

"We must get back for dinner." She began walking again, breaking the spell. "Papà will complain if we are late. Then, I must go to the medical center to attend work."

Mario laughed and clapped as Ivayla and I retold the story of the hero's greeting I received in the piazza. Even Paolo, who poured wine freely, seemed to take pleasure in it. No one appeared to think the celebration unusual. After Mario's dinner of roast pork and several vegetable dishes, Paolo showed off his culinary skills by whipping up dessert using some gifted fresh pears and red wine. He topped the poached fruit with creamy vanilla mascarpone cheese. I'd never had a more delicious home-cooked meal.

Ivayla left the table to freshen up before leaving for work. Mario and Paolo invited me to join them on the veranda for an after-dinner espresso. I was getting used to the coffee's sharp, bitter taste, and I looked forward to it.

"What is your birth sign?" Mario pulled out a computer tablet. Modern technology appeared out of place among the old-world architecture surrounding us.

Paolo sat back in a chair, crossed his legs, and opened a newspaper.

"I was born on May 25." I leaned over to peek at the screen he was looking at, some astrological site. "I think I'm a Gemini."

"Gemelli, duality, and indecisiveness," Mario recited.

Not the most flattering traits.

"Can't say I pay much attention to zodiac stuff." I shrugged it off.

Mario paid me no mind and continued.

"Brilliant, gregarious, and with a tendency to be serious."

"Allora." I leaned back in my chair, trying out the newly learned pause word. "I'll only believe it if it says strikingly handsome."

From behind the newspaper came a little snort of laughter, so quiet I might have missed it had I not been paying attention.

"Allora, let me read you this important information." Mario held up a finger; his eyes lit up. "Matches for Gemelli are *Ariete, Leone, Bilancia, e Acquario.*" Aries, Leo, Libra, and Aquarius. "I know the exact person to match you!"

"Mario, why you bother him with nonsense?" The newsprint pages crinkled as Paolo roughly folded them in half.

Mario opened his mouth to reply but was cut short when Ivayla dashed in to say goodbye. She leaned down to kiss each of her fathers' cheeks. Her scent whorled in, a presence of its own, tickling the back of my throat.

"Tomorrow, I will need to sleep in a bit, but Papà and Babbo will help you if you need anything." She bowed and gave both my cheeks a quick kiss, too, flooding my limbs with warmth.

I rose from the table and stood at the balcony railing to watch Ivayla zip off on her yellow scooter.

"*Bella noche.* Look at the beautiful view." Mario walked up beside me. "Have you ever seen anything so lovely?"

"Never," I said, only tearing my eyes from the road once Ivayla disappeared from sight. "I can see why people fall in love with this place."

"Come," Mario said, motioning toward the house. "We get you settled in your room, yes?"

I nodded and followed him. Paolo had disappeared. I suspected to his art studio somewhere on the lower level at the back of the house.

The bedrooms, except for the master suite, were on the third floor, accessible from a long open corridor that overlooked the water. Mario pushed open one of three louvered doors and motioned me into the spacious room with a large window that faced the south. Below, a meticulously tended vegetable garden spanned the whole side of the property. Neat, uniform rows of healthy plants sprouted from rich black soil.

I brushed my teeth in the shared bathroom next to my room. After changing, I climbed onto the room's large bed and sprawled across the fluffy white blanket, certain I would sleep well the rest of my nights in Positano. And I was tired. Not the kind of tired I had been those first few days after I arrived, but the kind you felt after putting effort into something worthwhile.

I checked my cell phone for reception and after seeing it had connected to the villa's Wi-Fi, I messaged Claudia.

Me: Hey! Crazy great day. Townspeople treat me like a hero for saving Franz (heart attack guy). Got invited to stay at Ivayla's house (hot doctor). It's a villa.

Claudia: Wow... but you don't know them. Is it safe?

She was such a mom, though not anything like my mom. Thank God.

Me: Constant threat of getting hit by flying Italian hands when they get talking. Willing to risk it. Reminds me a lot of you!

Claudia: haha

Me: Ivayla has 2 very chill dads, a gay couple. One father is Paolo Lo Duca, a famous painter here. If he kills me, it'll make the news. I'll be dead, but famous.

Claudia: Not remotely funny.

Me: Everybody knows everybody. Feel very safe. Wish you could meet them. Especially Ivayla. She's amazing.

Claudia: Sounds like you're really enjoying Italy. I knew you would! Any leads on Giovanni?

Me: Hired a local to help me find him. A goat farmer.

Claudia: That sounds helpful... Not.

Me: lol. He's eager.

Claudia: Wish you luck! Wish me luck too. I have an OB/GYN check-up this morning. This kid has got to come out soon! I'm a house. xxx

Me: Luck.

I leaned over the side of the bed and rummaged through my backpack until I found Mary nestled in a sweatshirt, along with my grandmother's letter. I set Mary on the bedside night table atop the letter.

"I didn't want to come, but I'm here," I whispered, staring through the darkness, sure Grams could hear me. "Everyone is so ... so Italian, but I kind of like it. I met this terrific girl, a woman really, and a Lo Duca, if you can believe it. You'd like Ivayla."

I thought about my grandmother, like Claudia, fretting about me staying with people I didn't know.

"I trust them," I said. Though I couldn't say exactly why, somewhere deep inside, I knew I could.

The light of the moon peeked in between the slats of the door, softly illuminating the room. The whisper of the surf carried on the breeze. Up this high, it surprised me to hear it, like it was special-ordered to serenade me to sleep. I closed my eyes and thought about the list of my zodiac matches that Mario had read off earlier: Aries, Leo, Libra, and Aquarius. Was Ivayla one of those signs? Not that it meant anything, even if she was.

Ivayla put me in the friend zone. As disappointed as I was by those bumper guards placed around her, I would respect them.

Chapter 8

THE MORNING SUN WASHED OVER my face. The simple white cotton curtain at the window danced with the gentle morning wind. I lay still, eyes closed, and tried to pick out the earthy scents that the breeze carried in. There were ripening fruit trees and colorful blooms of which I knew none of the names.

Just as I suspected, the bed had been comfortable, and fighting off the last dregs of travel fatigue, I was hesitant to get up. The aroma of coffee and bacon wafting upstairs from the kitchen, combined with my grumbling stomach, enticed me to peel myself from the sheets.

My foot hit something solid at the end of the bed. The family cat stared at me with a disdainful expression. I'd disturbed his sleep.

"*Scusami*, Romeo." I reached down to scratch him behind his ears, assuming his purr indicated I was forgiven.

I hopped into the shower. Minutes later, washed and dressed, I stood on the veranda outside my bedroom door. As the villa went up, the levels recessed and overlooked the lower tiers of the house. Below the bedroom level, the outdoor space laid out like a spa retreat: a lap pool, giant planters, exploding with colorful flowers and several groupings of furniture with jewel tone-colored cushions. Every space had a function. Nothing was random.

I envied Ivayla growing up in this paradise. In my childhood home, my mother spent very little time fussing to make the house look nice. Dinner was often nothing more than boxed mac and cheese, a favorite of both Ray and me. I was sure a lack of money, time, and sheer exhaustion had a lot to do with it. Since she'd moved in with Mike, our mother kept a clean house, spent time in the garden, and read books for enjoyment. She still didn't cook, but free of Ray and me, it was like she became another person. Now, knowing she'd lied to me all these years about my father, I felt betrayed, like I hardly knew her.

I walked the length of the terrace and went down a flight of stairs. Ivayla was nowhere in sight, but I found Papà Mario sitting in the kitchen reading something on his iPad, a pair of lime green reading glasses perched on his nose.

"Buongiorno, my young American friend." Mario took the glasses off and stood. His sunny yellow shirt mirrored his gregarious disposition. "Paolo still sleeps, and Ivayla has only now gone to bed. Just you and I, *amico*."

The cappuccino maker hummed, glasses, and dishware clinked. Mario set a plate of vibrant red strawberries and a frothy cappuccino before me.

I picked up a strawberry, big enough that it would take two bites to eat, and bit into it. Juice ran down my chin. I wiped my mouth with the back of my hand, rolling my eyes heavenward.

"Delicious," I said.

"Do like this." Mario kissed his fingertips and said, "*delizioso.*"

"*Delizioso,*" I repeated, puckering my lips and making a smooching sound, the same as him.

"*Molto bene,* Edoardo. You like I help you with words?"

"How about you help me with my Italian, and I'll help you with your English?"

"*Eccellente.*" Mario looking pleased and then added, "Luigi has called. For you, he has information. When you ready, I take you to his business place in town."

Luigi had an official office in town? My hope ratcheted up. Maybe the goat farmer *was* the real deal.

We zipped into town in Mario's little, bright orange Fiat. Just like his daughter, he drove like a daredevil, fast and fearlessly. I held the overhead strap, maintaining a death grip on it the entire ride.

We parked and walked down a street heavy with foot traffic. Overhead, clean laundry flapped in the breeze as it hung from lines that crisscrossed between buildings. Except for the modern clothes and hairstyles, it seemed like the passage of time had stalled there. Women hung out windows calling to children running in the street below. Storeowners greeted shoppers and invited them to taste samples.

Mario stopped several times to purchase fresh cheese and meats, and to say hello to people he knew. The conversations were fast and in Italian. I couldn't follow them. When he motioned to me, I'd smile and say, "*buongiorno.*" With repeated practice, the greeting rolled off my tongue and sounded more authentic.

Each time Mario stopped, I scanned the buildings, looking for Luigi's office. There were no banks, business offices, or anything like that. The stores were mostly food shops with displays of fresh vegetables and fruit in every color of the rainbow, cages stacked with live chickens and an assortment of dried sausages strung across counters. Aromas from the food filled the air. If Luigi's office was here, it was well hidden. Unsuspecting. A perfect cover.

A half an hour and several purchases later, I followed Mario into a bakery. It must have been an old business because the name on the storefront, whitewashed, was unreadable. A bell clanged, announcing our arrival. I sighed as the unplanned shopping spree continued. I wanted to hear what Delatorre had to say. Despite my frustration, the glass cases full of mouth-watering sugary confections drew my eyes.

"Caio, Anna!" Mario sang, leaning over the counter to kiss the dark-haired woman behind it.

While they conversed in Italian, I considered the rows of pastries and wondered what Ivayla might like. I didn't have to ask as Mario pointed to a lobster tail-shaped pastry.

"*Sfogliatelle*, Ivayla's favorite." Mario winked at me.

We bought half a dozen to bring home.

"We share one now, yes?" He motioned to the white bag.

Dying to try it, I dug into the sack and drew one out. The wax paper protecting it crinkled as I peeled it away. The air filled with the heady scent of the fresh pastry and its sweet ricotta filling mixture. I tore the crispy-layered pastry in two and handed half to Mario. We munched, sighing with each bite.

"That was so good," I said.

"My friends, welcome!" Luigi Delatorre appeared from a doorway behind the counter, dressed completely in white save for his shiny, black, creaky shoes. He wiped his floured hands on his apron and clasped Mario's hand, then mine.

"Signor Delatorre," I said, startled. "I didn't realize when Mario brought me in here that you're the baker."

"This is Luigi's store!" Mario lifted his arms and gestured to the space. "The Delatorre Family Bakery has been here for generations!"

"You must try my biscotti! It is best anywhere. Anna, biscotti *per i nostri amici*. Get our friends some cookies," Luigi said to the woman working the counter, and then rested a hand on my shoulder. "My office is in the back. Come. I have *informazioni*."

His office, though, appeared to be just a perfunctory place to do bakery paperwork. At first glance, the most prominent items were two framed pictures. The larger of them, a movie poster teasing the circa 1980s James Bond flick, *A View to a Kill*. The other, an oil painting of the Annunciation of the Virgin Mary in a gilded frame. Everything in the office, including the desk and the phone, looked to be from some bygone era. The only modern thing in the compact space was a miniature laptop.

Not accessories that inspired confidence.

Luigi tapped on the computer's itty-bitty keyboard.

"I have a friend at *Ufficio dello Stato Civile*, the Office of Vital Records. The office keeps track of births and deaths. Because you did not know Giovanni Lo Duca's actual age, I used a range of fifteen years." He beckoned me closer, to look at the compilation of names and dates on the screen. "I narrow list down to men who apply for travel visas in the 1990s. They come from all over Italy, and I know not where they travel, so you see I must sort through many documents."

He pressed a button on the keyboard. Behind us, a printer camouflaged under a pile of folded aprons spat out a page of written text.

"I give you a small list to work on, eh? These men are local, but no longer living." Luigi crossed himself and handed the printout to me. "It is a small list, so only a small chance your relative is one of them. You work on that, so I can work on a much longer list of living men. *Capisci?*"

I wiped my hands on my jeans and took the list from Luigi. There were five names on the list, all men. All named Giovanni Lo Duca. All deceased.

I stared at it and swallowed hard. "Thank you."

We left Delatorre's Bakery and walked back to Mario's car. I didn't talk.

"This shakes you." Mario patted my back. "You no consider your Giovanni gone?"

"No, I hadn't." The words stuck in my throat. I'd told everyone this man was a distant, obscure relative. My responses needed to stay in line with my story. I kept my silence until I could control my voice. "My family only found out about him recently. They'd be sorry to hear he's dead."

It was nearing the dinner hour when Ivayla came into the kitchen, her eyes unfocused and narrowed with the remnants of sleep, but smiling. From the counter where I sliced vegetables, tomatoes, peppers, and zucchini for Mario's dishes, I watched her stretch and yawn. Mario greeted her with a whispered endearment and a kiss on the top of her head.

"Are you helping cook dinner, Edward?" In a slow, lazy state, she bumped up against me and stayed there. Her sleep-warmed skin seared through the fabric of my shirt. It felt reassuring and protective, and I was unprepared for the way my body warmed in response. Our eyes met, and a kaleidoscope of butterflies took flight in my stomach. Her sleepy grin nearly buckled my knees.

"I... I... Yes." I gave in to simplicity. I reached behind me for the bakery bag and held it open for her. "While we were out, Mario and I picked these up. "

Ivayla peeked inside and smiled like a Cheshire cat.

"Sfogliatelle! I see Papà is teaching you well. To me, sfogli-atelle is more precious than gold." She took one out and bit into it. Her eyes rolled upward. "*Delizioso!*"

I liked that a simple pastry could bring her this kind of joy. It had me wondering what else I could do to bring that look of satisfaction to her face.

"Grazie, Papà. Grazie, Edward." She kissed his cheek, and then mine, again. "Now tell me, what did our signor Delatorre have to say?"

I pulled the printout from my back pocket, unfolded it, and handed it to her. She took the paper, but her eyes didn't leave my face. I returned to my cutting work.

"What happened? Tell me." Her strong fingers captured my chin and turned my face toward her.

She read me like a book. I'd never been good at hiding my emotions.

"The goat farmer, slash baker, slash private eye said Giovanni Lo Duca might be dead."

"Oh." Ivayla released me and sank, crossed legged, into a nearby chair to read the list. "Locating the families would be the next best thing, no?"

"I suppose so." I shrugged with little conviction.

"There is no supposing." She bounded to her feet, took my knife, and set it down. "Let's go. We have time before dinner."

"Go where?"

"To visit these families." She waved Delatorre's printout over her head.

"We're just going to waltz up to these people and ask if their dead Giovanni went to New York in 1990?"

"Yes, but without the waltz. Death is sensitive. I know how to speak with them to get your answers," she said.

My father was dead, or he wasn't. One way or the other, I needed to know. I trusted Ivayla to get the job done. I washed my hands and followed her out.

We traveled a few miles, and Ivayla parked her Vespa next to a row of connected houses. She rang a doorbell and spoke with a woman not much older than us. The two of them conversed in Italian, and I could only pick up a word here and there. Ivayla didn't attempt to include me, and she came away shaking her head.

"This family's Giovanni Lo Duca applied for a visa but never left Positano," she said. "They gave me some information about another family in Anacapri."

In just less than two hours, we visited all five addresses on the list and came away able to cross off every name on Delatorre's Dead Man list.

"Your relative is not on this list. I hope that brings you some comfort." Ivayla handed me the spare helmet.

"It doesn't mean he isn't dead. He's just not on *that* list." I pulled on my helmet, trying hard to maintain a neutral expression.

"This is true." She reached up to adjust my chin strap, her touch gentle as her eyes briefly held mine. "No matter what, we will find him."

Her devotion to my search stirred me up. But those mocha eyes kept tapping into me. I sensed she knew locating Lo Duca meant more to me than I was letting on. I straddled the motorbike behind her and wrapped my arms around her waist. The truth welled in my chest, begging to be told. The moped's hornet-buzz engine silenced me. The opportunity for me to talk slipped away as the Vespa rolled forward. I vowed I would tell her the truth about my connection to Giovanni Lo Duca soon, the next quiet moment we had alone.

The aroma of dinner filled the villa upon our return.

"Mario is a great cook." My mouth salivated as I climbed the entry stairs behind Ivayla, headed for the kitchen.

"Yes, he enjoys feeding everyone. I love to eat, but I have to be careful. I am getting fat." Ivayla grabbed her rounded hips to prove her point.

My eyes wandered a bit, but I didn't see a square inch that didn't look appealing.

"Ciao!" Ivayla's called out.

From the kitchen came an enthusiastic response, several glee club-like hellos. Ivayla ran ahead to greet them, kissing Mario and a middle-aged man and woman sitting with him. The woman, fashionably slim, wore a pair of brown cat-like retro-framed eyeglasses. The guy, the tall outdoorsman kind, had the pale tan of a northern European.

"This is our Edoardo." Mario clapped his hands on my shoulders. "From America."

"You are the one who save our Franz, yes?" The woman adjusted the peach-colored scarf around her neck. Under her eyeglasses, the corner of her brown eyes had wrinkles, the kind that came from smiling often.

"The one and only," I said.

Before I knew what was happening, she grabbed me into a tight hug and planted kisses on both sides of my face.

"Grazie! Thank you! I am most pleased to see you." She put a hand to her chest. "I am Mercedes, Mario's sister."

Unlike the way we'd say the German car in the states, she pronounced her name with a hard 'c', like the 'ch' in cheddar, giving it an Italian flavor. I could see the family resemblance, though her English was better than her brother's. She reached for the tall, square-headed man behind her and pulled him forward.

"This is my handsome German lover, Otto," she said, patting his chest with affection. "It is his father who you saved."

"I am Otto Schmidt. I am grateful for your actions to save my father." The man, a younger, healthier version of his father, clasped my hand in his enormous ones. His proper English wrapped in a thick, guttural German enunciation.

"It was nothing, really," I said, embarrassed by the continued praise. "How is he?"

"His health continues to improve," Otto said and gave my hand a final shake before releasing it.

The aunt, with her deep olive skin and an air of frivolity, and him with his stern poise and pale skin, made them an odd pair. I instantly liked them both.

Conversation halted as Paolo came into the room.

"Ciao, Paolo!" Mercedes stepped forward, greeting him with the customary kiss to each side of the face. Otto and he shook hands, but by the scowl on his face, it was easy to see Paolo's disinterest in the company.

"*Ancora? Non mi dire!*" he said.

"Babbo," Ivayla said, handing out plates and utensils. "While Edward is with us, it is excellent practice for us to use our English."

The great artist spared me a look. "Why has no one opened wine yet?"

Unruffled by her artist father's temper, Ivayla moved past me to pull a bottle of wine from the kitchen's state-of-the-art wine fridge. With swift adeptness, she released the cork and poured several glasses of red wine.

"Grazie, *cucciola mia.*" Paolo accepted a glass and a kiss on the cheek from his daughter and appeared calmer.

"My pet. An endearment," Ivayla whispered over her shoulder to me with a wink.

Everyone took a seat at the large dining room table. Each seat had a place setting with nice dishes and a cloth napkin. A vase of creamy white flowers drew the eye to the center of the table, and was surrounded by an assortment of fresh, hearty pieces of bread and dipping oils. Paolo claimed one head of the table, and Mario, the other. I sat next to Ivayla, inhaling the heavenly aroma of the food as I helped her finish handing out the glasses of wine.

"Risotto." Mario held out his hand for our plates. We passed them to him, and he returned them with a heaping portion of creamy rice.

"So Edoardo." Mercedes sat with Otto facing Ivayla and me from across the table. "Do you like men or women? Or both?"

I choked on my wine.

"So rude a question," Ivayla said.

"It is not a test, dear Edoardo." Mercedes laughed, shook out her napkin and laid it over her lap, untroubled by her niece's comment.

"I have no issues with same-sex couples, but I'm very much heterosexual," I answered.

Her gaze, made larger and more intense by the prescription lenses of her glasses, stayed glued on me.

"You have a girl, someone special back in the States?"

"Not right now." I shrugged.

Mercedes and Mario exchanged looks.

"Allora. You must have noticed our Ivayla is *bella donna*." She gestured to Ivayla with a sweeping hand and smiled. "Next time she gets up, notice those sturdy child-bearing hips."

"Oh, oh!" Ivayla threw her napkin at her aunt and laughed. "You are truly terrible."

"We try to marry her off, but she fight us," Mario said with a shrug. "We love bambinos. The clock ticks. This year, she turns thirty!"

Humor gone, Ivayla uttered something sharp in Italian. As effective as a slap, Mario and Mercedes fell silent. I made a mental note not to mention marriage or children to Ivayla. And definitely not her age.

"Mercedes and Otto, I tell them you look for Giovanni Lo Duca." Mario wisely chose another topic. "Ivayla and Edoardo take a list and go visit houses."

"We did not find him." Ivayla brushed a warm hand over my forearm. "We will keep looking until we do. Giovanni Lo Duca was dear to one of Edward's relatives—a woman who was intimate with signor Lo Duca."

That seemed to get everyone's attention, except for Paolo, who continued to drink his wine.

"Sex and love, they make all stories more interesting." Mercedes served Otto a large portion of the bruschetta antipasto, roasted garlic and a mixture of the olives and tomatoes, before adding anything to her own plate. "What you say, Edoardo, is this a love story?"

I shoved a forkful of food in my mouth. The conversation had taken a bumpy turn. I didn't think the disaster that called herself my mother had been in love with Giovanni. Before Mike, she'd tripped from one terrible relationship to the next. Each one came with its fair share of drama, but none of them looked anything like love. Not to my eyes. But I sure as hell wasn't about to share any of that.

"You and you brother, always such the romantics, Mercedes." Paolo waved a hand. "Who say love?"

"To want to find him after all these years? That sounds like love." Ivayla refilled my wine glass. "Who is this woman? Your aunt?"

Five sets of eyes focused on me. I writhed in my seat, my face hot.

"*Uffa!*" Paolo shot to his feet. The table trembled under his hammering fists. All heads turned his way. "We no discuss this while we eat!"

Unfazed, everyone else kept eating, and Paolo sat back down. They must have been used to such outbursts—but me? Not so much. I kept my gaze lowered, both grateful for the intervention, but also thinking I should apologize. Neither seemed entirely appropriate. I upended my glass instead. Under the table, Ivayla patted my thigh.

Mario served the next course of food and for several minutes, we all focused on the food being passed around. Paolo generously refilled our wine glasses. Everyone served, Mercedes' attention shifted to her niece.

"Allora. How is your friend, Ralph, Ivayla?"

"He is well. Grazie," she answered.

"I don't know how you can date him, Ivayla." The words left my mouth before I could think them through. Again all eyes turned to me, and I knew I needed to explain the comment. "You're gorgeous, and in case you haven't noticed, that dude's just old."

Mario and Mercedes let out full belly laughs. Otto raised his wine glass in my direction. Paolo snorted, his mouth curled in a conspiratorial smile as he signaled for me to pass him my wine glass, and topped it off.

"Careful, Edward from New York." Ivayla's thick eyebrows sloped inward as she pinned me with a darkened stare. "My opinion of you can change back to *ragazzo bello ma maleducato*."

Rude pretty boy.

"Rude, no. Truthful, yes!" Otto's hands cut through the air, adding emphasis.

"Mamma mia, Mario. You see, Vay's eyes, they are excellent!" Mercedes declared at an eardrum-busting volume.

Ivayla tilted her head. "What do you mean by this, *Zia* Mercedes?"

"When we meet your Ralph, we think, poor *ragazza*, her eyesight *non e buona*. Not good. But, your new friend, Edoardo, he *is* handsome. Robust and…" Mercedes winked at me. "Virile."

I nearly spit out my wine.

Mario put an arm around my shoulders. "Edoardo, you see, Dr. Monroe like our beautiful Ivayla, but he *divorzio*. He no marry again. No marry, no bambinos."

"Papà, you and Babbo raised me to be proud, to make my own decisions." Ivayla put her hand over Mario's. "I am focusing on my career. Ralph fits my life right now."

"*Dio, che noia!* He is boring. *And American!*" Paolo's frowning expression bared his displeasure.

I jerked back as if he'd slapped me.

"*Basta!* No more." Ivayla put her hands on the table, and leaning forward, gave everyone a stern look. At that moment, a mirror image of Paolo. "Dr. Monroe is a brilliant doctor. How unkind you all are to speak about him so!"

The table erupted; word bombs in Italian exploded, hands jabbed the air like swords. Across the table, Otto glanced at me, and with a shrug, continued to eat. He and I were the only two people at the table still in our seats.

I didn't know enough of their language to decipher the argument, but although I felt a tick of jealousy at the way Ivayla came to Monroe's defense, I watched on, fascinated.

Then, just as swiftly as it started, it stopped. Everyone resumed their seats, remarkably quiet. The silence, though, lasted only a moment before Mercedes and Ivayla giggled, and the rest of us joined in.

The night continued with Paolo opening two more bottles of wine and Mario bringing more food to the table. I didn't understand Paolo's negative impression of Americans. For a moment, I empathized with Ivayla's boyfriend. Whether we were nice or Ivayla liked us didn't appear to matter to Paolo. Our nationality put us behind the eight ball with him. I couldn't change where I'd been born any more than I could change the brown color of my eyes.

Even as I drank and laughed, it bothered me. Usually, people liked me. And, I liked that people liked me. I went out of my way to make it so. It was no different with the great Paolo Lo Duca.

Near midnight, I stood up and said goodnight to everyone. Ivayla had already left the table to get ready for work. With a belly full from Mario's delectable cooking and many, many glasses of Paolo's wine, my heart was happy but my feet, lazy.

Ahead, in the open corridor leading to the bedrooms, Ivayla came out from her room a few doors down, dressed for work. She stopped on the terrace overlooking the moonlit gardens below. I fumbled in my pocket for my cell, wanting to take a picture, a memory to hold, to help me remember Positano and this beautiful woman after I went back home.

"Don't move," I said, and she turned her face toward me. I snapped a few shots and slid the cell into my pocket. As I drew closer to her, I started humming a tune that sprung into my head from some obscure place in my memory.

"Ivayla, I just met a girl named Ivayla." I looped an arm around one of the white portico columns and arched toward her. My mind, arrested by the wine, let the silly song flow unchecked from my lips. "And she thinks I'm pretty, oh so pretty."

"I like your song. Is it well known in the States?"

"It's from *West Side Story*. I suppose you've never seen it," I said, and she shook her head. "You come back to the States, Ivayla, and I will find a performance, wherever it's playing, and take you to see it."

She rested her head against the column, smiling at me with her eyes. "You are sweet. And perhaps *alticcio*, a little tipsy, from the wine?"

"If I am, it's the Duke's fault. He kept refilling my glass," I said. "Strange because I don't think he likes me, and I think because I'm American."

"I apologize for that. That is Babbo's way. My fathers do not approve of Dr. Monroe. It is this way since they first met him. But you," Ivayla paused and brushed a wayward strand of hair from my forehead. "You, they like."

The gesture with the words felt intimate, and hoping for more, I closed my eyes and leaned into the touch.

"Buonanotte, pretty boy," she whispered close to my ear.

Her breath caressed my cheek and made my skin tingle. The air swirled with her scent and heightened my awareness of her. But when I opened my eyes, she was moving through the darkened corridor, away from me.

Chapter 9

I CAME DOWN THE NEXT MORNING, later than the day before, and looked down at the street level for Ivayla's Vespa. It wasn't there. She hadn't returned home from work yet. In the kitchen, I could hear Mario talking on the phone, his voice so loud the conversation carried throughout the house.

After last night's overindulgence, the thought of food made my stomach turn. Instead, I bypassed the main floor and descended another two flights of steps to the bottom level. A door on the side of the villa led out to the vegetable garden below my bedroom window. Passing through a row of neatly trimmed hedges, I found myself in the garden. Soaking up the early morning sun was row upon ordered row of tomatoes, cucumbers, long green beans, crisp-leafed lettuces, an assortment of shapes and different colored pepper varieties. Way more vegetables than I was familiar with. I stopped to admire the odd-shaped squashes growing from vines that climbed teepee-like wooden structures. Deeper into the garden, I heard a faint whistling. I followed it until I came across a wooden ladder leaning against the trunk of a squat tree. Paolo stood balanced halfway up the ladder, his torso hidden by the thick plume of giant green leaves. He worked steadily, his sure hands pulling fruit from one of several trees.

I stood next to the ladder and looked up. "Good morning."

He grunted an unintelligible reply and continued working.

"What kind of tree is this?"

"Fig," came the clipped answer.

I didn't go around checking out other guys, but I could acknowledge when I saw a guy whose looks were above average. I recognized Paolo as such a man. He had a wiry, lean, but sturdy build. The bright mahogany color of his eyes and cap of wavy blue-black hair were the same as the ones that first captured my notice of Ivayla. I hadn't asked her about her birth mother; it hadn't felt appropriate, our acquaintance so new, but she favored Paolo's striking visual genetics. She seemed to have his quiet confidence, and from the spike of anger I'd witnessed last night, perhaps his caldo temper as well. Whatever the case was with her mother, a past lover or a surrogate, if I had to guess whose DNA Ivayla carried, Paolo or Mario's, I'd bet it was Paolo's. A safe assumption since she also carried his name.

The artist came down the ladder, the pockets of his apron filled with plump, odd-looking purple fruit. "These figs are perfectly ripe."

He handed one to me. It was firm and warm in my hand. Despite his outburst last night, today he appeared okay with my presence.

"I've never eaten a fig," I said.

"No? You can eat that one, but they are delicious warm with goat cheese, walnuts, and a bit of prosciutto." I could practically taste the food from his description. With a rare smile, he kissed his fingertips. "Wait until you taste them tonight."

The hand gestures were typical of every characterization of an Italian I'd had ever known. However, now it felt less comical. It was a sign of exuberance, a zest for life.

"I can't eat right now. I'll wait until tonight." I gave the fig back to him and rubbed my temples. "Do you have aspirin or some kind of pain reliever?"

"You no feel well?"

"I don't, no. You must have a cast-iron stomach to be up and alert the morning after eating so late and drinking so much wine," I said.

"Espresso," he said. "It help you digest. Come, I make you a cup in my studio, and you see how much better you feel."

I was unsure about the espresso but was charged by the invitation to see the epicenter of his creativity.

He brought me around the back of the property to a freestanding cottage. A mass of flowering vines crisscrossed the stone walls;

thick with the same purple-pink blooms I'd seen throughout the town. Their sweet scent perfumed the doorstep.

"What kind of flowers are those?" I asked.

"Bougainvillea," Paolo said. "A favorite."

The door creaked when he pushed it open, revealing one large room, illuminated by sunlight streaming through the windows. Over the threshold, the familiar smell of paint and varnish greeted us. Streaks, smears, and dots of dried paint dirtied the earth-colored tiled floor. Cobwebs, glinting in the morning sun, traversed the corners of the room. The place was dusty, like what you'd expect of a brilliant mind too busy to clean. Stacks of tall canvases, some taller than me, leaned up against the walls. A solitary canvas leaned against the center of the back wall, jars of brushes, and tubes of paint littered the floor next to it.

A chill ran up my spine. I was standing in Il Duco's painting studio. How many people got to say that?

Paolo crossed the room to an area with a counter and sink that must have served as a kitchen at one time in the cottage's history. He put the figs in a basket and set to work, making coffee in the tiniest pot I'd ever seen.

"May I?" I put my hand on the closest stack of canvases.

"Sì." He waved a hand of consent and turned away to start our coffee.

The steady buzz of the bean grinder filled the studio as I reverently flipped through the canvases. Each painting was a landscape, each colorful and detailed in Paolo's distinct style. The last one in the stack made me pause: a trellised walkway with bright flowers. It was the same walkway I'd passed through on my way down to the water my second day in Positano. I gawked in wonder as I looked around the studio. While I admired the artwork, seeing the painted treasures and the rough-hewn studio of a master depressed me.

Paolo had the life I had dreamed of as a kid. That life had never been a reality for me, and because of that, I'd given it up. I didn't have any reminders at home. I kept busy and never thought about it. Here, it smacked me in the face.

I righted the canvases and stepped back. So much scenery, but no people. I had enjoyed drawing action characters, fighting, but then I remembered Ivayla last night on the balcony and framed that image in my head.

She would be more interesting to paint than muscled superheroes.

"Have you ever painted anything besides local landscapes, like people?" I asked.

"Sì, when I younger man." He pointed to a paint-speckled table tucked in the corner where an old leather art portfolio lay.

I moved to the table and opened the book; the leather binder crackled and winced with age. Laminated pages filled the book, each holding a sketch, some in watercolor, some charcoal, and some simple pencil renderings. I leaned in to smell the pages. They didn't smell anything like my art books back home. I detected faint traces of the aged mediums, an actual artist's journal.

The central theme was people on vacation or at play. The Eiffel Tower providing the backdrop for a couple having coffee, a crowd of people watching fireworks in a darkened sky, a couple riding bikes along a lakeshore, reminiscent of home. I stopped at one in particular, a lone woman reading under a tree. Paolo had painted the woman with her eyes raised as if she were looking at him. Maybe Ivayla's mother?

"Here, drink." He came up behind me and pushed a tiny cup of steaming espresso into my hand. I had to abandon the book.

We stood side by side, drinking the coffee while looking at his painting in progress.

"I start painting young. People, they are difficult. I switch to scenes of Toscana," he said.

"I haven't seen your Tuscan landscapes, only the ones of Positano."

"I paint Toscana no more."

"Why?" I asked and took a sip of the espresso.

"Better to bury the past." He kept his eyes on his painting in progress. I opened my mouth to question him, but then he asked, "You paint?"

"I used to." I scrolled through my cell and showed him the

images I'd taken of walls of my old bedroom of Conan, Spider-man, and the Mario brothers. "Kid stuff I did a long time ago. I have painted nothing since."

"Why this is?"

I slipped my cell into my pocket, feeling the weight of his attention.

"I lost interest." I shrugged. "Unless you're famous like you, there's no money in art."

"True expression comes from love. No money."

"That may be true but pursuing art as a career isn't realistic for the average person." Several years ago, I'd confronted Tom Rudack, the man I'd known as my father. Our meeting reshaped my priorities. "It wasn't realistic for me."

Paolo took my empty cup and walked away. Behind me, a cabinet creaked, and a drawer slammed shut. I stood trying to think of something to say, afraid I'd offended him until he pushed a sketchbook and pencils at me. "While here, you draw."

"Grazie." I accepted the gifts, overwhelmed by the sudden kindness. Maybe Ivayla was right last night when she'd told me her father's comments about my nationality weren't personal.

"Perhaps to pay you back, I can clean up your studio," I said. "I've gotten a lot of practice cleaning up after the guys on the construction site."

"You no need to pay back." He patted my shoulder and smiled at me. It was the best feeling, a sign that we were becoming friends.

"I know what I want to draw first—Ivayla," I mused aloud, from one artist to another. "She's got great lines."

I regretted the comment as soon as it left my mouth.

His hand on my shoulder twitched. "You no touch my daughter."

My face heated. "Signor Lo Duca. I would never disrespect Ivayla or you—"

"My daughter is *molto bella*, but I no have her carry on with American." He shook a finger. "No!"

His reaction deflated me, especially since the morning had started off so well. No matter what I might try to say now, Paolo would not listen. I took my gifted art supplies and skulked out of his studio, my head hung low. Maybe I wouldn't have minded so much if I *were* the American carrying on with his daughter. At least it'd be worth it. But no, Paolo just lumped me into a heap of disdain he had of Americans.

One step forward, two steps back.

I went back to the house thinking I needed to find out what the old doctor had done. And then avoid doing it. Whatever it was, he was ruining it for all of us *Americani*.

After breakfast with Mario, I sat down to Google-search the family in Anacapri, a city at the highest elevation on the island of Capri. I mapped out directions and planned my trip via bus and ferry.

Poolside, I sat reading *House of Medici*, fascinated by the wealthy banking family, a dynasty that shaped the early history of Florence and its art. I read uninterrupted until Ivayla came home. Her presence pulled my attention from the book like a magnet. She came to the foot of my lounge chair, and I had to use my hand to shield my eyes from the sun to look up at her.

"I stopped at the stables to take Alba for a short ride. But then, I hurried home because it is a good day for a road trip," she said, her cheeks still ruddy from her motorbike ride. "I'll take you to see Sorrento—"

"Or maybe we could go to Capri to find that Lo Duca family? The one we learned about yesterday?" I showed her the plans I'd worked out for the bus and ferry.

"Molto bene. We will take the high-speed ferry to Capri. I will show you around the island. On the way back, we will stop in Sorrento to walk Piazza Tasso and sample local limoncello."

"Ivayla, you don't have to keep going on these wild goose chases with me." I leaned forward and brushed her hand with my fingertips. "You worked all night. You should stay at home and relax. I'm planning to go tomorrow."

"Don't worry about me, Edward. I don't do anything I don't want to." She caught my hand and tugged my arm. "We go now. I can take a siesta on the ferry."

Her infectious energy raced up the length of my arm and spread over me.

"Okay, let's do this." I stood, revved for the adventure.

"Papà, Babbo, we are off to Capri! Edward and I will eat dinner out. Ciao, ciao, ciao!" Ivayla shouted up the stairs to her fathers. When she heard Mario respond, she took off down the steps to the garage on the street level. I had to sprint to keep up with her.

"Why do Italians say 'ciao' several times when they're leaving?" I asked, putting on my helmet. "Isn't one enough?"

"We are generous people. One is never enough," she answered with a sweep of her hand and started the motorbike's engine.

Helmeted, we raced through the streets on her Vespa. As we got closer to Sorrento, Mount Vesuvius, the infamous volcano where the ruins of the ancient city of Pompeii still lie, loomed in the distance to the east. On the back of the motorbike, I held onto Ivayla. My stomach was a little squeamish, but I kept my eyes open this time. I wanted to see everything.

Ivayla parked and secured her Vespa with a chain-lock near the ferry terminal. We bought tickets and boarded. Families and businesspeople filled the ferry. Sitting upright, Ivayla closed her eyes, taking her promised siesta.

"Here, lean on me." I shimmied closer and slipped an arm around her waist. Without opening her eyes, she rested her head on my shoulder. It was a little thing really, but the weight of her head on my shoulder made me inexplicably happy.

As she rested, I watched the Island of Capri come closer and closer. Shear walls of craggy mountains rose out of the water like the land time had forgotten. I'd read that some believed the view inspired Homer's scene in the "Iliad" when Odysseus hears the wail of the sirens.

Ivayla automatically woke up, ready to go, when the ferry docked. I imagined being a doctor; she taught herself to sleep on command. She strode with purpose, cutting through milling crowds, and led me to a funicular—sort of an elevator that moves sideways up an incline. The four-minute trip brought us up the hill, from the port in Marina Grande to the piazzetta in the town of Capri above.

Like Positano, everything was stacked, but if possible, on more of a vertical. Streets wound in loops, endlessly upwards. Unlike Positano, it felt like an exclusive vacation spot with fancy restaurants and expensive, posh designer clothing boutiques.

We stopped at an outdoor café for water and espresso. The table's umbrella gave us a brief reprieve from the hot sun while Ivayla consulted her cell phone map app.

"The Lo Duca family lives in Anacapri, the highest elevation on the island." She pointed up. "We can take the chairlift to the top of Mount Salaro. An easy way up, and something you should experience while you are here. To walk down is much easier."

Everything about Ivayla, from the way she spoke to the way she strode confidently into any situation, made me curious about the reason she spent her valuable time working on this with me.

"You're going to a lot of trouble helping me," I said. "Why?"

"You need help. I am up for the challenge."

"I don't think most people would see this, or me, as worth their time." I lowered my eyes. "You've been more than kind."

"I am pleased to help you." She smiled as she rested a hand atop mine.

"Thank you," I said.

"You are welcome." She pushed her chair out and stood. "Now let us go find the Lo Ducas of Anacapri."

We wandered up the narrow, winding stone walkways, through arches, and up steps, up steps, and up steps, to the chairlift she spoke of. A simple cable system carried a string of one-person metal chairs up and down the mountain. The chairs reminded me of the swing ride at the carnival, though I was certain those chairs had more safety features. Ivayla insisted I go first. Like a ski lift, the line of swings kept moving. A local assisted me as a slatted chair scooped me up, a thin metal arm swung down in front of me, and off I went. Behind me, Ivayla waved and hopped on the next chair.

"I'm texting you my brother's phone number in case I don't make it off this alive," I shouted back to her, across the distance between our swings.

We rode up the mountainside over what looked like and likely was, ancient land, pointing and hollering back and forth to each other.

One by one, the chairs deposited us at the top crest. A soft mountain breeze blew, cooling what the sun warmed. We spent some time admiring and marveling at the views, from the unreal zigzagging roads below to the intense blue waters that surrounded the island. Ivayla leaned on a stone wall where the mountain dropped away, pointing out boaters near the famed Blue Grotto. As beautiful as the scenery was, the graceful arch of her arms, the perfect bow of her lips, the bend of her knee, stole all my attention.

"Don't move." I yanked off my backpack and hopped on the large boulder nearby. I dug into the backpack and pulled out the sketchbook and pencils Paolo had given me. "I want to draw you standing there."

"I did not know you were an artist too." Holding the pose, she looked over her shoulder at me.

"I haven't drawn in a long time." My pencil moved across the page as I spoke. "The last thing I drew was a piece for... er... someone."

"Why do you say it like that?" She fixed her gaze on me.

"I drew something for my father. I worked hard on it." I shrugged. "But he didn't appreciate it."

"I am sorry for this. His opinion has stopped you from drawing?" she asked.

I hesitated before offering my lame answer.

"Yeah, but you know, kids are impressionable." I tried to laugh it off. "Looking back at it, I see it through different eyes. It wasn't very good."

"Still, it is not nice for him to have done that," Ivayla said, and her attention drifted to the water below.

I wished I hadn't shared that memory. That I'd given Tom's opinion so much power over me, especially since learning he wasn't my father, made me feel foolish.

I let the subject slip away and concentrated on the drawing; soothed by the soft gratifying sound of my charcoal pencil scraping the paper surface. Drawing Ivayla's contour felt nearly sensuous. My whole body warmed as my eyes and pencil narrated her shape. My hands and fingers worked in conjunction, a separate entity from the rest of me, moving confidently across the page, sculpting the lines of her silhouette.

Drawing felt like taking that first breath of mountain air. I didn't know how or even why I'd stayed away from it for so long.

Despite the breeze, the heat of the sun intensified at the top of the mountain. I didn't want to make Ivayla stand in the direct sunlight while I drew in the fine details of her face. My sketch had taken the shape of a woman enjoying a mountain view.

"Okay, we're done for now." I dropped my pencil in one of the backpack pockets. Released from the pose, she came over to look.

"Edward!" She put a hand on my shoulder and leaned in. "I expected a stick figure, but you are in truth, an artist."

"It's okay," I said, but the charge of her compliment spiraled in my chest. I closed the sketchbook cover and tucked the book in my backpack, already looking forward to working on it more as soon I could.

She started walking again, and for a moment I stood still, once again tracing her outline with my eyes and watching the sway of her hips. Realizing I wasn't in step with her, she spun and caught me watching her.

"What are you doing?"

"Studying your lines," I said.

"Why?" The slightest tint of red highlighted her cheeks.

"Because I want to draw you correctly."

"You need to keep drawing."

I smiled. "With you as a muse, it might be impossible not to."

"A muse?" She crinkled her nose.

"It's a person who inspires an artist to create," I said. "Like you do for me."

"I know what it means, but I think you are making funny of me," she said.

"It's '*fun*,' not funny." I laughed.

"Yes, I made a mistake. I go for long stretches without speaking English. I forget certain words." She waved a frustrated hand, then turned and started walking again.

"Hey!" I rushed to catch up to her. "I'm sorry. I wasn't making fun of you. The mistake was just so cute. You're always teaching me stuff, it's nice to teach you something once in a while."

"I am not upset about the mistake, Edward. It's just—" She sighed and dropped her chin.

"Just what?" I nudged.

"It is nothing. We should go before it gets late." Ivayla bowed her head to check her cell for the walking directions. "We do not want to interrupt family time by knocking on anyone's door going into the supper hour."

Drawing Ivayla made me even more conscious of her effortless beauty, the way she flicked her hair, the curve of her cheekbones, the thickness of her lips. I walked beside her to the residential part of the island, distracted by my sudden and strong awareness of her. Her reaction, though, made it clear she didn't want my attention—at least not in that way.

We stepped onto the brick walkway that led up to the front door of the Lo Duca family of Anacapri. My musings of her beauty hit a wall. The sharp edge of reality brought me back to the real reason for our trip. It could very well be another dead end, but as we made our way to the doorstep, saliva flooded my mouth, making me swallow several times in a row.

I might be about to meet my father.

I stood silently at Ivayla's side as she rang the bell. The white cement house, with rounded windows and doorways and a red tile roof, had a view of the water that suggested financial comfort. An older woman answered the door. Ivayla conversed with her in quick Italian. In its rapidity, I understood nothing. From the woman's scowl, waving arms, and sharp tone, our visit was nothing more than an irritating interruption.

I smiled at her, trying to appear friendly as Ivayla forged ahead, her tone respectful but insistent. After a bit, the woman sighed, and recited a list of names: "Marco Giovanni, Ricco Giovanni, Bruno Giovanni, Alberto Giovanni..."

Ivayla asked her another question and typed the answer into her cell phone.

"Grazie, signora." Ivayla touched the old woman's arm. "Buongiorno."

Miraculously, the woman smiled at her. We both waved and started back to the road.

"What'd she say? What'd she say?" I asked, my shoulder pressing into hers, sending a little tingle up my arm.

"Her father was Giovanni, and his name passed on to many boys in the family. She has a brother, a cousin, and a son named Giovanni, too," she said, and then added, "The brother is gone. Her cousin lives in Toscana but is too old to be the man you are looking for. Her son is the right age. He lives in Chicago."

"My Giovanni Lo Duca can't be a citizen of the United States," I said. "Before I flew here, I searched for him online. Nothing matched."

"Her cousin's name is Marco Giovanni Lo Duca. She said it wasn't uncommon for the boys to be given Giovanni as a second name."

"A middle name?" I clapped my hands to my face. "That might potentially quadruple the search radius."

"Or narrow it. An Italian second name is not so much like your American middle name. If you're given a second name here, we use it, like Anna Maria." Ivayla continued walking. "Call your grandmamma or this Diane and find out if your Giovanni had a second name."

"Diane can't help. She has no more information." I threw my hands in the air. "I'll never find him."

She stopped to face me. "It will redefine our search. Not a problem. Why do you get so upset?"

"Because my grandmother is dead, and Diane..." I puffed out. "And Diane isn't just a relative. She's my mother. I only recently found out she had the affair with Giovanni Lo Duca. He's my father."

She pressed her lips together and blinked a few times. I awaited the fallout from my dishonesty.

"Allora. I wondered why someone would try as hard as you have to find a long-lost family member."

We walked to the marina and waited for the ferry back to Sorrento, neither of us talking. Ivayla scooted away to take pictures with her cell. She didn't seem angry, but her quietness suggested my truth had changed things.

A long row of colorful rowboats caught my eye. Chewing my lip, I took out my sketchbook to draw.

Chapter 10

CONVERSATION BETWEEN IVAYLA AND I hit a standstill, making the ferry ride back to the mainland uncomfortable. Shame and embarrassment sat heavy in my chest. No one could have predicted we would spend so much time together. Least of all me. Had I known, I would have leveled with her about the identity of my father from day one.

However, once we arrived in Sorrento, the mood between us rebounded. We traveled by foot through Piazzo Tasso, the main strip, with Ivayla pointing out things of interest. At a small bistro, we decided on pizza. All the walking had worked up our appetites, and we ordered one pie each, hers with vegetables, mine with olives and prosciutto, both with thick, fresh slices of melted mozzarella.

Ivayla took a hearty bite. With a soft guttural moan, her eyes rolled heavenwards. Her uninhibited zest and enjoyment of food sent heat surging through my groin. I understood then how a weird fetish started. Just watching this woman eat was like foreplay.

"Looks like you enjoy pizza as much as you enjoy those sfogliatelle pastries," I said.

She mopped her lips with the oversized napkin and shook her head. "When it is made right, nothing rivals sfogliatelle."

"Nothing?"

"Nothing." Her lips twisted around a smile, and I was thankful the table hid the swelling effect she had on me. Then she reached out to touch my forearm. "I wish you'd have trusted me sooner that you are looking for your papà, Edward. Tell me more. I want to hear about your family, your life back in America."

The tension in my back eased. She opened a door to allow me a chance to redeem myself.

"Not much to tell," I replied. "I was born and raised in a small town. The man I believed to be my father left when I was little. It was just my mother, me, and my older brother, Ray."

I told her about my grandmother's death and her letter, segueing into how I learned that my deadbeat dad was not, in fact, my father.

"I recently moved into an apartment in my boss's house. His wife, Claudia, is my best friend." I finished the last of my slice and chewed thoughtfully before I spoke again. "That probably sounds a little weird."

"Why is that? This Claudia is an agreeable person who cares for you?"

"She does. She's the best. I almost didn't get on the plane to come here. Claudia gave me the kick in the ass I needed." I sipped my glass of wine, mulling over how Claudia's and my relationship had evolved over the last several years. I scrolled through my cell, found a family photo of Claudia, Toby, and the girls and handed it to Ivayla.

She took the phone and studied the photo. "A good-looking family."

"Claudia is very pregnant and about to pop out their third kid. I've had friends all my life, but I didn't have a best friend until I met her. I guess it's weird because, she's older, smarter. Like you."

"Watch it, Edward from New York." She shot me a look. "I am not *that* much older."

"Don't misunderstand me. I'm not saying you're old, not at all." My eyes traveled appreciatively over her face. "I mean you're like... sophisticated. Confident."

Her cheeks flushed under my compliment.

"I do not know her, but I need only to listen to how you speak of her. I admire her already." She returned my phone to me. "If I ever get to New York you will introduce us, yes?"

"Definitely." I sat up a little taller and grinned. "You come to

New York, and I'll introduce you to everyone I know and show you all there is to see."

"Deal." She put out her hand, and we shook on our pact.

A hum of energy ran up my arm, tempting me to lean in and press for more. The waiter came to refill our water glasses. I pulled my hand back; the interruption reminding me of where we stood. Ivayla and I had a friendship. That's what she'd called it, but every time she was near, I felt tempted to overstep that line. To torch it.

"Now, tell me about your mamma." She lifted another slice of pizza. "Is she married? Do you have a... what is it called... a stair father?"

"Step-father." I smiled.

"That's right. I was just testing *you*." She laughed, unashamed.

These little mistakes were small gifts to me. They, along with her sense of humor, made her approachable, relatable. Yet another thing to admire about this woman.

"Do you have a *step*-father?" she asked.

"There's been boyfriends, a steady guy now, but my mother never remarried after my father left... I mean, Tom."

She waited for me to go on. There wasn't anything to add. I took a bite of my pizza and chewed slowly.

"Ah, you don't wish to talk about her." Her voice softened as tightness flared in my chest. "I am curious about it. As you realize, I have two papàs and no mamma."

Her inflection warbled, just enough to reveal her struggle with the matter.

"Did you ever know your mother?" I asked, watching her expression.

"Yes." She stopped eating. "We were not estranged as you and your papà are. I would still be with her had a car accident not taken her life."

I put my pizza down and caught her gaze. "I'm sorry, Ivayla."

"I have some memories of her, but I was little, practically a bambino. I cannot be sure if they are my memories or moments stolen from old photographs." She straightened her shoulders and laid her hands across the tabletop. "But I am very fortunate. I have known little sadness since. Babbo and Papà were together when I was little. I shared time between them and mamma. When mamma died, it was an easy transition for me to live with them. They have always taken great care with me." She pushed out a smile.

I forged ahead and asked what I'd been wondering all along. "One of them is your biological father, right?"

"Yes."

"Which one?"

She smiled and shook her head. "That is something we do not discuss. Mamma loved them both. She asked them to help her have a baby. And Babbo and Papà loved her, not romantic love, of course. My conception took place through intrauterine insemination — but they both gave of themselves. So, you see, no matter the biology, they are both my fathers."

Despite a bead of envy of her having two fathers very much present in her life, I was happy she had them.

"I see Paolo in you."

"People tell me this often. It is our eyes and the color of our hair."

"Your hair is so black it's almost blue. And beautiful." I didn't tell her how often I was tempted to run my fingers through it.

"Stop, you flatter me. I think you try to butter me up." She pulled a thick bunch of her silky tresses through a hand and tossed it over her shoulder. "With my mamma lost long ago, I am very much interested in learning about your mamma."

"I'd rather not talk about her."

"Why is this?"

"Because there's not much I can say about her that isn't embarrassing." I laughed uneasily and looked away.

"No, no. That cannot be so," she said.

"It *is* true. Coming here made me realize how small my life has been until now. She didn't tell us to reach for our dreams. She lived a mediocre life and taught my brother and me to do the same." I didn't enjoy talking about my childhood, but Ivayla's sympathetic expression urged me on. "You told Mario I'm kind. You know why, Ivayla? Because I don't expect anything. And I don't ask for anything. I used to ask for stuff when I was little like every kid does. Toys, candy. Only, what I wanted more than anything were art lessons. My mother's answer was always the same, we couldn't afford fancy extras like other families because our no-good father left us. Wanna know what I did?"

The words tumbled out of my mouth, not giving her a chance to respond.

"I set out to find him, to find Tom Rudack and convince him I was worthy of being his son. When I started tenth grade, I found him online. He lived in Connecticut. I traveled three hours, took a ferry and a taxi, and staked out the coffee shop he tagged in his posts. I dressed in my nicest shirt and jeans and brought some of my best artwork with me. I really thought I could win him over, make him interested in knowing me."

I twisted my fingers together, remembering that painful encounter.

"He thought I was pathetic, called me a silly little kid with ridiculous dreams. It's been years since that day, Ivayla, but I can still hear the way he laughed when I told him I wanted to study art." I dropped my chin, remembering. His words left me untethered, and I hadn't known how to respond. "I couldn't get out of that coffee shop fast enough."

The man wasn't my father, but telling the story of that day was like stabbing an old wound.

"*Cuore mio*," she whispered, pressing a hand to her heart. Her chair scraped the floor, and then, she was beside me, her weight lightly pressing into my side, her warm hand over mine.

I tried to tame the fire in my chest, but her sympathetic tone and kindness were lighter fluid to white-hot coals. Heat roared up, flames scorching my eyes.

"God, I just... I need a moment." I pulled away from her, stood and strode across the dining room to the exit and out onto the road. I stood outside; fists curled and stared out across the piazza. I shouldn't have told her the damn story. It made my world look stupid and small, and worse, I'd shown this intelligent woman how much someone else's opinion affected me. The restaurant door opened behind me. Ivayla moved next to me, staying in my peripheral.

"Can I get you anything?" she asked but didn't touch me.

"I just need. A. Minute." I gulped air, blowing it out through my lips until I felt solid enough to speak again. "Okay. Okay. I'm good."

Chin raised and arms crossed, she narrowed her thickly lashed eyes at me. Fury thinned her full lips.

"Are you... *angry?*" I asked, dumbfounded by her expression.

"What you think, huh? You keep me in the dark about your parents. Now, I see you suffer from great sadness. Why have you held this back?" Her hands shot in the air, two punctuating exclamations. "Do you know anything? That I should not be offended, Edward?"

She leered at me for a long, tense moment. Surprised by her rash, abrupt anger, I stared blankly at her. She grunted, throwing her fisted hands in the air before turning and stalking off.

"Ivayla, come on!" I rushed forward, my neck prickled with annoyance. I caught her arm and blocked her way. "We barely know each other. You can't just expect me to come out and talk about something that personal."

"*We don't know each other?*" She yanked her arm from my grasp and threw her hair over her shoulder. "How can you say that?"

"We don't. But I'd like it if we got to know each other much, much better."

A frosty glare met my appeal.

I thought about Claudia's words at the airport. She'd hit me with a truth about myself that I hadn't even realized until she spoke it: It was easier for me to fit in than stand out. I wanted to be genuine with Ivayla. I wanted her to see the real me.

"Until a month ago, my mother let me believe my father was some loser who didn't care about me. Behind that lie, she hid the truth that my actual father is some guy in Italy who doesn't even know I exist," I spat the last sentence out through gritted teeth. I looked up, gnawing my bottom lip, waiting for the burn at the back of my eyes to cool.

"But Ivayla, I need you to know, I like you. I really, really like you. And what's more, I trust you." I lowered my eyes to hers and reached for her hand. "Meeting you has helped me deal with this, to make sense of it. Don't lose faith in me. Please, if you want to know more, ask me. Whatever you want to know, I'll tell you."

"Edward, Edward." Her tone softened. "Don't be foolish. I don't give up easily."

She put her arms around my neck and embraced me, the changeover in her mood so fast I felt whiplashed. Still, I pressed my nose into her hair and inhaled. Holding her, I felt the warmth of her closeness radiate through my limbs. The temptation to turn my head and find her mouth with mine overwhelmed me. I wanted to kiss her. So bad.

Ivayla Lo Duca with her natural grace, big-heartedness, and lightning-fast temper, made me want to be a better man. This woman, a stranger a few days ago, was turning my life on its ear.

Under any other circumstances, I would have kissed her, would have laid my heart on the line for a chance with her. It would've been so easy, but Paolo had issued a warning; Ivayla already had a boyfriend, and I would fly home in ten days. I couldn't see how to flip a situation with so much riding against me.

I needed to keep my emotions in check.

"The thing about my mother is, she's not a woman you'd admire," I said.

"You judge her." Ivayla grew rigid in my arms. "And you judge me."

I pulled back to look at her. "How am I judging you?"

"Tell me about her, Edward. Leave the judgment out."

I sputtered for a moment before I could think of something to say.

"Okay," I inhaled and took another shot at it. "When I was little, my mother's husband, Tom, skipped out on her. She had to raise two boys on her own. When my brother and I begged for something we couldn't afford, she'd blame our father for our situation. Ray and I grew up hating Tom. It was the only thing we had in common. She could have taken me aside, told me the truth. But she didn't. Not until a final letter from my grandmother forced her to."

"Maybe your mamma needed to make sure you and your brother kept close," she said. "And then again, maybe she didn't want you to feel different from Ray, that you didn't belong."

"I never thought of it that way." I leaned a shoulder against the brick wall of the restaurant. "She claimed Tom was already one foot out the door when she met Lo Duca. Apparently, he charmed the pants off her. Knowing my mother, that wasn't hard to do."

"Edward," she said with a reproving tone.

"Yeah, okay. Without judgment." This was proving harder than it should be.

Through the open windows of the restaurant, music streamed out, Bocelli's resonant voice melted into the evening air. It reminded me of nights with my mother, the two of us counting steps as we moved across the carpet in the TV room.

"She taught me how to dance." I straightened and held out a hand to her. "May I show you?"

"Yes, I would enjoy that." She stepped closer.

Sliding my left arm up Ivayla's right, I cupped her hand in mine. I laid the fingers of my right hand on her hip, just as my mother had taught me. Applying gentle pressure forward, I coaxed Ivayla to move with me.

"Lovely." Ivayla smiled, her steps sure as my own.

"Both my mother and grandmother believed a man should know how to hold a woman and lead her across the dance floor. When I was little, to get me to learn, they bribed me with treats, a piece of candy, a cupcake. I always liked to dance and probably would've done it without a bribe, but you know, cupcakes are awesome."

We continued to move, swaying to the song, her laughter warming my chest.

"Anyway, my mother said when she met Giovanni Lo Duca, his English was sparse, that of someone just learning to speak it, and most of her coworkers were too uncomfortable with the language barrier to approach him." I guided our steps, swaying, continuing to relay the story my mother had told me. "If I can say one positive thing about my mother, it's that she's friendly. She's kind to people down on their luck. She'd give a homeless guy the last dollar in her pocket. Giovanni was new in town. I guess my mother was lonely since her husband was stepping out on her."

"To be promised a life with family and then to find yourself alone?" Ivayla shook her head. "That must have been a difficult time for your mamma."

I stopped moving and stood, holding her.

"I've never really thought about it. But it makes sense why she looked elsewhere. She found out she was pregnant a month after Giovanni left the country. Hard to imagine, but back then, you couldn't just go on the computer and find someone. And for a woman on a limited income to locate a man she barely knew in another country? Wasn't going to happen. We were lucky we had a decent-running car parked out front. I don't blame her for not looking for Lo Duca. Just for not telling me when I was old enough to understand it. That was wrong."

"Yes, maybe." Ivayla tipped her head back to look up at me. "Your mamma got something right. You are proof of that. She raised a child who is a charming and kind gentleman."

A flash of heat raced through my body. "Thank you," I said, my voice a little too breathy for my liking. I cleared my throat. "I guess my mother did the best she could. Growing up, my life wasn't awful. She's not like other moms, but she's easy to talk to. And, she calls me honey bear."

"Oh, adorable." She pressed a little closer. "Now I *must* go to New York so you can introduce me to Claudia *and* your mamma."

"Will you really come to New York?" My question spilled out on a breath.

"Yes. When I was at medical school, I did not get to that part of your country. I would enjoy a trip to see the Big Apple and your island." Ivayla's fingers flexed, tightening their hold on me.

"Long Island," I said, smiling at her. "I would love if you came to visit me."

We returned late, with me mellow and smiling after several samples of limoncello. Ivayla took my arm and steered me up the stairs of the villa.

In the family room, Paolo watched television, an American movie dubbed in Italian.

"Ciao, Babbo!" Ivalya kissed his cheeks.

"Any luck?" he asked.

"No," I said and collapsed into the chair next to him.

"We have more information. We are not giving up," she said, her eyes catching mine. Again, she kissed Paolo's cheek and then kissed mine. "Now, I must go to sleep to rest for work tomorrow. *Buona notte.*"

We both watched Ivayla leave the room. Paolo went to the kitchen and took out two narrow, tall glasses. He filled them halfway with a yellow liquid from a clear bottle.

"Grappa," he said, and handed me a glass. "Salute."

"Salute," I responded and took a sip. It hit my throat like turpentine. My eyes watered as I coughed.

"Allora, you like Capri and Sorrento, Edoardo?" he asked, ignoring the way I struggled to control a fit of gagging.

I cleared my throat and mentally reset for another sip. "It was great."

"Did you draw?"

"Yes, sir." I picked up my backpack from the floor and took out the sketchbook.

"Good, good." He flipped through my sketches of the rowboats at the marina, appraising each page, but then stopped when he came to my rendering of Ivayla leaning on the wall overlooking Capri. He nodded his approval. "The shading and compositions are strong. *Molto bene.*"

The Duke thought my drawings were good. I let his praise sink in.

"Tomorrow morning, I go up the hill to paint. You come, too," he said. "Not late, early. *All'alba*, sunrise."

"Sì, grazie," I said and shoved my hands into my pockets. I didn't want him to see how nervous his generous offer made me. I'd not spent more than a few minutes alone with the man, and now I was being asked to spend the morning painting alongside him? I mean, what a tremendous offer, but I was rusty. My art wasn't up to snuff. And what the hell would we talk about?

Chapter 11

IT'D BEEN A LONG, EMOTIONAL day, and my whole body felt heavy as I climbed the stairs to the guest room. I fell across the bed. The weight of my body made a thumping noise. And now, I had the added burden of making a good impression on Paolo in the morning.

I plugged in my phone and checked my messages. My cell chimed with a series of incoming photos. Ivayla sending pictures she'd taken throughout the day, of me on the chairlift, gazing over a stone wall, stopping to try on a hat at a store, and a few of her and I together. Tourist shots—the kind that a foreigner in a foreign land would show his family when he got home from his trip.

I forwarded a few to Claudia, one of them, a shot of Ivayla and me in Sorrento. A moment later, my cell pinged with her response.

Claudia: Capri looks amazing. Best of all, you look HAPPY! This trip is good for you. Any news on Giovanni?

Me: Mostly dead ends. Losing faith that we will find him. On the plus side, got invited to paint with the Duke.

Claudia: Awesome!

Me: Nervous he'll find out I'm a fraud.

Claudia: You are NO SUCH THING. You'll rock it.

Me: Thanks. You always believe in me.

Claudia: Because I'm a fan. <3. Your doctor friend is vry beautiful! Nothing there?

Me: Niente — not for the lack of wishing.

Claudia: Maybe it's those shoes.

I laughed out loud.

Me: I'll wear my sneakers tmw and report back. You still pregnant?

Claudia: Expansively so. Having our girls talk to the little booger, and tell him he needs to come out. Could be any time now. BTW, Toby says to check your email. He found a house in Davis Park he's excited about. He wants to set up an appointment with the realtor to see it as soon as you get home.

Sure enough, when I opened my email, I found one from Toby. He'd sent information with photos of a two-floor bungalow on Fire Island—the rental house he wanted us to buy. It needed fixing up: a bathroom and kitchen, reno and landscaping. All stuff Toby, Ray, and I were capable of. It would feel good to work on something I owned. I replied with my permission to set up the appointment, that I was ready to provide my autograph wherever needed. I sent another email to Grams' lawyer, making sure Mr. Morris would release my inheritance to my bank account as soon as I returned to the states to pay for my share of the property.

I also emailed Luigi Delatorre, passing on what we'd learned from the old woman in Anacapri. The woman's information both capped and broadened the search for Lo Duca. I hoped Luigi could use it to figure out the next step.

The date on the email was a rude reminder that I had one week left in Italy. As it stood, looking for Giovanni Lo Duca could easily push past my allotted two weeks. Sticking around longer would put Toby and Ray in a tight situation, winterizing the rental properties. I knew the ropes, and I led a team. Toby was a friend and my boss. It would be shitty to leave him in the lurch. No matter how tempted I was to stay longer, when the week was up, I'd be on that plane. That meant if there was any chance I was going to find my father before the week was out, I had to put the pedal to the metal.

Something touched my shoulder, and I swatted it away.

"Edoardo, *andiamo.*" The quiet command came with a firm hand on my shoulder.

I opened my eyes and found Paolo standing at the side of my

bed. My mouth was dry and sand-paperish. Past him, night's darkness ebbed and hints of dawn peeked through the gauzy window curtains. Morning's stillness embraced the house. I'd fallen asleep, still dressed in my clothes from the day before.

"I meet you downstairs," he said and slipped out of my room.

Today I was going on an art expedition with a genuine Italian artist. I sat up and framed Claudia's words in my mind.

"I'm going to rock this," I said aloud, and then I whispered, "Thank you, Grams."

Paolo and I took our morning cappuccinos out onto the veranda. He lit a cigarette and crossed his legs. The early morning quietness was pleasant. With neither of us compelled to talk, we drank in companionable silence. His gaze drifted out over the nearby rooftops. Tobacco smoke curled around his paint-stained hand. I hated smoking. Both of my grandparents were lifelong cigarette smokers. Grandpa had bladder cancer on top of a heart condition. Grams had emphysema. It was likely doing irreparable damage to Paolo's health. We'd only recently met. I didn't feel like I had the right to lecture the esteemed artist about the detriment of the habit.

As soon as we finished, he motioned to me to follow him. We walked through the narrow streets of the still sleeping town, to a passageway that led up a hill. The sun, emerging from the water, tried to break free of the horizon. Its soft yawning rays lit our way. Paolo's steps were agile, even loaded down with two canvases and a satchel of brushes and tubes of paint. I trudged along behind him, half-awake, my own art pack slung over my back.

A long set of old cement steps twisted upwards and ended onto a grassy terrace of a park. The open space had a fountain and a bench, but little else. A beautiful view lay at the edge of the park, but Paolo turned and cut through a thick section of trees that bordered the clearing. A wooded dirt path took us up another hundred feet to a small clearing hidden away from the casual eye. It was here that he stopped and put down his supplies.

We were steps from a sheer drop where, in the moments before sunrise, the houses and village below were darkened blots on a darker, endless incline. With practiced motions, Paolo set up the easel and arranged his paints and brushes. The view—the open sky, land falling away—called to me, whispering for me to come closer, to walk to the edge, but fear hummed in my chest. I stood gaping at the view, unable to talk or move. Paolo's rough fingers closed over my arm, and he drew me forward. I held my breath and let him take me to the edge.

"Fear is here." He tapped his head with a paint-tinted index finger. "Concentrate. Breathe."

He inhaled, a crooked smile etched on his lips, and nodded for me to do likewise.

I inhaled, sipping the dewy morning air through my lips, and filled my lungs. He released me, patted my back, and went back to finish setting up.

After several breaths, I left the edge and joined Paolo where he had set up two folding chairs a few feet apart. The breathing exercise settled me far more than I would've expected. My stomach growled with hunger, but I ignored it, sat down next to him, and took out my sketchbook.

From his chair, Paolo reached over and took the pad from my hands.

"We look first." He motioned to the horizon. "See. Feel. Then, we draw."

He pulled out a paper bag and a small knife from his satchel. Without saying a word, he cut bite-sized pieces of dried sausage and small wedges of cheese and handed some to me.

We ate in silence, our eyes following the slow rise of the sun.

I sketched, and he painted, silently, side-by-side. A few times, I opened my mouth to speak, but when I saw those brows set in concentration, the absolute focus to his work, I swallowed back the unimportant chatter. Watching him work mesmerized me. He dipped a large brush in blue paint, and with broad confident strokes, he colored the sky. His arm moved like an orchestra conductor, poetry in motion, large sweeping motions, then smaller, controlled ones, each movement competent and effective. He pulled and pushed the paint, blending it with an assortment of brush sizes, thick, thin, large, until the smudges of paint became clouds, an ocean, and houses. The houses became a village with trees and bushes. Depth came in highlights and shadowing, making the scene come to life before my eyes.

Inspired, I refocused on my work, moving the graphite pencil across the page, contouring the forms, outlines, and shadows my eyes captured. I concentrated on sections of the city, the cathedral, the shops, and a curving road, filling many pages of the sketchbook he'd gifted me.

At noon, he dropped his paintbrush, stood up, stretched, and said, "*Noi mangiamo.* We eat."

Fingers smudged with our day's labor, the two of us collected our things and retraced our steps down the path and through the park. At the street level, instead of turning left toward the villa, he turned right, into town. We walked down a narrow cobblestone path, slick with runoff water. Through the many doors open to the narrow passage came murmurings of people talking in the native tongue, the sounds of clinking dishes and of running water, and Italian music. The aroma of cooking onions and garlic made my stomach growl.

Paolo entered a doorway and stopped to unload his canvas and painting tools on shelves on the back wall of the room. He motioned for me to do likewise.

Unburdened of our supplies, we strode past men in white kitchen aprons and caps to the front of the restaurant.

"Ciao Paolo! Ciao Edoardo! Welcome." Mercedes extended her arms wide, greeting him, and me, with a hug and a kiss. "You are hungry, yes? I will serve you something extra special."

She brought Paolo and me to a corner booth by the window, away from the rest of the tables. I figured the private spot was Paolo's regular table, saved for VIPs. She didn't ask us what we wanted. Perhaps Paolo got the same thing each time. He seemed like that kind of guy.

Mercedes came back with a bottle of wine and filled our glasses. "Do you enjoy dancing, Edoardo?"

"I do," I said.

"There is a wonderful night club nearby, *Mosse Notturne.*"

Bottle in hand, she started dancing, an impromptu box step. "You and Ivayla must come out dancing with Otto and me!"

"Mercedes, *non piu*." Paolo waved a hand at her.

"Ah, he is no fun. I embarrass him." She laughed. "It's okay. I know he loves me. Right, Paolo?"

He grunted, eliciting another laugh from her.

"We are childhood friends from up north," she said. "Both misfits among our families. I am a divorced mother living with my boyfriend. Paolo, he is a talented artist, but a very grumpy homosexual, married to my little brother."

Mercedes smiled and disappeared into the kitchen. I expected her indulgence to annoy Paolo, but he seemed unruffled by it. He read a newspaper while I sipped my wine, an easy silence between us. A while later, Mercedes returned with two other servers, each carrying several plates. They covered the entire surface of our table with food.

"Mercedes, too much," Paolo said, tossing his folded newspaper on the seat beside him.

"Edoardo is a new guest and a local hero. I am honored to have him in my restaurant. Eat what you can. I will send the rest home with you for Mario and Ivayla. *Mangia.*" She showered the tops of the dishes with cheese, grating it fresh from a wedge of Parmigiano Reggiano. Before leaving the tableside, she topped off our wine.

I stared at the food. Should I start with the *caprese insalata*, thick creamy slices of bufala mozzarella over vine-ripened tomatoes married with dark fragrant basil leaves, or perhaps the golden brown arancini, stuffed rice balls, coated in crunchy breadcrumbs and fried to perfection? Then, there was the saltimbocca, thin veal cutlets rolled with herbs and topped with salty prosciutto, and finally, the *ragù alla bolognese*, flat pasta noodles in a meat-thickened tomato sauce.

I went for the pasta first, spooning a sizeable portion on my plate. Anticipating the first bite, I twirled the light noodles around my fork and popped it into my mouth.

Heaven.

"So, you, Mercedes, and Mario grew up together?" I reached

for the dish of rice balls.

"Mercedes and I go to school together." Paolo took small portions from several plates. "Mario was little. I no pay him too much attention back then."

"When did you first… notice him?" I was curious, but more so, I wanted to keep him talking.

"I leave to travel a few years. When I come back, Mario a grown man." Paolo watched people drift by the front of the restaurant. When his attention returned to the table, he smiled with his eyes. "He *flirta*."

"He flirted with you? Did you know he was…" I didn't know how to finish my question. Personal questions were an uncharted conversation between us.

"*Omosessuale?*" He looked at me. "Sì. It why I avoid him. I no want to be like that. Families no want us to be like that. Not accepted."

I chewed my food, thinking about what that must have been like. My mother didn't support my dreams, but she never told my brother or me who we could date or be friends with. Ray and I had grown up ignorant of prejudices. My mother made lots of mistakes, but as far as I was concerned, her easy, open acceptance of others was something she got right.

"What changed your mind?"

"Love," he said.

Ivayla stood at the kitchen counter, her furball, Romeo, cradled in one arm while she paged through my early morning sketches with her free hand. I hovered over her shoulder, proud at how easily I'd filled half the book with renderings of that morning's sunrise over Positano.

"It couldn't have been a more amazing day! It was like I couldn't *not* draw. I had to!" My belly was still full from lunch. My brain mellowed with the wine.

She nuzzled her chin in Romeo's fur and smiled at me. "Babbo has really taken to you."

"You think so?" I folded my sketchbook closed, wanting her words to be true.

"Allora, I've never known him to take other artists to his secret painting areas to draw with him," she said. "And then, to take you with him to eat? How can this not be so?"

I bowed my head, basking in that knowledge.

"I have a little present for you." She held out her hand. In her palm sat a gum eraser, square and thick, the kind many artists used. "Babbo uses this when he sketches. I think it will be helpful to you, too, in case you have to erase a few lines to make a better picture."

Heat flared behind my eyes. I curled my hand over hers, interlacing our fingers. With the eraser between our palms, I brought our hands to my chest.

"Thank you," I whispered, wondering if she had any idea what her small gesture meant to me. "This may have been the best day of my life. Ever."

"It isn't even over yet," she said, a soft smile on her face.

"No, it's not," I agreed. "When I saw Mercedes earlier, she invited us to go dancing with her and Otto. What do you say we take her up on it?"

"Oh yes, let's do that!" Ivayla squeezed my hand. "Mercedes and Otto are such fun!"

The way our eyes held made me feel dizzy. I had to resist the pull she had on me. She wasn't free to pursue.

"I guess you should ask your boyfriend to come?" Dropping my gaze, I released her hand.

"My boyfriend?" She blinked.

I shoved my hands into my pockets. "You know, fidanza-to-Ralph?"

"No, no." She repositioned Romeo in her arms. "Dancing is not something Dr. Monroe enjoys. Besides, he is away at a conference in the U.K. this week."

My gut tightened. No boyfriend meant no buffer between her and this one-sided infatuation of mine—*for an entire week!* I hoped a night of dancing with her didn't make my head explode.

Ivayla stroked the cat's head, unaware of my internal struggle.

"What do you think, Romeo? Someone who dances, sings, and gets up at sunrise to draw—jumps at the chance to visit unknown places? Does this sound like a person I should spend so much time helping?" She turned the cat around and wiggled its furry little paw at me. "Romeo thinks you are special. He says anyone who sees you as we do, would agree that helping you is worth their time."

"Romeo is a very perceptive cat." I rubbed the top of Romeo's head, grinning. Damn, she was making it impossible not to fall head over heels in love with her. "Go put on your dancing shoes, pretty lady, 'cause I'm going to take you out on the town."

I splurged on another pair of shoes from Riccardo at the men's store. He recommended a pair of stitched cap-toe oxfords in saddle brown leather with thin-lace ties. That night, Ivayla and I met Mercedes and Otto at Mosse Notturne, a local nightclub. The four of us drank, laughed, shouted over the too-loud music, and danced, danced, danced.

In the early morning, we hugged and kissed the other couple goodbye and parted ways.

"Up for a walk on the beach before heading back?" I asked.

"Yes, I love the beach at night." She slipped off her heels and pulled a sweater over her shoulders.

The fall weather was creeping in. The nights had grown cooler than when I'd first arrived.

"Does it get much colder?" I asked.

"Oh yes, but not like the cold of your States." Her shoulder bumped my arm. "It is refreshing."

"I'll have to come back and see for myself."

"Yes, you must come back." She stopped and faced me. "Will you?"

She reached up to adjust the collar of my shirt, her eyes on the task. A tantalizing sensation stirred between my legs, followed by a familiar bone-deep, achy need.

I wrapped my hand around her wrist, gently tightening until she looked up and met my gaze.

"I will if you want me to."

My cell chimed, once. Then again, several times in a row.

"Someone wants you." Ivayla held my gaze for a long moment before her eyes dipped down and she pulled her hands away. "You must check your mobile."

Was there a breathiness to her voice or had I imagined it? Were we having a moment? Damn the messages—but they kept coming, relentless, until I conceded. I pulled the cell from my trouser pocket and impatiently swiped the screen with my thumb.

Half a dozen messages from Toby.

Toby: Lucas is here! 9 lbs, 1 oz!

Toby: Claudia is doing great. She's amazing.

Toby: Our son, Lucas Donato Faye. When are you coming home? We can't wait for you to meet him.

Photos followed, a string of them, showing a chubby, red-faced infant. A tired, smiling Claudia in a hospital bed; she and Toby holding their new son.

"Claudia had the baby," I told Ivayla. A garble of laughter stuck in my throat, and my vision blurred. A strong wave of homesickness swept over me. "It's a boy, a big boy, named Lucas."

"This is wonderful news," she said. "Awww. Look at you. You are crying happy tears for your friends."

She put her arms around me, face pressed into the crook of my neck, and squeezed me. I felt her warm breath against my skin.

Our heights complimented each other, our fit natural and easy, and I curled my arms around her waist. Bowing my head, my lips ghosted the side of her face, near her temple, where her heartbeat thrummed through her skin.

"I am happy. So happy. Their girls, Julianne and Beatrix, are so much fun. I love spending time with them," I said. "I can't wait to be a father someday, for that to be a part of my life."

She pulled away. "This is a nice thing to want."

With the physical space between us, the air cooled immediately. I cringed, remembering her reaction at the dinner table a few nights earlier. I had vowed not to bring up marriage or babies, but my response, wanting kids, was an honest one.

We walked silently up the hill toward Villa Campanella. On the veranda, we said goodnight and went to our separate rooms. I lay in bed, inhaling the cool early morning air, attempting to brush away my disappointment. From the first moment I'd laid eyes on Ivayla, I had been attracted to her, but today, there'd been several instances where I believed she'd felt something more than friendship for me. Of course, we could never act on it as long as fidanzato-Ralph remained in the picture.

The next morning, Ivayla slept in while I got up early and worked alongside Paolo and Mario, picking the last of the season's ripened vegetables in the garden. I steadied myself, ready to come clean as I'd done with Ivayla in Sorrento.

"Mario, Paolo, I wasn't completely honest when I first came to your house and told you about my search for Giovanni Lo Duca. He's not only a relative... he's my father."

I plucked a ripened plum tomato from the vine and waited for a response.

"You lie?" Paolo stopped working and aimed his laser inquisitive brown eyes at me. The intensity of his gaze felt like a police investigation spotlight.

"I was honest about never having met him."

"Ivayla knows?" the artist jabbed in return.

"Yes, I told her." I waited, knowing how protective he was of Ivayla, expecting his anger.

His mouth clamped shut, Paolo's gaze swung to Mario. The men exchanged glances, using a language I imagined they'd honed over their many years together.

"I'm sorry. I respect you both, and I didn't mean to upset anyone." I rushed to defend myself. "It's embarrassing to have to tell people that I don't know my father. It's worse explaining that I didn't even know he existed until a few weeks ago."

"Of course, it is." Mario patted my back, as usual, taking it better than his partner.

My cell buzzed in my pocket. I glanced at the screen. Delatorre. A call I was both dreading and eager to get.

"Excuse me. I have to take this call from signor Delatorre. He has information." I handed Mario the basket and stepped clear of the garden.

"The information from the woman from Anacapri proved helpful. I find her cousin in Tuscany." Luigi sounded breathless.

"You found him? You found my father?" I paced across the grass, pulling at my hair.

"Not yet, but I have spoken to his sister. She tells me same dates and travel information you give me. Workplace and city. It matches," he said. "It is several hour drive. Tomorrow, I pick you up early. We drive to meet them."

Tomorrow? I wanted to leave now.

I sucked in a breath. I'd waited this long. It could wait another day. "Okay. Thank you. I'll be ready."

I thought about messaging Claudia, but she was up to her ears in motherhood. Needing to tell someone, I rushed up the steps to the bedroom level and rapped on Ivayla's door.

She answered smiling, though half-awake, barefoot and wrapped in a short white robe that gave me an eyeful of long, smooth tan legs. She was beautiful even without makeup and her hair in a sleep-tangled ponytail. An intense flame sparked low in my belly.

"I have to go to Tuscany." I kept my eyes on her face. "Luigi tracked down the cousin of the woman from Anacapri. He thinks this is *the family*. I'm leaving first thing tomorrow."

Her eyes flew open, and she grabbed both my hands. "This is fantastic news!"

"Well, it is, and it isn't." I held her hands loosely. "As much as I'd like to continue to stay here, go dancing with you, tear through the countryside on the back of your Vespa, if Luigi is right about this family, I'll be spending the rest of time up north until I fly home."

"What?" Her lips turned down in a pout, and she withdrew her hands from mine. "You are planning to leave me behind?"

"I don't want to leave you, Ivayla. I've had a wonderful time staying with you and your fathers. You've been so kind and generous, but I really feel like this is it, that I'm about to meet my father. I promise I'll stay in touch."

"Oh sure, sure." She crossed her arms. "No, I will come with you."

"You're a doctor. You have important work."

"Edward!" She swatted my shoulder. "I have put a great deal of effort into finding your father with you. You cannot ask me to stay back. Allow me to see this through."

"I would love that, but can you take the time off from work?"

"It is already approved," she said.

"You took the time off? Before knowing?"

"Yes, because it is your last week. There is much you haven't seen. I have been thinking, no matter what happens with your father, I will be a proper guide and show my American friend the city of *Firenze*. It is one of my favorite places. I could not let you go home without seeing it. That would be criminal. I shall call signor Delatorre and tell him to meet us there."

"This is way more than I expected. Grazie, Ivayla," I said, without an ounce of regret, and my stomach doing crazy little backflips. I would agree to anything this woman proposed. Better still, I didn't have to say goodbye, yet.

"Good. We must not waste time. We must pack and go." She took my hand and pulled me out to the veranda. Obedient, I let her lead me to Mario and Paolo in the kitchen, washing their fresh-picked vegetables.

"Papà, Babbo, Edward and I are off to Toscana!"

"You stop in and see *Nonna e Nonno* in Siena," Mario said.

Paolo grunted. "Why you bother her with them, Mario?"

"They love her. It is us they don't want to see," he replied and looked at Ivayla. "You go."

"I don't think we will have the time, Papà." Ivayla took my hand. "We must concentrate our efforts on finding Edward's father."

"Sì. Of course. I will make you food to carry. Go." Mario waved her off, and Ivayla raced up the steps to pack, leaving me alone with her fathers.

"Mario, Paolo, thank you for letting me stay at the villa. I will not be back. I'm hoping to spend some time getting to know my father and his family."

"Oh, how we will miss you!" Mario caught me in a bear hug and nearly squeezed the life out of me.

Paolo, less expressive, put a firm hand on my shoulder. "I

enjoyed our time. You will keep doing your art, eh?"

"Yes, I will. Thank you for giving it back to me," I said, and shook his hand.

"Sì, sì, you are welcome, my friend." With a rare smile, he clapped my back.

I climbed the steps to my bedroom to pack with a lump in my throat. I would miss this place, these people.

When we came down, Mario stood and fussed with the collar of Ivayla's jacket.

"Your horoscope says now is favorable time to explore!" He pressed something into Ivayla's hand and folded her fingers around it. Looking at her, he whispered something to her in Italian and kissed both sides of her face.

"Oh, Papà, your gift is unnecessary." Ivayla shoved the item into her shoulder bag lightning fast.

"It's in the stars, *vita mia*," he said, giving my shoulder an affectionate pat. "Better to be safe than sorry. This is said in America, true Edoardo?"

"True, sir," I answered.

"What's that, Mario?" Paolo nodded to Ivayla's bag.

"Just some Euros, Babbo. As if I need it!" Ivayla waved a hand and kissed Paolo's and Mario's cheeks. "I will call you later. Ciao, ciao, ciao!"

Paolo's eyes caught mine. "You remember what I say, Edoardo."

All eyes turned on me. The skin under the collar of my shirt prickled. Whatever was going on, somehow, it had to do with me and Paolo's warning.

"Go. Have fun!" Mario twitched, unable to contain his glee.

Ivayla caught my hand and pulled me toward the stairs. I looked over my shoulder one last time. Paolo's suspicious gaze followed me out of the house.

Chapter 12

WE TOOK A TAXI TO the piazza in town, where we boarded a bus. The same bus line that had brought me into Positano would now take us out. The bus coasted along the winding roads through the Amalfi coast, and Ivayla pointed out landmarks.

I held my tongue for the hour-long trip, but once we had our tickets and found seats on the train to Tuscany, I couldn't contain my curiosity any longer.

"What was going on between you and Mario? He didn't give you money, did he?"

"No," she said, her voice without inflection. She dug into her handbag, pulled out a small box, and held it out for me to see. The writing was in Italian, but the logo and brand name were immediately familiar: Durex.

"He gave you... Your *father* gave you condoms?" My face reddened under my tan. "Surely he doesn't think you and me..."

Now Paolo's suspicious gaze made sense. He'd caught on to Mario's matchmaking. I'd been warned not to mess around with his daughter.

"Papà is comfortable speaking of sex. Babbo is more reserved. Don't tell, but sometimes I avoid telling Babbo things that will upset him." She tossed the box into her bag, sat back, and closed her eyes. Her breath softened in sleep.

Sitting beside Ivayla, I stole long looks at her as she slept. There was so much more I wanted to—no, *needed* to—ask her. She looked so peaceful, and I held back, resisting the temptation to wake her. Working the overnight shift must have exhausted her.

I, however, fidgeted in my seat, unsure how she could be so

offhand about the condoms. Had she given Mario the impression we would need condoms on our trip? I'd spent the week being saintly as all hell around her, curbing any wayward thoughts. I'd kept the vibe friendly between us. It wasn't because I didn't want her. The woman was freaking beautiful. But those condoms in her possession blew my restraint out the window. Unfiltered thoughts ransacked my brain, thoughts of what I could do in a hotel room with a box of rubbers and Ivayla, naked and willing. The possibility of touching her, how her skin would smell when I pressed my lips to the long column of her neck, how her curvy body would feel under my hands, how it would feel up against mine.

The whole of me buzzed at the prospect. Three major hiccups, however, were messing up my hot fantasy.

First: Ralph, the dinosaur boyfriend. Even if Ivayla didn't talk about him much, Dr. Ralph Monroe factored into the equation, making me the third wheel. Two's company. Three was definitely a crowd. And I didn't like to share.

Second: Paolo's aversion to Americans. However, the further we traveled away from Positano, the less weight that one held. With the likelihood that I'd never see the artist again, that one could be scratched from the roster.

If only it weren't for the third and most important hitch: Ivayla, always kind and helpful to me, had given no indication that she was interested in me *like that*. Even now, with condoms in her purse getting me all hot and bothered, she appeared above it, ambivalent. Uninterested.

Who was I kidding? She was a multilingual doctor. I was a small-town guy with not a hell of a lot going on.

I sat back in my seat and squeezed my eyes shut. I needed to put the condoms out of my mind. They were nothing more than one of Mario's fanciful hopes of *amore*.

Once we reached our destination, Ivayla immediately reactivated. I grabbed our bags, and as we exited the station, I let Ivayla take the lead. She hadn't said a word more about the condoms. It was dead in the water. A part of me felt relieved. I needed to focus on the reason I was here. To meet my father.

It was late afternoon in Florence when we arrived. A quick taxi ride took us from the train station to the hotel on the Arno River where Ivayla booked us rooms. Unlike Berto's hotel, this one was air-conditioned, and the concierge greeted us immediately. We should've been travel-weary, but the energy of the city hit us like a shot of adrenaline.

We dropped our bags in one room and headed out to the street.

"Come, Edward." Ivayla took my hand. "Now I show you the most magical city in the world, Firenze!"

The book I'd been reading about the Medici family described how the Basilica of Saint Mary of the Flower took 140 years to complete. The sheer size of the massive white *duomo,* trimmed in green and pink Carrara marble in person, floored me.

I stared, eyes raised in awe, as I followed Ivayla down the cobblestone streets to the *Galleria dell'Accademia*. The Galleria housed one of the world's most well-known sculptures, Michelangelo's David. I'd seen and read about the famous statue in the pages of my art books. Admiring it on a flat page, though, was nothing like standing before The. Actual. Statue. I spent a good part of an hour studying the marble figure, overcome with rushing emotions. David's musculature, the veins in his arms, the precise etching of each toe and finger, were strikingly lifelike.

I was still humming with an art lover's high when Ivayla whisked me into the heart of the city, to Piazza della Signoria. Here, reigning tall over the square's grand fountain, a marble King Neptune greeted us riding a chariot drawn by sea horses and flanked by mystical creatures.

In an open arcade to one side, another dozen statues stood on a platform under gothic arches. One of them was a bronze medieval folklore sculpture of Perseus holding the head of the slain Medusa.

I wanted to linger, but Ivayla had an agenda, and my tour guide hurried me onwards, to the Uffizi Gallery.

I had been looking forward to seeing this museum the most. The Uffizi housed a vast amount of Renaissance art from the greatest masters: Raphael, Michelangelo, Caravaggio, Rembrandt. I felt a little like a kid about to go to Disney World.

Ivayla and I stood side-by-side looking at Leonardo da Vinci's, *The Annunciation*. Da Vinci had finished the biblical painting in 1475 when he was only 20 years old.

"Madonna art is a popular theme," I said. "Why do you think there is so much art dedicated to her?"

"The Blessed Mother portrays to us a person of indomitable spirit and immense faith." Her gaze remained on the painting as she spoke. "Mary understood her child would not be her own, but a gift to the world. When I see her hand raised, as it is here before the angel Gabriel." Ivayla motioned to the painting. "I can hear her promise to God to be faithful. Even after Jesus's death, she continued to live in faith. We revere the Blessed Mother for her courage, her holiness. It is an example to us all."

I turned to look at her, rapt by her worldly knowledge and obvious confidence in her belief.

"She makes me think of my grandmother," I said, and told her about the little statue in my backpack, how my grandmother had given it to me, and insisted I take it to Italy with me. "It's like having a piece of Grams with me."

"I like your story. It is sweet, like you." Ivayla curled her hand around mine and squeezed it.

"She left me money to go to art school," I said.

Ivayla pressed our joint hands to my chest. "She knew your heart."

"Better than I did. I forgot how much I love drawing, painting... creating." I twisted to look at the art students who sat on nearby benches, sketchpads propped against crossed legs, pencils moving across the matte paper. "Until I came to Italy."

"You are good at art. Even Babbo says so. You should do it."

"I can't. I'm using the money to invest in property instead."

"Oh, Edward, no." She looked up at me. "You will change that, yes? It was your nonna's wish for you to follow your dream."

"I can't change it. I made a deal with Toby." I smiled and tugged playfully at her hand. "But don't worry, I'm sure after being here, I'll keep on drawing."

"Good." She grinned in return. "Now let us go find more Holy Mother paintings. There are many."

After an hour, we'd only scratched the surface of all there was to see. However, hunger pangs drove us out in search of food. We found an open-air restaurant with an unobstructed view of the piazza. Ivayla insisted we order the local specialty, lampredotto sandwiches, but waited until I said I liked it before she informed me that the meat was cow stomach.

We laughed and drank wine. Nearby, an elderly local played the accordion and sang in Italian. I felt warm, relaxed, and right in every way. Being in Italy with Ivayla, a good friend, made life, for that moment, perfect.

"The amount of artwork in this city is incredible, it just blows my mind," I raved. "I don't think you could see it all in even a few weeks. If only I had more time."

"Why rush to go home then? Stay longer." She gazed at me from over the top of her wineglass.

Oh, to stay and spend an unlimited amount of time studying Renaissance art compositions, colors, and brushstrokes. I sighed. That would not happen.

"I made a deal with Toby, and I promised to be back to winterize the rental houses," I said. "I can't go back on my word."

"Do you miss it?"

Other than Toby's email, I hadn't thought about work at all.

"I don't think anyone grows up dreaming of being a guy on a construction crew," I said. "But I'm good at what I do."

"Tell me, Edward, if you could pick anything, what would you like to do?"

I took a sip of wine and leaned my elbows on the table. "I'd move here and eat my way through the country and become a fat old man."

She snorted, almost elegantly, and slapped my arm. "Be serious."

"I would move here." I glanced over my shoulder at the statues in the darkening piazza before turning back to her, where those warm brown eyes magnetized my line of vision. "I need more of this."

"When you do, you will fulfill nonna's wish for you, and we will have lots of time to know each other better." She said it like it was a done deal.

With her by my side, I could imagine a life in *bella Italia*. The vision created a little pull in my belly.

If only it were possible.

"Why wait?" I shrugged, playing along. "Let's start now. What do you want to know?"

"I see this jagged scar, here." She leaned in and brushed the tip of my chin with a fingertip. "It looks recent. I am curious to know the story behind it."

"This scar is a short story. You sure you don't want to know how I hit a home run to win a Little League pennant?" I asked. "Or that I gave my girlfriend, Ashley, a ring in fifth grade because I planned to marry her?"

"You proposed marriage?" Her brows raised.

"Yeah, most sincerely, with a spider ring from the bubble gum machine," I said, grinning. "It was a really cool glow-in-dark ring, but she still dumped my butt."

"Boo-hoo." She laughed in that musical way of hers, her bottom lip rolled out in a pout, and then, pointed to my chin. "They are sweet stories, but now, you tell me about the scar."

"I got drunk after my mother told me about Giovanni Lo Duca and had it out with a table. The table won. The end." I covered the scar with my hand. "The way I figure it, every handsome guy needs a flaw. Just a small one to offset his perfect good looks. This one is mine."

I laughed despite my self-consciousness.

"You joke. But, you *are* a handsome man." She gently tugged my hand away. A warm, pleasurable sensation rippled up my torso. "I find it… annoyingly adorable."

We held each other's gaze. I took her hand. She didn't pull away. Despite the breeze and all the distinct scents, I could smell her, the salt on her skin, the floral notes of body lotion, the lemon of her shampoo. Her scent roused all my senses, infecting all of me, and rendering me speechless for a moment.

"Ivayla." I fingered the gold bracelet on her wrist. "To get back to what we were talking about earlier."

"We have talked so much. What is it you wish to return to?" She leaned back in her seat and sipped her wine, allowing me to continue to hold her hand.

"Those *things* Mario gave you," I said, peeking up at her. Did she feel me tremble?

"You are very interested in them." A soft smile of amusement curled her lips.

"Uh, huh." I chuckled softly. "So, humor me. Tell me why he gave them to you."

"You see," she said with a sigh. "I am an *Ariete*, Aries. Papà believes we are *scritti nelle stelle*, written in the stars, that our match is inevitable."

"And what do you think?"

"I am not one to discount the beliefs of my ancestors." She looked at me. "If the stars say our signs are an excellent match, intellectually and physically, I suppose they just might be."

"Intellectually and physically? Hmmm, curious," I said, and slid closer, pressing my leg to hers. Heat spiked up the length of my thigh. "It doesn't bother you that I am younger than you?"

"What? You are but a few years younger, yes?"

"Twenty-six."

"A man, not a baby. And anyway, age does not matter to the stars. It does not matter to me either. As you know, Ralph is many years older."

"Believe me, I noticed. What do the stars say about you and old Ralph?"

"Our signs are not compatible." She lifted a shoulder in a careless shrug. "It matters little, though."

"Why not?" I swept my thumb over her knuckles. Her fingers were long, her wrist slender and delicate and her skin warm to the touch.

"Because," she said, "it is done."

"Done?" My heart skipped a beat. "You mean you aren't together anymore?"

"This is correct. I spoke to him last night."

I wanted to jump up, whoop and cheer, but refrained. "Are you upset?"

"No." She shook her head. "I wanted to end it after Sorrento."

"Why Sorrento?" I asked, hoping she'd been feeling what I'd been feeling.

"I have never spoken openly with Ralph as I did with you that day. Our relationship was one of convenience. Dr. Monroe is someone to go out to dinner with, to talk about work with. And best of all—" She smirked. "I enjoyed how he annoyed Papà and Babbo. My fathers, they meddle too much."

"They just want you to be happy," I said.

"I was until recently." She pulled her hand from mine and raked it through her thick hair. "Now I am in much more trouble since a new, more terrible man has taken his place."

"You met someone else?" I blew out a terse breath. "You've got to be kidding me."

"Stop it." She bit her bottom lip. "No pretending you do not know I am speaking of you."

My brows went up, and I leaned in. "Ivayla, are you saying you like me? Like, *like me*, like me?"

"I am sure I don't know what that nonsensical sentence means, but if you are asking me if I like you, the answer is yes."

"In more than a friendly way?"

"Mamma mia. *Yes*." She bowed her head, hiding her blush beneath a curtain of hair. "Edward from New York, you make me feel embarrassed, like a schoolgirl."

I laughed despite myself. "How about I say something about you that embarrasses me?"

"Okay, I am listening." She rested her chin on her hand.

"My knees literally wobble every time you touch me," I said.

"Really?" She reached out to caress my face, her lips stretched with an impish grin. "Like when I do this?"

The touch sent shivers down my neck, my torso, firing up my libido.

"Ivayla," I groaned. "Do you know how much I want to kiss you?"

She leaned forward, hand on my leg, and whispered, "What are you waiting for?"

I grabbed a thick handful of her hair and drew her mouth to mine. Her arms curled around my neck, allowing me to feel her soft purr of pleasure vibrate against my chest. A surge of electric energy raced through my torso and limbs.

I pulled away only far enough to catch my breath, our noses still touching. Applause and cheers of approval erupted from the three waiters who watched on.

Heads ducked, we both threw down Euros to cover the dinner check, and left the restaurant. Holding hands, and stealing looks at each other, we headed back to the hotel on foot. A push of air came from busy restaurants along with milling voices, and here and there, Italian music floated out from the entranceways to us.

At the bridge near our hotel, the Arno River's dark waters below sent up a cool burst of fall air. Ivayla shivered, and I stopped to pull her close, angling her head and bringing her mouth to meet mine again.

She wound her fingers in the hair at the nape of my neck, and she kissed me back with an urgency I would have never expected.

"I've wanted to kiss you since we met at your father's gallery. The same night you taught me how to drink espresso properly." I leaned my forehead to hers; my heart pounding in my ears.

"The feeling was mutual." She snaked her arms around my waist, head tilted back, and she smiled at me. "I think tonight, we do not need two hotel rooms."

My mouth popped open in surprise. "Are you sure?"

She eyed me. "Do you not wish to spend the night with me?"

"Ivayla, oh, my God, yes." I nodded, holding her tighter. "I want to be with you, but I also don't want you to feel rushed."

"All week we behave, denying what is between us. I don't wish to wait any longer." She kissed my chin and took my hand. "As I have told you, Edward, I don't do anything I don't want to."

Together we crossed the street to the hotel, and she marched up to the concierge desk, with me trailing behind. After settling the room matter, she led me to the elevator where a couple exited just as we arrived.

Alone in the elevator car, she leaned back against me and tilted her head. I lowered my head and trailed my lips over the exposed

creamy expanse of her neck. She purred, spiking my unmistakable arousal. Instead of shying away, she pressed her backside
firmly against me.

"Whoa!" I wrapped my arms around her waist and leaned low
to whisper in her ear. "You are an evil woman."

Her answering giggle told me she was aware of how she was
affecting me. The elevator delivered us to our floor, and intoxi-
cated with each other, our steps faltered, interrupted by the need
to kiss every few steps, our hands fumbling to touch and explore
each other.

At the room door, Ivayla worked my neck with her mouth as I
fumbled to get the card key in the slot, my fingers clumsy in my
rush to get her inside. We practically fell into the darkened room.
Before the door shut, I tugged her blouse from the waistband
of her pants, following the contour of her ribcage until her soft,
rounded flesh filled my hands. She moaned softly in my mouth,
her hands over mine, encouraging me to keep touching.

I pressed my hips into her, moving her back until we bumped
against the wall. Ivayla panted with pleasure but raised a hand
to hold me back. She grabbed her handbag and rooted around in
it until she came out with condoms in hand and tossed the bag
aside. We pulled at each other's clothing, tugging and pushing
fabric aside. She tore the square packet open and, with her eyes
locked on mine, adeptly sheathed me.

"We are *scritto nelle stelle*, Edoardo."

Not interested in the soft bed only steps away, she tugged me
against her and pulled at my hips until our bodies melded together
as one. My lungs emptied of air.

Her slick heat swept over me like pure silk, stealing my ability
to focus beyond the heat surging through my torso and limbs like
an invading alien life force. Our mouths locked together in a hungry kiss, ratcheting up the speed of my movements in sync with
my heartbeat. I moved with an urgency I couldn't contain—nor
wanted to. Against the wall, with our breaths in tandem, we came
together in an explosive release.

I carried her to the bed where we shed the rest of our clothes,
the two of us ready to continue our exploration of each other.

She encouraged me in whispered Italian, the exotic sounds of her native tongue thrilled me in a way I could've never expected. I complied, slowly teasing the curves of her body with my hands and mouth until neither of us could resist the need to unite our bodies once again.

Other than the bedding, sheets and pillows pulled and tossed about during the night's wild foray, the hotel room remained unstamped by our presence. The open window shades allowed the morning's rising sun to creep in and chase night's darkness from the hotel room. Our limbs rendered useless from lovemaking, we'd passed out tangled up in each other.

I lay awake for some time with Ivayla curled around me. I didn't dare move. The world felt alive with possibilities, my life in complete alignment. This feeling often came with a new lover—the unexplored novelty held its own allures—but something about Ivayla made it different. I felt a deep-rooted contentedness like we were meant to be. Though I couldn't say exactly why.

Lying still I watched her breath and sleep, combing her hair away from her face with my fingers and kissing her forehead.

"*Scritto nelle stelle*, Ivayla," I whispered.

Whatever this thing was between us, it differed from my past relationships. Solid. Special. Like we could build a life around it.

I gave myself a mental shake and forced myself to stop thinking of a future with Ivayla. I was going home soon, and considering the circumstances, it made no sense to think like that. It reeked of a setup for disappointment.

After a while, Ivayla sat up in bed and stretched like a slinky, sexy cat.

"Good morning, my love." She ran a hand over my stubbled cheek. A rush of goosebumps tore down my spine, spiking heat between my legs. She gave me a brief kiss and reached for her cell phone. "I have work messages I must respond to. Would you mind much?"

"No, go ahead." I blew out a breath and leaned back against the pillows.

For a split second, I thought about tossing her phone aside and making her pay attention to me. But as I watched her, my eyes following the contours of her face, discriminating between the light and dark shaded areas, I became mesmerized. The light played on her cheekbones and nose, on the deeply dark spot just under her mouth, and where her bottom lip, full and thick, jutted out.

I hung over the edge of the bed and rustled through my knapsack. Mary bumped against my knuckles. I took out my sketchbook, flipped to a blank page.

"What are you doing?" She glanced back over her shoulder at me, fingers still tapping out a message on the phone's keypad.

"Just go back to what you're doing," I said, sweeping the pencil across the page, capturing the way the folds of the sheet fell away from her, darkening the area where the roundness of her breast created shadows. I drew her chin pressed to her bare shoulder and outline of her face, and I tried to capture the way her eyes looked. The way they looked at me.

"Don't, I look horrible." She Italianized horrible, silencing the h and rolling the r's, rendering it *orr-e-bel*.

Sexy-freaking-adorable.

"Yes, so *orribel*," I mimicked, my pencil still moving. "I can't take my eyes off you."

"Edward, you've made my life truly impossible, sneaking in my head when I try to work. And sleep. And eat. You are an impossible man."

I closed my eyes a moment to draw in a deep breath; sure my heart would burst with happiness. Then I continued my sketch, eyes open, and limbs tingling.

"You shouldn't have waited so long to make your move." I swung my gaze from her to the sketch, filling in her dark eyebrows and impossibly long eyelashes. "You know the first time I saw you up on that horse, I thought, 'That is a *magnificent* creature.'"

The apple of her cheeks rose with her smile. "Is that so?"

"Yes." I grinned down at my artwork. "I don't know horses very well, but Alba is the most beautiful mare I've ever seen."

A bed pillow hit me in the head. I tossed the sketchbook aside, threw back the covers and flung myself atop of her.

"*Ragazzo bello ma maleducato,*" she taunted, giggling, and tried to push me away.

"I'm back to being a rude pretty boy, huh?" I grabbed her wrists, shook the phone loose from her grip, and pressed her hands into the mattress. "If you had to decide right now between sfogliatelle or the rude pretty boy, what would you choose?"

"Oh, Edward from New York, do not make me choose between you and sfogliatelle. You will lose." She laughed and lifted her hips to press against me. "Lucky for you, I am hungry for something much more substantial."

A wildfire of heat ripped through my body, testing every ounce of willpower. With significant effort, I held myself apart from her; overcome with the raw wonder of her.

"Ivayla." I lowered myself to my elbows and tangled my hands in the waterfall of glossy black hair cascading over the pillow. "Is this real?"

She hooked her legs around my back and smiled.

"Kiss me and find out."

Chapter 13

AN HOUR LATER, FACES FLUSH and eyes still glowing, we met Luigi Delatorre in the piazza closest to the hotel. He greeted me with an enthusiastic handshake and Ivayla with a kiss on both sides of her face.

"The house, it is not far. They have agreed to speak to us." Luigi rushed his words, his face ruddy with excitement.

His unsettled state reminded me of the strangeness of the expedition we were about to embark on. Questions filled my head—spawning many uncertainties. Had we found the *right* family? And if it were the right family, would my father accept me?

So many things could go wrong. Luigi ushered us to a small white car similar to Mario's, and the three of us squeezed into it. I had the front seat next to Luigi. My stomach rolled with nerves as we zipped up into the rural hills of Tuscany. I tried to stay calm by keeping my eyes fixed on the sights.

Unlike the stacked houses of Positano's landscape, vast terraced properties, trattorias, and wineries dotted the rolling hills of the Tuscan countryside. It was good that we had a car. It was not a place you'd find public transportation.

"The name of the woman I speak to is Rosa Lo Duca," Luigi said, relaying the phone call he'd had with a woman at the residence. "Rosa tell me her brother, Giovanni, traveled to America in 1992. While there, her brother work as a gardener."

A bubble of hope grew at the narrative that matched my mother's. Luigi strongly believed the woman he'd spoken with was Giovanni's sister. Which, if it were so, would make her my aunt.

Aunt Rosa.

Today, I would possibly meet an Italian person I was related to, the first truly legitimate step to fulfilling my grandmother's dying wish. This was the reason I'd come to Italy. I watched the scenery go by. The view offered me a sense of serenity, the innate sense that I was welcomed here, that I belonged here. It would be nice to know I didn't imagine this, that I did indeed have a connection to this land; that this was where the other half of my family lived.

"This is exciting." Ivayla reached between the seats to squeeze my arm. "I knew one way or the other, we would find him."

I didn't respond. My mouth was dry, my tongue twisted. Why was it that when a person's most ardent wish was about to come true, it was so damn scary? I pressed a hand on my backpack in my lap. Knowing Mary was inside calmed me. With the importance of this event, she had to travel to Tuscany with me.

Luigi pulled off the main road and drove up a long dusty driveway to a house hidden behind scraggly olive trees. The house was old, battered and bruised from years under the Tuscan sun. Bright flowers grew near the house, the only area that seemed to be tended to regularly.

The three of us got out of the car and stood awkwardly looking at each other. Luigi took off his hat and folded it nervously in his hands.

"Please stay here. I first speak to the family. Then, I introduce you," he said.

Ivayla and I nodded our silent agreement. We watched Luigi approach the front door and ring the doorbell.

I had an overwhelming sense of déjà vu. I was about to put myself before my father, a man who was a stranger, in hopes he wanted to know me.

A woman wearing a crocheted shawl over her shoulders and a liberal dose of gray in her black hair answered. Her gaze lifted over Luigi's shoulder to us. She came outside and pulled the door shut behind her. The woman was plain-faced and without makeup. It made it difficult to guess her age.

Luigi gestured for us to come forward.

"What the hell am I supposed to say?" I whispered to Ivayla.

"You will know," she said, intertwining her fingers in mine.

I swallowed back the lump in my throat as Ivayla and I moved closer.

"Signora Lo Duca," Luigi said, sweeping his hand from her to us. *"Signorina Ivayla é signor Edoardo."*

"Buongiorno," Rosa said with little enthusiasm for her company. Her eyes latched onto me, and I stood still under her scrutiny until she motioned to the side of the property, north of the house. *"Andiamo."*

The austere greeting was unlike any other I had received during my stay. I hadn't exactly expected to be hugged, but I had hoped for more. An acknowledging smile perhaps.

We followed her around the corner of the house where lines of clean clothes and linens flapped in the morning breeze. Past the clothesline, an elderly man stood bent forward. As we drew closer, it was apparent he wasn't bending. His back was rounded, hunched with age.

"Papà," Rosa called out sharply and touched the old man's shoulder. He glanced her way, unaware of us until she spoke again. This time, he turned slowly; his gnarled hand curled around the handle of a wooden cane.

"If all is proper, this is your nonno, Giovanni Lo Duca," Luigi said in a low voice.

My grandfather.

"Edoardo Lo Duca. *Lui viene dall'America."* Rosa spoke to him. *"Dicono che è il figlio di Giovanni."*

"He is from America. They say he is the son of Giovanni," Ivayla whispered the translation, though I understood the vein of what Rosa had said.

The old man eyeballed me for a long, awkward moment.

"Vieni qui," he said and tapped his cane on the ground.

Luigi put a hand on my shoulder and prodded me forward. My gut in a vise grip, I let go of Ivayla's hand and stepped in front of the senior Giovanni Lo Duca, close enough to hear the light wheeze of his breath. The whole outdoors seemed to go quiet—everyone silent and waiting. Old milky-brown eyes set deep within wrinkled skin studied my face. I searched his face, too, but saw nothing of myself in him. Would he see something familiar in me? My father's nose? The Lo Duca forehead?

I didn't resist the knobby-knuckled finger that pushed at my chin, impelling me to turn my head so he could view my profile. With a grunt, he released my face, his mouth curled down in a gummy scowl.

"*Impossibile! Ma mio figlio è morto.*" He turned away and threw up a hand in dismissal.

I glanced at Rosa. She lowered her eyes.

"What does that mean?" I turned to Luigi. "Is this my father's family or not?"

"I think, yes," Luigi said, once again twisting his hat. "But there is trouble."

"Why? What exactly did he say?" My gaze bounced from Luigi to Ivayla.

She and Luigi exchanged a look before she answered, her expression wrought with despair. I inhaled; steadying myself for the bad news I knew was coming.

"He said it is impossible—his son is dead."

I'd come this close, only to learn my father was eternally out of my reach. I bowed my head with the grave weight of that understanding.

I inhaled and drew on the strength that at least I had them. I stepped back in front of the old man.

"I'm sorry. I had hoped to get to know him. But I am your son's son. That makes us—" I gestured between them and me. "That makes us family. *Siamo una famiglia.*"

"No! *Va' via, impostore!*" The old man shook his cane threateningly at me, his voice sharp.

Surprised by his anger, I stepped back, concerned he might strike me.

"Oh, Papà!" Rosa cried out and scurried after her father as he moved away. The two, with their backs to us, conversed in a sharp, quick Italian.

Rosa gestured toward us, seeming to plead with her father. Who could say why—perhaps for being so bad-mannered? For treating me like a criminal instead of his long-lost grandson?

Unmoved by her plea, he pushed past her and entered the house. Rosa followed him, and the door shut with a thud behind them.

My throat went dry. A breeze kicked up. Swirling dust in the air stung my eyes, and my vision blurred. I shot past Luigi and Ivayla, making my way back to the car. I stood outside the passenger door overlooking the property.

It was as if I was being disowned before they'd knew me.

To come this close only to be pushed off a cliff —

Falling without a landing in sight.

Ivayla's arms came from behind me, wrapping around my waist and hugging my back. She said nothing. A minute after her, Luigi came hustling over and shoved his cap on his head.

"I very much apologize, Edoardo," he said, breathless.

I scrubbed a hand across my chin and looked up at the sky. "You couldn't control his response, Luigi."

Ivayla grabbed my hand. "Signor Lo Duca was so awful and terribly rude! I have a mind to go back and speak with him."

The vision of her telling the old man off made me smile despite it all.

"No, Ivayla." I shook my head. "Think of what he must have been feeling about our visit. I mean, to have a stranger walk up to you and say they are family you never knew about."

"You are too kind, Edward," she said.

"No." Again, I shook my head. "I just... I get it."

The rejection felt uncomfortably familiar. Very much like that day I ambushed Tom Rudack in the coffee shop.

The interaction with Tom had left me stung and wordless. Head low, I'd gone out to the parking lot to catch the bus toward home. Outside the door, my foot nearly slid out from under me on a sheet of paper littering the ground. The paper was dimpled and torn from the store's foot traffic. I knew right away it was my artwork. The drawing I'd given to Tom.

He didn't want anything to do with me.

Then, like now, emotions pushed and pulled at me. I felt lost and unable to react.

"I'm going for a walk." I tugged my hand from Ivalya's. "I'll meet you back at the hotel later."

"I will come with you." She started after me.

I held up a hand to stop her. "I need to be alone for a bit."

I was grateful that she didn't argue the point. Instead, she pressed a kiss to my cheek and left with Luigi.

Walking blindly across the field; up a steep slope surely no car could climb, I forced myself to focus on the surrounding view, and not unpack the events that had unfolded. The beautiful vistas, and the charm of the medieval hilltop towns of Umbria, held a sense that time stood still.

In the distance, further up the hill, everything turned green and thick with trees. I didn't know how long or how far I'd walked when I came to an old church. It stood by itself, alone with no houses or plowed fields around it. Its brick façade was worn and sun-washed. In a few spots, cracks in the brick showed signs of recent repair, the patches like ragged veins of scar tissue. Old, but cared for.

I walked around it twice before stopping in front of the entrance. Its thick, worn, wooden door stood propped open by a large, heavy stone. The last time I'd been in a church was for Toby and Claudia's wedding, at the christening of their daughters. This one wasn't like the churches around the neighborhoods of Long Island; and was far more humble than anything I'd seen in Italy. Intrigued, I poked my head inside and listened. Discerning no manmade noise, I stepped inside.

A pungent sweetness—incense and candles—permeated the cooler air and blended with the scent of many bygone centuries. A dozen lit candles flickered in the vestibule, though there wasn't a soul in sight. Sunlight streamed through stain glass windows in streaks of blues and greens. On the walls were religious frescos, a narrative, birth to death, dark to light, most of it fire and brimstone. The artwork was reminiscent of the religious paintings that appeared in many of the duomos throughout the area.

A large, faded statue of Mary dominated a corner of the church. I could tell time and sun had depleted the statue's original colors. The whitewashed pigments, pure white and a serene, pale blue, seemed fitting for what I'd recently learned about the Blessed

Mother.

I meandered down the main aisle and slipped into a wooden pew, worn soft and smooth from use. How many bodies had slipped into and out of those pews during the many years of daily and weekly prayer? How many had sat here in celebration of milestones, births, and marriages, or seeking refuge while grieving the loss of loved ones?

Since my very first days in Italy, in all the places I'd traveled, away from the hustle and bustle of tourists, that feeling of stilled time, of family, of tradition, abounded. The churches had both a strong sense of welcoming and an undeniable insistence for respect. The Italian people viewed religion with reverence, unlike at home, where most people I knew didn't go to church because they didn't want to get out of bed early on Sunday mornings to listen to antiquated Biblical messages they couldn't connect with.

I envied the Italians their history, for the familiar belief that enriched life and made them more certain of their place on this spinning globe.

With a sigh, I took out my cell. Up in the hills, as I suspected, there was no service. I typed out a message to Claudia, anyway.

Me: We found my father's family in Tuscany. Today, I met my grandfather and aunt. They say my father is dead. I don't know what happened to him. My grandfather is overcome with grief and doesn't accept me. I'm at a loss for words. Not even sure how or what to feel.

I saved the message to send later and pocketed my cell. I leaned back in the pew, and sighing aloud, finally let my wayward thoughts tumble forward.

I had come to Italy bruised and alone. Empty. One chance meeting at the hotel changed everything. My optimism in finding my father had spiraled upon meeting Ivayla. Ever since, I spent every waking moment strategizing the next move.

Still, I knew very little about my father. Even my mother only had a few months of memories of him. She'd painted him as quiet and with a strong work ethic, alone in a foreign country. Exactly like my current situation. I snorted at the irony.

As hope had taken over, I envisioned what Giovanni Lo Duca

might be like. A man who no doubt would be surprised at my existence, but who would welcome me into his life. Because I was his son. And because from what I'd seen so far, that was the way the people were here.

That dream was over. My mother had cheated me by waiting until Grams passed to tell me about him. If only she had leveled with me years ago, maybe then there would have been a chance. But now, I would never meet my father. I'd never look in his eyes and have him know me as his son.

Death had beaten me to his door.

"No!" I slammed my fist on the back of the pew in front of me.

The scornful sound pierced the silence and bellowed through the church. Tears stung the backs of my eyes. I squeezed them shut, determined to stuff the weakness back into the dark hole it had come from. A low growl vibrated in my throat.

I put my shoulders back and looked up again. In front of me, the solemn statue of the Madonna stood, hands outstretched. Throughout my time here, the Virgin Mother seemed to follow me everywhere—in hotels, in the stores, and shops, in Mario and Paolo's house, and now, here, in this dark moment. Sitting there, I felt her presence as if she, together with my grandmother, were watching over me, telling me to keep the faith, to have courage.

I breathed slowly. The heat from the back of my eyes moved lower, to my neck, and settled finally in my chest.

I thought about Grams' letter. She'd sent me here for a reason. Maybe that reason wasn't to meet my father.

My grandmother must have known I'd have a slim chance of finding him. She wouldn't have made me come, knowing I'd likely be disappointed. That wasn't her style.

I'd only ever known life in my small hometown, where most things remained the same, day in and day out. More likely, Grams wanted to challenge me to step outside my comfort zone, to see more than what I expected of the world.

I'd arrived in Italy, a pathetic guy with two blackened eyes, angry because my mother kept the truth from me about my real father, and full up on self-pity because I had no palpable plans for my future. I panicked at the unfamiliar, but eventually, I opened to it. I looked forward to whatever new experience the day had in store for me. And in the process, I'd met a kind and beautiful doctor named Ivayla Lo Duca, an Italian artist and his gregarious husband, a family who let me stay in their beautiful villa—opening a whole new world of sights, colors, and flavors to me.

Whatever my grandmother had in mind for this trip, I had found more. Much more. And the best part of what I'd found awaited me back at the hotel.

I strode down the hill and through the streets, impelled by the sheer need to see Ivayla again. Like my father before me, I had found comfort in the arms of a woman in a foreign land. Memories of our night sent a soft, evocative buzz through me.

I wondered if Giovanni's feelings for my mother had been anything like what I felt for Ivayla, how much I thought of her and wanted to be with her.

They couldn't have been. Otherwise, how could he have ever left her?

Just inside the hotel doors, Ivalya paced the lobby. I stood still and ate up the sight of her, my heart hammering against my ribs.

Ivayla saw me and stopped mid-pace. With a piercing gasp, she ran at me and threw her arms around my neck. Her fingers raked the back of my hair while she showered my face with kisses.

My face heated under the loving assault, but it felt so good—to be missed, to be loved—like coming home. I didn't stop her.

Thank you, Grams. Thank you for this.

"Cuore mio," she said in a breathless whisper and pressed her mouth firmly to mine. She pulled back and framed my face with her hands. "I am happy to see you."

"You missed me?" I asked, the corner of my mouth ticked upward.

"Very much so." Continuing to hold my face in her hands, she searched my expression like she was trying to gauge my mental temperature. "Are you well?"

"I'm fine." I pressed a kiss into her palm. "Don't fuss."

Her eyes held a flicker of doubt.

"Luigi has left. He promised to find out what happened to your father. He sends his apologies. He feels terrible about all of this."

"He shouldn't. Luigi said he'd find my father, and he did," I said. "It just so happens, he's dead. That's not Luigi's fault."

"No, but I am sad about that."

"Me, too. My feelings about it caught me off guard. I didn't expect it to hit me so hard. But last week, my view of the world changed."

I took her hands and pulled her closer. The scent of her exploded through my senses, and I had to take a breath before I could speak again.

"You happened, Ivayla. You came into Berto's hotel and pushed me aside. Even if I never find out what happened to my father, I'm glad I came to Italy. I'm grateful my grandmother made me come. Because it led me to *you*." I pressed my lips to her knuckles. "I'm not the same guy who stepped off that plane in Rome. You are a big part of that change, and I want to thank you for that. I can't even tell you how much it's helped me to have you and your fathers in my life. You've made me feel like I belong. It's been a long time since I felt that way."

"You need not say more, Edward." Tears pooled in her brown eyes.

"But I want to because you've given me something I've never felt." I brushed my lips against hers. "You might think it's weird because we've only known each other a short time, but since that first day when you grabbed my wrist and I looked into your eyes, I've been falling in love with you, Ivayla."

Future be damned, that was the truth of it.

"How impossible you are! To make me so happy when I am so sad." A couple of fat tears broke loose and rolled down her cheek. She swatted my shoulder and sniffled.

"Ivayla?"

"What?"

"Do you…" I paused, drawing on deep courage. "Do you feel sort of anything like that about me?"

"What do you think? That I come here and sleep in your bed just to be nice?" She dug unceremoniously into her handbag and pulled out a fistful of tissues.

After she wiped her nose, I tipped her chin up.

"Tell me then."

"I love you," she said, the words brisk, like a cursory obligation.

"You didn't have to say *that*. I wasn't fishing for those words."

"It is true."

"That's not possible. It's too soon."

"No, it is not." She shook her head. "I love you because you were kind to the man who asked you if you knew his cousin in Florida. Because you cry at the birth of a friend's baby. Because after such a terrible disappointment, you say you are grateful for the experience and happy your grandmother made you come."

She pressed into me, her warm espresso eyes summoning me. *Come,* they said. *Fall,* they said.

If I went, there'd be no escape. Whether she intended it, she'd have all of me.

My breaths came noisily and uncontrolled. Letting myself fall meant trusting my heart to a woman I'd known less than two weeks.

"Take me up to our room now. I will show you." Her hand slid down my spine and over the curve of my backside.

Heat surged south; my thoughts clouded. Pressing needs demanded action. I grabbed her hand and took off for the elevator. I jabbed the call button twice.

"Ivayla, tomorrow, can we go back to Positano?"

"You don't want to see Rome?"

I shook my head. "My heart isn't in it."

"Of course, Edward. I will tell Papà and Babbo to expect us."

"One last request." I took both her hands in mine. "No more talk about my father. I don't want to think about it anymore."

Paolo said it was best to bury the past. And that's what I would do.

Chapter 14

WHEN WE CHECKED OUT OF the hotel the next morning, the cool air outside made us stop to pull on sweaters. The leaves of the palms rattled, clicking and rustling, making noises unlike anything at home. We boarded the train headed back to Positano. Quiet, I stared out the train window. Winter was coming to this paradise. I found myself interested in knowing what the season would bring to the region. I wished I could stay and see it all.

Ivayla didn't stress over travel. She slept, and in much the same way as when we went to Tuscany, she dozed off on the way back to Positano. I watched her sleep, studied her features softened in rest, with my artist's eye.

My fingers itched to draw her again, but instead of giving in to it, I scrolled through my cell phone and found a missed message from Claudia.

Claudia: I'm sorry about your father. Sometimes the only thing to do is sit with it. Sending you hugs xxx. Call your mother.

My mother? I slipped the phone into my backpack. That woman caused this royal mess. She was the last person I wanted to talk to.

In Positano, Ivayla and I hired a taxi to take us up the mountainside. We walked through the house's gated entryway, and a great sense of relief washed over me. It wasn't my home, but being in a foreign country, Villa Campanella felt like a sturdy fortress against my recent wave of disappointment.

"Ciao, Babbo! Ciao, Papà!" Ivayla called out to her fathers as we entered the villa's contemporary dining room.

"Come, prego! Sit my loves." Mario rose from the table where he and Paolo sat eating dinner and came across the room to hug us both. "I will get you something to eat."

He rushed off to fetch additional table settings. I lowered my backpack to the floor at the wide breezeway into the room. As usual, Mario overloaded the table with food. The tempting aromas of pasta and vegetables, shrimp, and bread dangled in the air. Paolo pointed to the chair across from him, motioning for me to sit. I stayed on my feet, inhaling deeply. Though I wasn't hungry, I'd missed this.

"Tell us, have you found your Giovanni?" Mario inquired, silverware clinking as he set the table with the added dinner dishes.

Ivayla silenced him with a subtle shake of her head.

"No, no, they should hear about it." I gave her shoulders a gentle squeeze. "You can tell them. If you'll forgive me, all I want to do is go up and shower and go to bed."

"Did you draw?" Paolo asked.

I met his eyes and nodded. "I did. Maybe some of my best work."

"Good." He winked, egging a smile out of me. *Buona notte.*

Among a chorus of good nights, I dragged myself up the stairs. In the bathroom, I stripped and then got under a spray of hot water. I stayed in the shower longer than usual, letting the steam loosen my tense muscles. Dragging my tired limbs back to my bedroom, I changed into shorts and a T-shirt and fell across the bed. The soft, airy blankets ballooned up around me, cradling every inch. It was heavenly. The only thing that would've made the bed better was if Ivayla were beside me. My mind wandered as I drifted off, remembering the best part of the last few days— my time with Ivayla, loving her.

The door gently creaked open, spilling the room with moonlight from the hallway portico. Ivayla's silhouette crossed the room with the soft patter of her footsteps before the mattress dipped under her weight.

"You shouldn't be here," I said, but reached for her just the same.

"I know. I will stay only a moment." She lay down beside me and took my hand.

I laced her fingers through mine. Hers were strong and elegant hands, smart if hands could be smart.

"How are you feeling?" she asked.

"Tired, but happy to be back here and be with you and your fathers." I rolled onto my side, threaded my fingers through her hair and kissed her cheek. I wanted to ask again *Is this real?* But I didn't want her to think me stupid and unsure—which, for maybe the first time in my history of dating, I totally was.

Because she mattered more than anyone who'd come before.

"I was thinking," I said. "So what if I never got to meet my father. You grew up without your mother and look at you. You're amazing. As I figure it, I'm better off having a dead father than believing my father is a deadbeat asshole who couldn't be bothered with me. I'm... okay, or I will be. Don't worry about me."

"Allora, you cannot stop me from worrying about you. You are in my heart, Edward." She twisted toward me and stroked my face. "I am not working tomorrow. Perhaps you would like to take a ride to Pompeii to see the ruins?"

"Sure. Seeing people who had it much worse off than me will really cheer me up," I said with a snort.

"I must return to my room, but I am sad for you." She hugged me. "You will be okay?"

I nodded, and she pressed her lips to mine for a lingering kiss that spoke of future promises. She left, departing as quietly as she'd entered. The door closed with a soft click. I sighed and rolled over, already missing her.

After some deep breathing, my mind quieted, and I dozed off.

The bedroom door popped open again, but this time with more gusto. A whoosh of air ruffled my hair and the sheets on the bed.

"Get up!" came a growling command.

I sprung upright with a start, the time of night unclear. Paolo stood in the doorway, his hand on the knob. It was too dark to see his face, but the moonlight outlined his profile and the tight set of his stance.

"Is everything okay?" Alarmed, I threw my feet over the side of the bed.

He flipped the light switch, throwing the room into brightness I wasn't ready for. I rubbed my eyes.

"You tell me what this is." He came at me, shoving a book in front of my face, and pointed to a page.

I blinked several times, trying to get my eyes to focus only to realize he had my sketchbook in his hand. It was opened to a portrait of a nude young woman sitting on a bed, a blanket draped over her midsection, breasts exposed, the feminine form skillfully shaded by my very hand.

I was a good artist. There was no mistaking the shape of the face and eyes, the long dark hair—Paolo knew the drawing was his daughter.

"Paolo." I started tentatively, taking the drawing pad from him and closing the cover. "I meant no disrespect. Ivayla is very beautiful, and… we've grown close."

"I told you 'no.'"

"I know. You did, and I'm sorry, but I love your daughter." The admission came without preamble, but the words connected with my heart. I sat up taller and repeated it with more force. "*I love Ivayla.*"

We locked eyes. The deep-set wrinkles around his eyes intensified.

"My daughter not be with you." He shook a condemning finger at me. "No American, no!"

It was like talking to a wall. I sprung to my feet, eyes narrowed.

"What the hell do you have against Americans? I thought you liked me. You took me up the mountain to draw."

"I have reasons. I no need explain to you. Pack your things and get out," he snapped and left the room.

I sat on the bed and rubbed my face, thinking of Ivayla. She'd be sleeping soundly, unaware of the turn of events. I shoved my stuff into my duffle bag and stepped out onto the portico. I glanced toward Ivayla's bedroom and thought about calling out to her. Maybe Mario would wake up, too. No doubt they would be on my side. But Paolo hovered in the dark shadows, arms crossed.

"You can send me away, but it won't change how we feel about each other," I said.

"Out." He pointed to the steps.

I turned and started down the stairs. Paolo followed. Though he was several steps behind, I felt the press of him forcing me out. We exchanged no further words. I left the villa quietly, pulling the door shut behind me.

Berto sat behind the check-in desk watching an Italian television show when I stepped up to the hotel counter.

"Signor Rudack, prego!" He stood and made a slight bow in my direction. "It is such a pleasure to see you again."

"Berto," I acknowledged him and wearily dropped my bag to the floor.

"Will you be needing a room again?" he asked, and I nodded. "One night or more?"

"One night, but maybe hold it open in case I need it for more, okay?"

He nodded. "Of course. You are always welcome here, my friend."

I clomped up the stairs, unlocked the door, and threw my bag on the floor next to the bed. The room was stuffy. I tore off my clothes, punched the flat pillow until it submitted, and dropped my head onto it.

Unable to sleep, I took out my cell phone and sent a message to Claudia.

Me: I need to talk. Things have gone from bad to worse. Text me when you're available.

Claudia: I'm up. Nursing Lucas. What happened?

Me: The Duke is a stubborn, insufferable old coot. Threw me out.

Claudia: Wow, what did you do?

Me: He doesn't like Americans... And I drew a naked picture of Ivayla.

Claudia: Did she pose?

Me: Hey now! Not a pervert!! I'm into Ivayla, in a big way.
Claudia: Well then, she really MUST be something!
Me: She is. She's amazing.
Claudia: What'll happen when you come home?

What was I going to do? Now that Ivayla was part of my life, I couldn't think of going forward without her.

Me: Need to figure it out. Otherwise, this one will roll me. FOR REAL.

Claudia: Oh, wow. THAT serious already?

I knew what she was thinking: We'd known each other for less than two weeks. How could I feel this strongly? It sounded impractical. Only teenagers fell in love so quickly. I'd dated a lot of girls but being with Ivayla made me feel different. Being with her filled a space in my heart that had been empty. If I tried to explain it, I'd come off sounding like an infatuated idiot. But the thing was, I wasn't interested in trying to convince Claudia, or anyone else, of how I felt. I didn't care what they thought.

The cell binged with another message.

Claudia: Did you speak to your mother?

My mother, *again*. Annoyance rattled in my throat.

Me: No and don't want to.

Claudia: She's still your mother. She worries about you.

I tossed the phone on the night table without replying. Claudia was 'moming' me. My friend was a good person and a great mother. She was nothing like Diane Rudack. My mother didn't sweat the small stuff. From experience, I knew mom wasn't losing sleep over my situation.

I lay there, staring up at the ceiling, too angry to sleep. Ivayla was a grown woman. Paolo had no right to dictate what she did or who she did it with.

Narrow-minded old Italian.

It was *his husband* who encouraged us. The condoms Mario had given Ivayla had set off the tempest of sex that had followed.

It made little sense that Paolo and Mario could hold such differing opinions of me. At first, I thought it was that moody artist thing, but now I knew it was more. Paolo viewed me as a threat. But a threat to what? I was sure part of the answer lie in my being

American.

Ivayla was strong-willed, and I was certain when she found out what went down between Paolo and me, she'd be livid. She'd have it out with her father. She would aim that fury of hers, the one I'd only sampled, full force at Paolo. Hell knew no fury—and all that.

But for what? A short-term romance? Was a doomed relationship worth driving a wedge between her and her family?

I had fallen in love with Italy, with the food, with the people. I'd fallen in love with its art and its history. But mostly with an amazing woman. Still, it'd be insane for either of us to think we could continue this thing long-distance, thousands of miles apart, seeing each other maybe every few months—at most, a handful of times a year.

My heart ached, heavy with the narrow list of undesirable, and likely, not sustainable, options that lay before me. Before us.

I squeezed my eyes shut. No, none of it really mattered. A world away, my old life awaited my return. In three days, I was going home to the United States.

I must've dozed off because the sound of the doorknob jiggling startled me awake. I yanked the sheet up to cover my nakedness; eyes pinned on the door.

"Grazie, Berto," came Ivayla's hushed voice from the hallway.

The door squeaked, rotating on its hinges. It clicked shut, followed by the thump of her bag hitting the floor.

"I'm sorry I had to leave," I said, unsure of what else to say.

She glided toward the bed, into a shaft of moonlight that shone through the curtains. The light caught her and illuminated her with an angelic glow.

"You left without telling me," she said, her tone accusing. The mattress dipped under her weight as she sat down on the bed next to me. "Did you think I would not notice?"

"Paolo kicked me out. He found my hotel room drawing of you," I said. "The naked one."

"You did not think to wake me? That I would care to know?"

She rested a hand on my chest.

"He's your father. It's his house. I didn't want you to take sides."

Her eyes stayed on mine. "You assume I would not choose your side?"

"I didn't want you to have to choose. They're your family. And we're…" I grunted. "We're, I don't know what, hanging onto the possibility of something that may not have a future?"

She tipped her chin down, lowering her eyes from my sight.

"For years, Papà and Babbo have been wanting to marry me off. You hear them. They cry, *'oh boo-hoo, Ivayla. We grow old waiting for you to give us bambinos to bounce on our knees.'* They think I resist them because I am too involved with my work, but that is not true. I want to marry and have babies. It is just that I have not found someone who is both kind and honest. And who also makes my pulse race." She lifted her gaze, her eyes locking on my face. "Not until you, Edward."

My heart thumped hard in my chest. "Ivayla, are you saying…"

She peeled back the sheet, revealing my nudity. With a smile, she trailed her fingers up the inside of my bare thigh, eliciting an involuntary moan from my lips.

With her hand lying teasingly close to the most sensitive part of my anatomy, I fought a rush of adrenaline that coursed through my veins. She stood, and in one smooth motion, slipped her dress over her head and dropped it to the floor. Lucky for me I was lying down because the sight of her standing there in nothing but a skimpy pair of undies would've brought me to my knees. Straddling my hips, she lowered herself onto her elbows and cradled my face between her palms.

"*Ti adoro,*" she whispered, moving her lips over my mouth. "*Ti amo.*"

I woke to find Ivayla moving quickly about the room. Dressed, with her hair swept up in a long, neat braid down her back, she appeared ready to rock-and-roll.

"I must go to see Alba. The stable has messaged to say she injured her leg. They say not so bad, but I must go to talk with the veterinarian."

"Do you want me to come?" I asked.

"It is unnecessary. Stay in bed. Sleep." She finger-combed my sleep-mussed hair and brushed a kiss across my lips. "We will talk to Papà and Babbo when I return. Smooth things out, yes?"

"Ivayla, wait." I arched forward and grabbed her hand. "I want to smooth things out with Paolo, but we need to talk about what happens when I go back to the United States."

"This is not a problem, Edward. You will apply for dual citizenship. Italy's offices are not quick to process paperwork. That part will take some time, but Signor Delatorre can help you. Once you have your citizenship, you can live and work here." She moved a few feet toward the door and looked over her shoulder. "I am quite confident I can persuade you to stay."

She batted her eyelashes at me, but I was trying to process the information.

"I will call you and tell you when I leave the stables. We will meet on the street and go in to talk to Papà and Babbo together." She strode to the door, turning to throw me a kiss. "All will be right. You will see. *Ciao, ciao, ciao, amore mio!*"

I snatched the kiss from the air and fell back on the bed, smiling. She swept from the room; her laughter following her out. Stirred by her movement, her scent lingered in the air. A warm sensation tickled the back of my throat.

With the memory of Ivayla's warm body next to mine, I catapulted into fantasy, skipping dreamily down the yellow brick road. I imagined a life with Ivayla, the two of us living together, facing the mornings with espresso, eating, arguing, making love, and falling into bed each night. I pictured us, years from now, married with kids. We'd known each other only a short time, but envisaging a future with her warmed me through and through. Except, a reality check quickly flattened my high. I'd be leaving my friends and family and moving to a country where I could barely speak the language, not to mention I'd be coming without a job or much money.

How long would an intelligent career woman hang on to a guy who had so little to offer in return? And then, what would I do?

I dressed and went into the piazza for breakfast. The fruit stand lady gifted me her most beautiful, ripe pear, and Giorgio at the café refused to take payment for my cappuccino. The attention embarrassed me, but I knew enough to accept the gifts graciously. These were proud people.

I returned to the bench overlooking the beach, the same one I'd slept on that first night in Positano when the days ahead had been uncertain. I held the uneaten pear in one hand and sipped the hot coffee. A soft wind of sweet sea air ruffled my hair.

Even as I admired the beautiful view, the truth crept up inside me. I had to set things straight with Ivayla. Any idea of a future was a fantasy. The sooner we acknowledged that, the better.

That meant leaving Positano as soon as possible. Truthfully, I didn't want to have a face-off with Paolo, anyway. The thought of it made my stomach clench. I would let the thing with him lie. Whatever his reason for hating me, I'd concede.

Once I left the Amalfi Coast, I'd never see him again, anyway.

I went through the steps, planning my departure: check out of Berto's hotel, buy a train ticket north, and then talk to Ivayla.

At the edge of the piazza, the crowd parted to let someone through. Luigi in his bakery whites stopped only briefly to scan the area before his gaze settled on me. His footsteps beat their way to my bench.

"You are here," he said as if I hadn't known my own location.

"But how did you know I'd be here?" I had told no one where I was going.

"I am good at finding people!" he said, and we both laughed. "I have a message from Rosa Lo Duca. She ask to see you."

The coffee cup shook in my hand. Caramel-colored liquid dribbled down my chin. I quickly sat up straight and wiped my mouth with the back of my hand.

"Rosa wants to see me?" I asked.

The jowls of Luigi's fleshy face jiggled with his quick nod. "Sì. She wishes to explain family to you."

I gulped down the rest of my cappuccino and took a taxi to the horse stable, a long depot-like building set beside a fenced paddock and shaded by several thick trees. Halfway down the interior herringbone-bricked walk, Ivayla stood in the open doorway of one of the dozen wood and steel-barred corrals. Inside the enclosure, Alba butted her head against Ivayla's shoulder, whinnying until her owner reached up to rub her muzzle.

"How is she?" I asked, noticing the bandaged leg.

"She needs sutures. The veterinarian has gone to get supplies for the procedure. But it is not so bad." She tipped her head, resting it on the side of the horse's face.

"I have news," I said and told her about Rosa's request to see me.

"I cannot go with you. The injury has made Alba very uneasy. I am the only one to calm her. But you must go, Edward."

"Ivayla," I murmured, pausing to inhale. "After I talk to my aunt, I'm going to Rome."

She smiled. "As soon as I am able, I will take the train to meet you there."

I wanted to tell her about my plans to leave. Before Delatorre showed up this morning with his news, though, I had a few days to work up to this final moment, to prepare for what I would say. But now, I no longer had that buffer. I tried to psych myself up, telling myself it would be hard, definitely painful, but necessary. The sooner the better.

My pulse drummed loudly, white noise in my head, drowning out the neighing of horses and other sounds around us. I opened my mouth, but nothing came out. It felt too rushed. Too unkind.

Oh, God. I just wasn't ready.

Instead, I heard myself telling her, "I'd love to do Rome with you."

"I am happy you will finally get your answers." She wrapped her arms tightly around me and kissed the side of my face. Her embrace stirred something deep inside me. Knowing I'd spend my last few days in Italy, enjoying Rome with Ivayla made my spineless procrastination worthwhile.

"Here, give this to Alba." I handed her the ripened pear I'd gotten earlier. Then I left and went directly to the bus station.

It wasn't long before I boarded the bus north to meet with my estranged aunt, once again.

Chapter 15

M Y THOUGHTS BOUNCED FROM ONE idea to the next during the train ride to Tuscany. I was unsure of how to feel about this meeting. Excited. Nervous. What did Rosa Lo Duca want to tell me? Was she ready to connect and get to know me? Would she and my grandfather accept me as part of their family?

Off the train, I hailed a taxi. The driver dropped me at the beginning of the driveway that led up to the Lo Duca's house. I strode up the incline, my stomach twisting tighter with each step. The wind blew in gusts. I pulled the hood of my sweatshirt up to keep my ears warm. The grounds were quiet. No sight of the old man or the woman—my grandfather or aunt. I stood at the front door and steadied myself. Then, I knocked, three times, hard, to make sure someone heard.

The door creaked opened slowly. Rosa's face appeared slightly pinched with annoyance. As her eyes alighted on me, the hard expression melted away and morphed into something softer. And way sadder.

"*Buongiorno*. Luigi Delatorre *parlarmi*." In rough Italian, I told her that Delatorre had spoken to me. With neither the old man nor Rosa able to speak English, and me familiar only with common Italian phrases, communicating would be difficult, making the visit even more daunting.

"*Vieni dentro*." She pulled the door open wider and invited me inside.

Filtered daylight, the only light in the house, came in through the draped windows. Faded carpet runners muffled our footsteps as we passed rooms styled in that old-world way, furniture and decor from another era. Despite the oldness to it, the rooms were tidy and had a scrubbed clean feel. A cool, earthy smell of brick and damp plaster ghosted under the scent of pungent herbs and spices.

Rosa, dressed in a black sweater over a drab floral print dress, brought me into a formal living room and motioned for me to sit on a gold upholstered couch. A large framed painting of an Italian landscape hung on the wall behind it. I sat down and laced my fingers on my lap. Somewhere down a hallway, a clock sounded out seconds in loud ticks.

From a stack of padded books, she selected two. She slid them soundlessly onto the surface of the carved legged coffee table, then, with an exhale, sat down across from me. The memory books' worn and faded leather-like covers hinted at their age. Without looking up, she opened one and leafed through pages of photographs locked uniformly behind protective sheets of cellophane. A low whine accompanied each turn of the yellowed and crinkled pages. She stopped when she found what she was looking for and turned the book in my direction.

"*Mio fratello*, Giovanni." *My brother*, she said and tapped a faded color photograph. I wanted to look at the photo, but her eyes latched on to my face, making it difficult to look away. Her hand curled on her lap like she wanted to touch me. "*Sei come lui.*"

I punched the sentence into my cell phone for translation: *You are like him.*

My fingers froze. I would see for the first time what my father looked like. I inhaled and lowered my gaze.

The retro color of the image looked like Kodachrome colorization used a half a century ago. The same type used to develop the images from the first half of my mother's life.

The photo was of a guy in his late teens to early twenties. Tight white pants and T-shirt clung to a wiry, thin build. I had the exact same build throughout high school—I had even worn my pants tight, too. A nest of wavy opaque black hair crowned his head; its length long, hitting his shoulders. Impeded by a thick mustache and beard, it was difficult to discern the shape of his face. I, too, could grow facial hair easily enough but had always preferred a clean-shaven chin. Though it didn't make sense, something about his eyes seemed familiar.

"Why did he go to America? For work? *A lavoro?*" I asked.

"*Mio papà—a vedere il mondo.*" She moved her arms in a circular motion. "*Una grande vita.*"

I'd picked up enough Italian to understand. "Your father wanted him to see the world, live a big life. Yes?"

"*Sì. Mio fratello, Giovanni* — America. *Incontrò una donna.*" She turned a page and pointed to a photo. "*Papà era molto felice.*"

Her brother, Giovanni, went to America, met *una donna*, a woman, and his father was *molto felice*, very happy. My skin prickled with goosebumps. The story fit. The photo of a young couple dancing was the absolute proof I'd been hoping for. Though younger, with fewer lines around her eyes and mouth, I recognized my mother's face. My face and eyes burned, a telltale sign I was about to lose my shit. I inhaled, attempting to pull myself together, and scrolled through my cell phone images to a recent photo of my mother.

"The woman is my mother." I showed the image to her, repeating my words in Italian. "*La donna è mia madre*, Diane."

Rosa leaned over to look, her fingers grazing mine, her hand shaking a little. Over the cell, her eyes met mine. She nodded thoughtfully and sighed.

There was more to come. With the translation app open on my cell phone, I motioned for her to speak into it.

"Giovanni *tornò arrabbiato*. Papà *e* Giovanni *litigarono.*" She scowled and raised her hands, curled into fists. "*Papà non piaceva il suo stile di vita.*"

I glanced at the translation. Her father disapproved of something in Giovanni's life, and the two of them had fought about it.

"What *stile di vita?* What did Giovanni do?"

"*Amedeo.*" She flicked the back of her right ear, her eyes cast down at her lap. "*Amor platonico.*"

The gesture meant something, but I did not understand what. I repeated the words to my phone, but the translations of 'Lover of God' and 'plutonic relationship' didn't offer clarity.

"*Non capisco*," I said, shaking my head.

Rosa dug into the large, sagging side pocket of her sweater, her cheeks flushed, and pulled out a curled photo. She caught my eyes for a moment before she pushed the photo into my hand.

The photo was of two young men, embracing near the edge of a cliff overlooking a body of water. In the dim light, I could hardly see their faces. The decorative table lamp next to the couch threw out a weak shaft of light, and I leaned toward it to see better. It was slightly out of focus, but I could see one man was Giovanni. He was older in the photo, his beard gone, and his arms around the other man suggested a close bond.

"*Due uomini.*" She held up two fingers and then shook her head. "*Non una donna.*"

Two men. Not a woman.

"You're saying they were together?" I looked up the word '*together.*' "Giovanni and l'uomo, *insieme?*"

"Sì," she said.

Giovanni and the man were together.

I stared at her with a blank expression. It made little sense. He and my mother had been lovers. I was proof of that.

"No. *Non capisco*," I said, but I feared the more she tried to make me understand, the more lost I would be.

She motioned to the wall behind my head. I turned slowly; praying whatever it was would give me some insight on the situation. It was the painting I'd noticed on the way in—the huge fresco of what appeared to be the Tuscan Hills.

Sure, it was good, but it meant nothing to me.

She waved her hands at it.

"*L'artista, Il Duco*," she said, her mouth turned down.

The artist: the Duke.

I could see it was Paolo's work, the brushwork his distinct style. By her sneer, Rosa didn't like the painting. But why the hell were we discussing artwork when I was so close to getting answers about my father?

I turned back to Rosa. "*L'artista,* Paolo Lo Duca?"

"Sì, *mio fratello.*"

"Oh, you have two brothers—*due fratelli*—Giovanni and

Paolo?" I held up two fingers, desperate to move on.

She made an impatient noise in the back of her throat. Her attention returned to the photo album as she briskly flipped its pages. Emitting another guttural noise, she rotated the book in my direction and snapped her finger at a black and white baby photo.

Handwritten under the photo was Giovanni Paolo.

"Whoa, wait." I sputtered like someone had lobbed a cannon-ball into my chest. "Your brother's name is Giovanni Paolo? *He's my father?*"

"Giovanni Paolo Lo Duca—*l'artista.*" She crossed her arms and gave me a firm nod of her head. "Sì."

The famed ill-tempered artist of Positano, Paolo Lo Duca, and her brother, Giovanni Lo Duca, was the same man.

I gripped the arm of the couch and squeezed my eyes shut to stop the room from spinning.

I'd not only met my father, but I'd been living with him for almost two weeks.

Paolo evidently didn't use his first name anymore, probably because his family disowned him. But he'd known I was looking for a man with his name—Giovanni. He knew why I'd come to Italy. Did he know he was the father I'd been looking for? I felt a spike of anger rise within me, still bitter at the way he'd thrown me out of the villa, but I could afford to give him the benefit of the doubt. As my mother had attested, he hadn't known she was pregnant. He knew nothing of me. It was likely Paolo was as oblivious of our connection as me.

I blew out and opened my eyes to study the photo in my hand, to study Giovanni's beardless face and those eyes that looked so familiar. They were definitely Paolo's.

Rosa tapped the photo again. "*Sposato.*"

Spouse. Married.

The photo Rosa hid in her pocket captured young male lovers and explained why the snapshot wasn't inside the album with the rest. My grandfather disapproved of a gay lifestyle. The senior Giovanni Lo Duca had said his son was dead. What he'd meant was his son was *as good as dead* to him.

Facts unscrambled, I recognized the other man in the photo, too. Though thinner, he still had a full, round face and that telltale gregarious smile.

"Mario," I said.

"Sì, Mario Mancini." She nodded.

"Oh my God," I groaned, dropping my head into my hands. Ivayla's father was my father!

Rosa's warm palms sandwiched my face as she gently guided my gaze toward her.

"*Siamo una famiglia,*" she whispered, her eyes glossy with tears.

We are a family.

"Sì." I covered her hands with mine, emotion clawing the back of my throat. "*Zia Rosa.*"

Aunt Rosa.

We smiled timidly at each other until the gruff, commanding voice of my grandfather bellowed through the house.

"Rosa!"

My aunt visibly stiffened. With tears in her eyes, she shushed me with a finger to her lips and pulled me to my feet. Reaching down, she quickly dislodged the photo of Paolo and my mother from the photo album and pressed it into my hand.

"*Mi dispiace.*" She hurried me to the back door. "*Devi andartene ora!*"

She was sorry, but I had to go. My grandfather apparently wasn't ready to accept me.

"*Grazie mille, Zia Rosa,*" I whispered and squeezed her hand.

She squeezed my hand back before letting it go. Then she closed the door on me.

I tucked the photo into my backpack and started down the driveway with a strong feeling it would not be the last time we'd see each other.

I made my way to town through the rural streets, full of noisy local kids just let out of school. I stopped at an overlook, the beauty of the view muddied by the barrage of thoughts and emotions unfolding inside of me. I'd found what I came to Italy for, my father. But now that I'd found him, he would blight the memories of the very relationship that had held me afloat during my time in Italy. Because if Paolo was my father, that meant Ivayla and I shared his blood.

Brother and sister. Half siblings—but still siblings.

What had been beautiful yesterday was now taboo.

Forbidden.

My stomach heaved, and I bent over, sure I would puke. Nothing came, but as I stood, a heavy malaise settled on my shoulders.

At the train station, my phone chimed with a barrage of incoming messages. All from Ivayla expressing her concern and desire to know the outcome of my meeting with Rosa.

I couldn't find it in me to call her. She deserved to know the truth. Just not yet. I sent her one simple text.

Me: Stay in Positano.

Chapter 16

I NEGOTIATED THE TRAIN SYSTEM, TO the bus, and back down the Amalfi coast. My cell rang with a call from my mother. I fidgeted for a moment, considering what I'd say to her, what I'd tell her about Paolo, but decided instead to let it go unanswered.

I'd deal with her after I spoke with my father.

In the gray of the early morning, the bus hugged the winding roads, bringing me closer to my fate. Here, the clouds that had merely loomed threateningly up north, released a small squall by the time the bus pulled up to my stop in Positano. Without an umbrella, attempting to stay dry was a futile effort. I pulled up the hood of my sweatshirt, set my eyes on the walk, and submitted to the rain.

Ivayla might be home, but one way or another, Paolo would know the truth. And I would be the one to tell him.

The rain drenched me. My hair stuck to my face, my sweatshirt, completely saturated, hung heavily on my frame. Thanks to the torrent of rainwater rushing downhill in every passageway, my shoes made sucking noises with each step toward the villa.

Outside the gated entrance to my father's house, I twisted the doorbell several times, harder than necessary. It chimed through the house above me. The door swung open to reveal Mario. His eyes and lips went round and wide at the sight of me. I opened my mouth to talk, but his meaty hand caught my arm and dragged me through the door.

"Edoardo," he said, sounding breathless and troubled. "Why you leave us? I worry."

I swiped water from my face. "Paolo didn't tell you?"

Mario shook his head.

"Where's Ivayla?" I glanced past him, but the house seemed quiet.

"She go to visit the horse," he said.

"Good." I nodded; relieved I didn't have to face her yet. "Where is Paolo? I need to speak to him."

"Sì, of course," he said, motioning to the stairway. "Come inside. Dry off. I get you something to eat. And a hot drink."

"No food, no drink. Just Paolo." I needed to say what I had to say and not get shifted off track.

We reached the main floor. Mario bustled to the nearest bathroom and came back with a stack of towels.

"You and Paolo grew up in Tuscany, huh?" I asked.

"Sì. Our families still there. We no bother with them. Ivayla say Luigi call you to go back there. We think you find family," Mario said, watching me dry my hair and face. "All day Ivayla *schizzinosa*, fussy, and no tell us more. She barely speaks to us, especially Paolo."

Mario looked at me as if I could help him understand her mood, but I pressed my lips together, refusing to talk.

"He's outside having after-breakfast *sigaretta*." He signaled to the veranda.

"Thank you." I handed Mario the damp towel and squared my shoulders.

Paolo sat in the same place as the day I'd met him. With his back to me, an elbow perched on the tabletop, smoke curled in the air around his head from the cigarette, nearly burned down to the nub, between his paint-stained fingers.

"I tell you no come back," he said without turning around.

The gauntlet had been thrown. There'd be no civilities.

I approached him at the table. Neither of us looked at the other. The dense rain filled the air with moisture, causing the acrid smell of the burning nicotine to hover. The steady fall of thick droplets smacked the open floor area, providing a backdrop of white noise.

"I'm not here because I want to be. I'm here because there's something we need to talk about." I took out Rosa's photo of my mother and Paolo from my backpack and dropped it on his lap. "That's my mother."

He picked up the photo, but instead of looking at it, he sat back and met my gaze. "What is this? I don't know your mother."

"Yes, you do." I thrust a finger at the photo. "Look at it damn it. Her name is Diane. You had a relationship with her when you were in America."

"Paolo, this is true?" Mario asked from behind us.

We both turned to look at him. Neither had known he was standing there.

"No." Paolo shoved the photo back at me.

I put my hands on the table and leaned forward. "There's no denying it, Paolo. I have proof."

For the first time, his eyes swiveled to my face.

"What is this you have?" Mario came forward.

"Niente." Paolo rose to his feet and vigorously stubbed out his cigarette in a glass ashtray.

"It's hardly nothing, Paolo. I spoke with your sister, Rosa. She told me how you went to America to please your father. He thought you'd sow your wild oats, and it would fix you, didn't he?"

"Sì, sì, sì!" he yelled, a vein in his jaw pulsing. "But it not a choice. And he no accept."

"Paolo and his papà, no love between them. I know this." Mario's face reddened. "Why this matter, Edoardo?"

"Twenty-seven years ago, my mother had an affair with an Italian man named Giovanni Lo Duca. A month after he returned to Italy, she found out she was pregnant. She didn't know how to get in touch with Giovanni. She could never tell him about the birth of his American son." I slid the photograph into the center of the table. "Rosa gave me this photo. It's a picture of Paolo in America—with my mother."

Mario leaned in to look.

"Look at her, Paolo." I jabbed at the photo. "You have to remember her. She worked in the same greenhouse you worked in, the only one who spoke to you."

"Sei pazzo." Paolo waved a dismissive hand at me and took a

step in the direction of the door.

I flash-backed to that day in the coffee shop, all those years ago. Tom Rudack had denied me as his son, but Paolo couldn't deny me. I wouldn't let him.

I moved in front of him, blocking him from moving away, my gaze tight on his.

"I'm not crazy. Rosa called you by your full name, Giovanni Paolo Lo Duca, *l'artista, Il Duco*. My mother told me about how she met you. How she was nice to you. All the pieces fit together. It has to be you. You are my father."

Next to us, Mario made a moaning noise and fell back a step. Paolo's eyes went wide and dark, and then his hands were on me, tightening around my throat, constricting my airway. My breath sputtered as fear rushed through my limbs. I clutched his wrists, pulling uselessly at his angry grip.

"Paolo, no!" Mario was on us, too, yanking at Paolo's hands.

A blaze of rage engulfed me, obliterating the fear. I grabbed the wrists restraining me and tore them away. But something snapped inside me. I lunged forward, hitting him in the chest, roundhouse with both fists. I was both younger and in better shape. The force of my fists sent him careening backward. He slammed into the patio railing, his motion jarringly interrupted. The railing emitted a sharp wail of protest before Paolo finally toppled to the floor in front of it.

Paolo clutched his chest, his expression morphing from hostility to surprise. My anger evaporated, immediately replaced with concern.

"Is it your heart?" I rushed to him and dropped to my knees. Without waiting for an answer, I began undoing the buttons of his shirt near his throat. "Mario, call Ivayla."

Mario stabbed the buttons on his phone and yelled, "*Presto! Vieni!*"

Come! Quickly!

He tossed the phone aside and nearly tumbled to the floor next to us, his fussing hands touching and prodding his husband.

"Stop!" Paolo slapped at both of our hands. "*Sto bene, Mario.*"

He said he was fine. I sat back on my heels but kept watching him. His breathing was normalizing, his color returning.

"*È vero*, Paolo?" Mario asked holding Paolo's hand. "Edoardo's mamma?"

Mario had asked the fated question: *Is it true?*

The rain paused, almost as if holding its breath in anticipation of Paolo's answer.

Paolo squeezed his hand but lowered his eyes. "Mario, *mi dispiace. Ti amo.*"

Paolo was apologizing. He and Mario had been together for a long time. From the photos Rosa had shown me, likely before Paolo met my mother. Could he have not told Mario about the affair?

Downstairs, the door smashed open, and the stairwell rattled with the sound of rushing footsteps. Ivayla burst onto the veranda, breathless, her cheeks reddened, her dark, beautiful hair matted to her head.

"Babbo, where does it hurt?" She pushed in between Mario and me to kneel at Paolo's side. She grabbed his arm and pressed two fingers to his wrist.

"*Sto bene, cucciola mia,*" he said, his eyes soft on her face.

"I will determine whether you are fine," she said stiffly. We all kept quiet for a minute while she monitored his pulse. She released his wrist and checked his eyes. Satisfied, she stood. "Edward, help me get him into a chair."

With Mario looking on, Ivayla and I assisted Paolo back into the chair he'd been sitting in when I'd arrived.

"Good," she said and looked at me. "Now you, tell me what happened."

Obviously, I was the odd person in the scene, the one who didn't belong.

"It's my fault," I said. "I pushed him."

"I no blame you! Paolo have hands round your neck!" Mario crossed his arms and gave Paolo a defiant stare.

Ivayla's expression softened as she came to me. She took my face in her hands, her doctor's eyes assessing my state of agitation.

"Edward, what have you done to cause such problems, huh?

You were supposed to wait for me to talk to Babbo and Papà."

Her voice was soft, but as her lips drew closer, I stiffened and pulled away.

"Ivayla, no."

I couldn't let her kiss me.

"Papà and Babbo." She took my hand firmly in hers. "You will not keep us apart. I love Edward."

Something in my body broke, my knees nearly buckled under me. I retracted my hand from hers and collapsed into a chair. "I wish that were all it took. But it won't work. Paolo is right. You and I…" I shook my head. "We can't be together, Ivayla."

She stared at me, dumbfounded. "Why do you say this?"

I locked eyes with her. Mario and Paolo stayed silent in the background.

"Because *he's my father*," I said.

"Babbo? *Your father?*" She blinked several times before folding into the seat next to me. "You are certain?"

"We'll need a paternity test to prove it, but after what Rosa told me, and with this photo," I reached across the table, grabbed the snapshot, and gave it to her, "kissing cousins have nothing on us. You and I can never touch each other again."

She considered the photo several long moments before speaking again.

"Babbo with your mother. Oh Babbo, you are so young and handsome. I have seen so few photos of your early life." She laid the image down and took my hand in hers. "This tells us much but, it is no problem for us."

"No!" Paolo and Mario shouted in unison. "*Non puoi!*"

"Mamma mia." She stood and turned her attention to Paolo. "I love you, Babbo. You are *mio padre* in every caring sense of the word, but you and I do not share blood."

"You are mine?" Mario took a tentative step toward her. "How you know this?"

"Do you think I would not be curious about my own DNA, Papà?" She smiled. "You forget, I am a medical doctor. I have access to these types of tests."

"Ah, *bella ragazza!*" Mario rushed at her, arms stretched wide, with the biggest grin I'd ever seen on his face. "In my heart, I know this, always!"

Father and daughter embraced. It didn't solve all our problems. I was still going home, but I felt a huge sense of relief knowing Ivayla and I hadn't tripped into a disturbing brother-sister relationship.

I caught Paolo's eyes. He regarded me coolly. There would be no embrace for us.

Chapter 17

IVAYLA INSISTED PAOLO GET CHECKED out, despite his grumbles. We all squeezed into Mario's car and went to the medical center. Ivayla spoke with the emergency room doctor, presumably ordering tests, then stepped away to leave Mario and Paolo alone.

She came to sit with me in the waiting area and leaned her shoulder into mine.

"How are you?" she asked.

"I don't know. This is kind of surreal." I shrugged, keeping my hands to myself. "Why didn't you tell me your father's name is Giovanni?"

"Giovanni is Babbo's given name, but for us, Giovanni does not exist." She made a slicing and tossing motion with her hand. "Since Babbo and Papà adopted me, I have only known Babbo as Paolo Lo Duca. You must know, when you told us your Giovanni had an affair with an American woman, I never suspected Babbo. As a little girl, I could see how much Babbo loved Papà. Mamma always said they were *scritti nelle stelle.*"

No wonder Paolo had not told Mario about my mother. Admitting to the affair might've meant losing the trust of someone he loved very much. A heavy price to pay for trying to please a father who wanted him to be something he wasn't, a straight man.

"You never knew about Rosa or my grandfather?" I asked.

"I do not know Babbo's side of the family. He does not permit us to speak of them. Bad blood. Now, I understand why." She looked up at me and squeezed my hand in hers. "I am sorry, Edward. I wish I could have told you. It would've saved you much time."

I thought about the rides we took on her scooter, the miles we'd traveled, the sights we'd seen during our search. "Yes, but it wouldn't have been near as fun."

"This is true. I find it interesting, now that I know, I see Babbo's features in you. The shape of your chin, the slope of your nose." With her free hand, she traced my chin and nose with her fingers. "But the likeness is not so much that it is immediately perceptible."

"Too bad. It could have saved us some trouble." I shook my head.

"What trouble is this?"

The trouble of having to say goodbye.

"If you thought I looked like your father, you wouldn't have wanted to kiss me. Then, we would have stayed friends. Just friends."

"Why do you say this? Do you wish us different now?" She stared at me, those inquisitive brown eyes trying to unfold the layers of my emotions.

"No," I said, squeezing my eyes shut. I meant it. I didn't wish our night hadn't happened, that I knew what her body felt like wrapped around mine, and what her lips tasted like. I blew out, driving down my body's hardening reaction. "I'm really glad you're not my sister."

"Not even a little sad there isn't any possibility, huh?"

"No, not even a little sad," I said and kissed her.

She brushed the hair from my forehead and met my eyes. "I have an opinion I would like to offer you."

"Lay it on me," I said.

"Call your mamma."

I pulled away and shook my head. "Did you talk to Claudia? The two of you seem bent on me calling her."

"Edward, you must tell your mamma you have found your papà," she said.

"I know. I will. Later," I said, still not ready to deal with my mother.

Paolo's tests came back normal, and we all breathed easier.

Ivayla suggested Paolo and I go to the lab to have the inside of our cheeks swabbed for a paternity test. We both consented.

Ivayla stayed back at the medical center to push the test along, but Mario, Paolo and I returned home, the three of us quiet.

The rain had stopped, and I left the two of them to talk. Outside, I walked through the garden, reaching out with my hands to stroke a few wet leaves of plants starting to fade with the cooler weather. At the end of the garden, a fence lined the property, with a similar view of the town and ocean below as the veranda.

I dialed my mother's number. One ring and my mother answered.

"Oh my God!" Mom squealed into the phone. "You had me worrying, Eddie. I thought something happened to you."

After almost two weeks of responding to Edward and Edoardo, Eddie sounded like someone else. Someone I was not.

"I'm fine. But Mom, I found him. I found Giovanni Lo Duca," I said. There was a long beat of silence. "Hello?"

"You… you found him?" Her voice sounded a little wobbly.

"Yeah, and he's a famous local artist," I rushed out. "He lives in a villa, up in the hills."

"How did he take finding out about you?"

"It was a shock to us both," I said, rubbing my neck where Paolo's hands had been.

"He—" she paused. "He accepts you as his?"

"Not exactly. We had a fight when I told him he was my father because the thing is Mom, he's gay."

"Gay?"

"Yes, with a husband. But the facts are there. His sister gave me a picture of you and him," I said. "We just took a DNA test, and when we get the results, he won't be able to deny me. I'll tell you more when I get home."

"So you're not staying longer?" she asked.

"Do you think I should?" I toed the grass and waited for her to tell me what to do.

"I don't know," she said, sounded slightly put out. "Do whatever you want."

"Right." I swatted at a leaf near my face. A little guidance from
her would have been nice. A convincing reason to stay. Or go
home. But my mother was exactly who she'd always been—
unreliable.

I missed Grams.

"I'll be home Saturday," I said and hung up.

I returned inside, to the kitchen where Paolo attempted to make
soft appeals to talk to Mario, only to be met with silence. Mario
refused to look at him and strode off to the bedroom. Paolo disappeared to his art studio. I felt guilty for bringing this situation into
their home, but I couldn't change what had happened.

And I couldn't change that the father I'd been searching for
was Paolo. This couldn't be the end of the road for us. I wouldn't
let it be.

I went downstairs and followed the path through the vegetable
garden to Paolo's painting studio. Through the window in the
door, I could see him standing in front of an unfinished canvas.
He wasn't painting, though, just standing in front of it.

I knocked and poked my head around the door. "May I come
in?"

"Sì, prego." He didn't bother to turn around.

I took up the spot beside him, and like him, stared at the painting before us.

"It miss something," he said.

It was rows and rows of houses.

"A stronger focal point?" I offered hesitantly. "The houses are
well-drawn, but I'm not sure what's at the heart of the piece."

I glanced at him to see how my opinion went over. His mouth
twitched, and grumbling in Italian, he pulled a sheet over the
painting but said nothing. Instead, he moved around the small
counter area, shuffling and banging stuff as he made espresso.

"You speak with mia sorella, Rosa?" he asked over his shoulder.

"Yes, Luigi found your sister and your father, too," I said.

"Amazing they talk to you," he said. "We no speak in long
time."

"Ivayla told me. But your father didn't say much. He took one look at me and told me you were dead." I hedged a quick look at him. He appeared neither surprised nor bothered. "But your sister asked me to come back. She was nice. I think she misses you. Maybe if you reached out to her, she might, you know, be interested in seeing you again."

"Eh, we see." Paolo waved a hand.

I stayed where I was, toeing the tile floor beneath my shoe. "I just spoke with my mother, to tell her about us."

"She is well, yes?" he asked.

"She's doing okay. Living with a guy that treats her good." I nodded. "Finally."

With his back still to me, he put his hands on the counter. His shoulders lifted and lowered with his labored breathing.

"Are you all right?" Concerned, I moved closer, but he waved me off and shuffled past me.

He opened a long drawer at an old wooden desk, rifled through the stack of drawing books inside before pulling one out, and determinedly flipping through its pages. He stopped at a particular sketch, stared long and hard at it before offering it to me.

"I draw this of her," he said.

My hand trembled as I took the artwork from him.

On the thick sketchbook paper, yellowed with age, I saw a likeness hard to deny. The shape of my mother's young face, her eyes, her kind smile. The drawing, highly detailed, complete with shadowing and highlights, told me she must have sat for Paolo.

"It many years ago," Paolo spoke, his eyes not on the drawing but on my face. "My family, they see I love Mario, and they no happy. I go to America for them. I no like it. When you show me that picture, memories come back. I remember your *madre*. At work, we call her Dee. She is a good person. Kind. She make my time away from home tolerable."

At a challenging time in his life, my mother had left an impression on Paolo. A good one.

"You helped make that time tolerable for her, too. She only has good memories of you," I said. It wasn't love, but my life had begun as an act between two people who helped each other through a difficult time. I could live with that.

With nothing else to say, I started for the door.

"Edoardo." He put a hand on my arm, stopping me. "I am sorry. I do not know about you. That year, it was *un brutto momento*—a very dark time. I never look back."

The painful tenor in his voice rattled me.

"My mother wanted to tell you," I said, a hitch in my voice. "She didn't know how to find you."

"We each go back to life that is not easy. Your mother, she have terrible time at home. And I..." He grappled to find the words. "I have love for Mario, and I miss him very much. It built much anger in me, for America, and for my family."

"Is that why you don't want Ivayla to be with an American?"

"Ivayla spend years at the school in America. When she come home, she talk about it. All the time. I worry she will go back. She will leave us."

"I can't imagine why she'd want to leave. It's amazing here. So amazing, I wish I could stay," I said, and meant it. I pulled the door open, then turned to say one last thing. "Paolo, speak to Mario. It was so long ago. He loves you. He'll understand."

"Sì, sì," he said, nodding. "Let us hope you are right."

I left the studio, leaving the door open behind me.

I tried to stay out of the way, avoiding Mario and Paolo and any common areas in the house, in hopes they'd work things out. I heard nothing for a few hours. But near dinnertime, pots, and pans clanged in the kitchen. Just under the clamor, I could hear Mario singing. I found both men in the kitchen. At the stove, Mario worked his culinary magic, the aroma of that night's feast wafting dreamily through the house. Paolo hummed, corkscrew in hand, as he selected a bottle of wine from the refrigerated chiller. The air between them seemed better. Possibly the ship had been righted.

I went in and, without being asked, went to the shelves for dishes to set the table, but all movement in the kitchen halted at the sound of the Vespa and the door shutting below. In the ensuing silence, our gazes bounced off one another. Moments later,

Ivayla came in with the printed lab results, cheeks flushed and lips curled in a heart-stopping grin.

She went to Paolo, kissed both of his cheeks, and handed him the papers.

"Congratulations, Babbo, it's a boy!"

He bowed his head and began reading the papers. A swirl of unease took flight in my chest. But when Paolo raised his eyes to me, they were wet with tears.

"You show me picture. Tell me truth. And still, to believe I have a son, *un ragazzo,* I know nothing about? No, not possible!" He shook the papers in the air, his voice heavy with emotion. "But it is true." He closed the distance between us and spread his arms. "*Mio figlio.*"

He called me *his son* and roughly pulled me to him, giving me a tight, exuberant bear hug. A hug. From my father. His arms tightened around me, and my throat thickened. Something inside snapped, and I tipped into a rushing tide of emotions. I leaned heavily into my father, and suddenly, I was crying so hard, I couldn't breathe.

"*Va bene*, Edoardo. It is good," Paolo murmured soothingly, bracing my weight and patting my back. He pulled a handkerchief from his pocket and handed it to me. "Wipe your face."

I wiped my face as told, smiling at the dad-like way he said it.

Behind us, glasses clinked as Mario poured flutes of sparkling wine.

"I am most happy to have bigger family!" Mario handed two glasses to Paolo, tears gleaming in his eyes, too. "We drink to our many blessings."

Paolo passed a glass to me, one arm slung over my shoulders. He lifted his glass and said, *"Siamo benedetti. Salute!"*

We are blessed. Cheers!

We moved into a huddle to clink glasses. Paolo hugged Mario, the two talking in hushed Italian. From the looks of it, they would be fine.

Ivayla pulled me aside.

"A strange day for you, *amore mio*. What you must have been thinking when you heard the truth." She put her hand on my neck and gently rubbed the skin there.

My sigh dragged my shoulders low. What hadn't I been thinking—and feeling? The anger. The implications. But now, with her standing close, all I could think about was that I hadn't held her in my arms for two days. An eternity. The way her gaze lingered on my mouth, I sensed she felt the same.

"I am a little sad that we are not related," she said, her grin poorly concealed behind pouting lips. "I always wanted a little brother."

Her eyes, alight with mischief, spurred a torrent of heat to tear through my body.

"Not funny, Ivayla," I said, but I laughed anyway. I glanced over at Mario and Paolo to be certain they weren't listening before I continued. "If your fathers weren't home, I'd take you upstairs and thoroughly convince you of the advantages of our current relationship, exactly as it is."

Her eyebrows rose with a hint of interest before she smiled and hit my shoulder playfully.

"Oh, Edward, you are terrible for putting thoughts in my head," she whispered, rising onto her toes to cover my lips with hers.

The warmness of her kiss hit me like a shot of pure adrenaline. I took hold of her shoulders and firmly placed her at arm's length.

"Not that I don't want to kiss you, but as things stand, I've got enough of both of your fathers' attention."

She didn't even bother looking to see if Mario and Paolo were watching us. "*Our* fathers need to get used to seeing us this way."

"Our fathers," I repeated. Even though I was going home, with the test results irrefutably tying us together, I would have a future with all of them.

I held her face in my hands, stroking the soft skin of her jaw with my thumbs. I wanted to kiss her again. She looked at me, lips slightly parted, wanting it too, but I held back.

"I'm sorry. I have a lot on my mind." I kissed her forehead.

I needed to tighten my resolve and draw a firm line between us, so the inevitable separation would be easier.

Chapter 18

I GOT UP EARLY THE NEXT morning and headed to the bathroom. I had one day left in Italy.

The bathroom door was slightly ajar, and I pushed through it, finding Ivayla still in her nightgown, brushing her teeth. With her eyes, she invited me inside. I felt the pull, but I resisted.

"I'll come back," I said, but before I could move away, she rinsed her mouth and tugged me inside.

She locked the door and pressed up against me, her hands riding quick and needy over my chest and moving lower at a rapid pace.

"Ivayla, I'm barely awake."

"I will wake you up." She sank to her knees in front of me, her hands tugging at the elastic of my boxers.

She'd woken my body, and from the look on her face, she was ready to devour it.

"Ivayla." I grabbed her hands and pulled her to her feet. She pressed into me, weakening my resolve tenfold. "God, please stop."

The tension in her hands slackened. She rested her chin on my shoulder and went stock still. The lack of movement unnerved me.

"You are going home. I know this," she said, her voice saturated with emotion. "Is it wrong to want to give you something to remember me by, to come back to?"

"Ivayla," I whispered her name, strangled by a rip of grief. I hugged her as tight as I could. This woman had become food for my soul. "I don't need anything more to remember you by.

You're branded on my heart."

She bunched the front of my T-shirt in her fists, her body stiffening.

"Then why go back? To a job you don't love?" She pulled away from me and crossed her arms. "Edward, do you want life to continue to pass you by? You must break up with your past. If you go back to it, you will grow old regretting it."

I tugged my boxers up and slumped against the vanity.

"I wish it were that easy," I said.

"No, it is not *easy*." She yanked the door open and turned her hardened gaze on me. "You think I go to America to study medicine because it is easy? No. Life and love. They are about the chances we take. But if you don't grab the opportunities offered to you. *Pouff*, they disappear."

She left the room. The door snapped closed behind her.

Showered and dressed, I walked into town, the whole time feeling bruised by Ivayla's parting words. The woman might be incredibly intelligent, but she was wrong about this one. When she went to the States, it had been a short-term residence, and part of her medical career trajectory. But for me to pick up and move to another country, it was more complicated. Where would I stay? What would I do? At home, I had a job and was on the verge of becoming a property owner. Toby had already scoped out a rental property, contacted the realtor, and was waiting for me to return so I could see it.

That was where my future lay.

I made my way to the Delatorre Bakery. The private investigation work was over. Luigi had delivered the goods as promised. I patted my pocket, making sure my wallet was still on me. Time to settle the bill. And make my credit card cry. After buying two pairs of Italian shoes, it was getting used to singing the blues.

The doorbell clanged as I entered the bakery. The scent of sweetbreads hit my nose and made me sigh. There were worse ways to spend your days than baking delicious-smelling goods. And Luigi was a damn fine baker.

As usual, Anna was behind the counter.

"*Ufficio.*" She smiled and motioned to the back. I went around the counter and down the short hallway to the bakery office.

"*Buongiorno amico!*" Luigi's sung out in happy greeting.

"*Buongiorno!*" I echoed and embraced his frame for a short hug.

The office had a different feel. He had painted the walls a fresh dove gray. The old, tired furnishings had been replaced.

"I like the changes you've made." I motioned to the sleek modern desk with a larger upgraded laptop.

"Sì, *un cambiamento!* It's sexy, right?"

"Yes, very." I smiled and nodded. "Just your style. I like it—*mi piace.*"

"Grazie." He patted my shoulder. "Now, what can I do for you? You need more people found?"

"No." I laughed. "I came to pay my bill. *Il conto.*"

He waved a hand. "It is settled, *amico mio.*"

"No, Luigi. A deal is a deal. I want to pay you for your service."

"Allora, it is taken care of," he said.

"What do you mean?"

"Paolo, he paid me," he said and pointed to the wall behind me.

Where the old James Bond movie poster had been, in its place hung an original painting by the Duke.

I stared at the landscape. Paolo paid my bill.

"Oh," I mumbled, blindsided by a mess of unruly feelings.

Paolo was taking care of me. Like a son. My eyes grew hot. I'd bawl if I didn't leave right away.

I stuck out my hand and said, "Thank you for a job well done."

Luigi shook my hand with gusto.

When I met this guy up on Goat Hill, I hadn't expected his efforts would amount to much. How wrong I'd been.

I stopped to see Anna on my way out and buy pastries to bring back to the villa. I bought some sfogliatelle for Ivayla, too—even if she wasn't talking to me.

I walked back to the villa, wondering how I would say goodbye to all of this: to this town, to Luigi, Mario, to my father... And to Ivayla.

The villa was quiet. I put the white bakery bag on the kitchen counter and went outside to Paolo's studio. He was painting. I knocked and poked my head in.

"Prego. Come." He motioned me in.

I stepped up beside him and admired the way his brush skillfully moved, in confident strokes, across the canvas.

"You paint, too. Canvases there." He gestured across the studio to a stack of prepared, gessoed canvases in an assortment of sizes.

"Not right now." I shifted my weight from foot to foot. "I just got back from Luigi's. I intended to pay him for his work. He showed me the painting. You didn't have to do that."

"It is nothing. He wished for artwork. We made a deal." He kept working. "He gets painting. I get son."

The force of his words sucked the air from my lungs.

"Paolo, I..."

He dropped his arms and looked at me. "I sorry I put hands on you yesterday. I get excited."

"I'm sorry I pushed you."

"No. It is good," he said. "Make me proud you stand up, protect yourself."

I scratched the back of my head, smiling despite myself. Maybe I could be a fighter *and* a lover, too.

Paolo seemed to think a moment. He set his paintbrush and palette down, pushed back the sleeve of his tunic, and unbuckled his watch.

"You have this." He took my arm and laid the watch over my wrist. "It belong to me nonno. It good watch. Very old. Well made. I wish you to have it."

"Your grandfather's watch? Paolo, I can't."

"Sì, you great-grandfather. *Il tuo bisnonno.*" His fingers worked efficiently, securing the strap to my wrist. Then he smiled and patted my cheek with his warm, thick hand. "You family! Edoardo, *mio figlio.*"

The tears I'd been holding back flooded my eyes. Embarrassed, I burrowed my face into the crook of my arm.

"Thank you, Paolo," I choked out.

"You call me Babbo, eh?" He pulled my arm away and cupped

my face in his hands. "And you come back."

I nodded. "I'll visit again, as soon as I can."

"No visit. You go home. Get things and come back. You stay, live here." He gave my arm a slight squeeze. "You my son. You welcome here."

He held his chin up, proud and sure as I looked into his face.

Live in Italy? With my father? The offer was surreal and extravagant, the offer of a buffet to a starving man who merely expected a piece of bread.

"That's very generous." I nodded, beaming. "You sure you're not just trying to keep Ivayla from following me?"

"Allora, I would be foolish to think she stay only to keep her papàs happy." He winked at me. "Think it over. Ivayla teach you language. Mario teach you to cook. I teach you how to love you art. You fit good here."

My father wanted me to come back. I swallowed hard and cleared my throat.

"Thank you," I said.

An offer like that presented a variety of opportunities. Things I didn't have time to consider at that moment because, from outside, Mario called to us. He had invited Luigi, Mercedes, Otto and his father, Franz to visit with me, one final time before my departure.

Chapter 19

THE MORNING I LEFT POSITANO, everyone came to see me off. Mercedes, Otto, Paolo, and Mario all fussed over me, each taking a turn to wish me a safe trip and give me a hug. They stepped back as Ivayla came forward.

"Promise you will come back, yes?" She framed my face with her graceful hands and smiled through her tears.

Her sad smile twisted like a knife in my gut.

"Ivayla, come to New York. You said you wanted to see it." The offer came out without thought but bloomed with a life of its own. "I can't leave without knowing when I'll see you again. Come to New York. Come to me."

"Yes, Edward, yes." She threw her arms around my neck.

"As soon as possible." I pulled back to look at her.

"I will."

"When?"

"January?"

"Early January."

"Yes."

"Okay then." I held her at arm's length and traced her every feature with my eyes, committing to memory the shape of her eyes, lips, nose, and cheeks. "I'll see you in the New Year."

I hugged her tight and kissed her one last time, then boarded the bus. Knowing I would see her in a few months was the only way I could let her go.

Through the bus window, the twisty, winding roads of Amalfi zipped by, already making me miss them.

My first weekday back on Long Island, I took the afternoon off to settle up with my grandmother's estate planner, a bittersweet moment that reeked of finality. A farewell to Grams.

I deposited the money into my savings account, and to honor Grams, I went to the nearest hobby and craft store and purchased art supplies. A new sketchpad and several graphite drawing pencils, a pack of pre-gessoed paint boards, an assortment of paintbrushes, thick and thin, round and flat. I stood in front of the paint display staring, the same way I'd done as a kid, in awe of all the colors. I chose a set of basic primary colors, then selected another dozen tubes in whatever color called out to me.

Thank you, Grams.

I left the store, whistling.

Toby called his realtor, and the next day we viewed the Fire Island rental property, inside and out. Ray tagged along as we sized up the house's potential. The home needed updating, interior and exterior, all stuff Toby, Ray and I could do.

"Our next step will be to notify the realtor we want to place a bid, then sign a contract and put down a good-faith deposit," Toby said after the walkthrough. "The house is solid, a good investment. I'd like to move on it right away so we don't lose it, but this is a big decision for you. Take the night. Sleep on it. Let me know what you want to do tomorrow."

After years in the business, Toby had an eye for this kind of investment. It would be his second venture property. I trusted him to know what was right for us.

"I don't need to think about it. I'm in. Call the realtor." I shook hands with Toby and walked over to a house on Bay Walk to finish up a job, replacing a section of cedar siding on the outside of a rental.

"Are you sure you know what you're doing?"

I turned surprised to see my brother had followed me. "What, buying that house?"

"Yeah." He came up next to me, unwrapped a stack of wood shingles, and held one out to me. "Grams wanted you to use her money for art school, not a rental house."

"You used Grams' money to buy your house. I'm using mine for a rental." I took a shingle from him and nailed it in place. "Kind of the same thing. Toby knows what he's doing, Ray. All I need to do is follow his lead."

"No, Eddie. It's *not* the same." He yanked the hammer out of my hand, forcing me to stop and listen. "Because you're not Toby. Toby's father was a craftsman. It's in his blood. He loves this work. You? You don't love this. It's just a job to you. You're good at that art stuff. Always have been. I always wondered if you stopped doing it because of Tom."

"T-tom?" I stuttered.

"Years ago he called the house and left a message. Said you made an unannounced trip to Connecticut to see him." He leaned against the side of the house and kicked a rock near the tip of his work boot. "Mom never heard the message. I deleted it. He was such an asshole to treat you that way. I wish you'd told me what you were planning. I would've talked you out of it. You were just a kid. You didn't deserve that."

"You didn't deserve a father like that either, but it's whatever," I said with a shrug. "I've moved on."

"Good, good." He turned his head to look at me. "I'm glad you found your real father. And, all I'm saying is, you should consider your alternatives. You're the son of a famous artist. Maybe that art stuff is in your blood."

My brother's perception of my life left me without words.

"I have to head over to a job on Ocean Walk." He pushed off the house.

"I deposited the check today," I said, wanting to share this bit of information with my brother. "I used some of the money to buy art supplies. I'm going to draw again."

"That's a step in the right direction." He smiled and began to move away. "Hey, Mom keeps bugging me about you. Don't be such a loser. Go see her already."

My brother's words passed over his shoulder, and I blinked several times before his parting request registered.

"Hey!" I shouted after him. "Why's it so important I go see Mom?"

"Maybe 'cause good or bad, she's still the only mother we've got?" He shrugged and kept walking.

Ray's answer made me chuckle, but he was right. She was the only mother we had. I'd been putting off seeing her not wanting to deal with her drama, but I couldn't keep avoiding her without feeling like a horrible son.

As I worked, I thought about the other things Ray had said. My older brother had never been easy on me. We were opposites in every way. And, I always assumed he didn't think much about me or about my dreams. Apparently, he had some ideas of what I should and shouldn't be doing. Buying the property still seemed like a solid investment, but he was right. I should use the money Grams had left me for something else. Something I wanted, as Grams had intended.

After work, I drove to my mother's house. Her car was the only one in the driveway. When I knocked, she opened the door, smiling when she saw me. Package tucked under my arm, I entered the den, the very location my mother divulged the truth about my father.

"When will Mike be home?" I asked, shutting the door on the chilly air outside.

"Don't worry. He's working overtime."

I nodded, not admitting my relief aloud. A phantom pain vibrated down my nose at the thought of my last run-in with my mother's boyfriend.

I jingled my keyring, unsure where or how to begin with her. She pulled the belt tighter on her worn, oversized black sweater, unable to maintain eye contact with me.

I worried my bottom lip with my teeth until I realized how stupid our silence was. She was still my mother. She'd done what she'd done. I could hold a grudge and step out of her life. Or I could step up and forgive her.

I stood the package up next to the coffee table and pulled out my phone.

"Would you like to see some photos of Italy?" I asked.

Mom nodded, and I sat down on the couch, assuming my place next to Whiskey. The dog lifted her head, her tail thumping on the cushion as I reached out to stroke her smooth fur.

Mom sat down beside us. I focused on my phone, scanning the stream of images, and stopping on the last one. I enlarged the photo with my fingers, pulled in a breath, and held the phone out.

"That's him," I said.

Mom slipped on a pair of glasses. The black-framed readers made her eyes huge and magnified the fine wrinkles around the outer edges of her eyes. I'd never seen the glasses before. Or the wrinkles.

With the briefest hesitation, she took the phone from me.

"Giovanni," she whispered, staring at the image of Paolo and me, father and son, side by side, his arm resting over my shoulders. Her head tipped to one side as her shoulders rounded down. "He aged well."

Her response held an air of sorrow. But at what? At the lost opportunity to be with my father, or was it sorrow that my father's life had blossomed in comparison to her own?

"I knew you resembled him, but I never realized just how much." She lowered the phone to her lap and lifted a hand to my cheek. "You're handsome just like your father."

"Do you wish it turned out differently for you and him?" I asked.

"Oh no. Those were hard times. We were just trying to get through it," she said. "I really only remember bits and pieces of our time together."

I let my mother talk, let her retrace the steps of how she met Paolo that year, how she empathized and connected with the foreigner who seemed as lonely as she'd been. I hadn't let her do that the night she'd told me about him. I'd been too angry about her deception, but now, hearing her side of it made me less annoyed with her.

"So, tell me about your father. What's he like?" She smiled. "Tell me everything."

"He's amazing." Pride filled my chest. I met her gaze, smiling, and took the phone from her. "Here, let me show you his husband, Mario."

The photo I showed her next was of Mario, taken at the villa.

He had an enormous grin on his face, hands in the air, gesturing excitedly as usual. I leaned over while she held my cell and finger scrolled through the images until Ivayla's face filled the screen.

"That's their daughter…"

"You have a sister?" Mom put a finger to her mouth. She hadn't thought of that possibility.

"Only in name. Ivayla is Mario's biological daughter."

"Oh." She nodded and continued to flick through the photos, stopping at one of Ivayla and me at Capri.

I remembered the day we'd taken the photo, remembered the thrill of having her shoulder pressed against mine, the warmness of her skin under the Italian sun. Peeking up, I caught eyes with my mother.

"She's very beautiful," she said, eyes narrowed with that observant, assessing look of hers.

"She is." I nodded, looking away.

"Italy has changed you," she said. "You seem different."

"Different how?" I asked.

"Different, good." She smiled. "Effervescent."

Her description made me grin.

"Italy was—" There weren't words to describe what Italy meant to me, what it had done to me. "This trip changed my life. Every single moment of every day, I think about Italy."

"It's the girl, Mario's daughter. You like her, don't you?"

"Yeah, Ivayla's great," I mumbled.

"No, you *like her* like her," she pressed.

"No, Mom." I looked down at my shoes and growled. "I love her."

My mother's hands turned my face to look at her.

"Oh honey bear," she whispered, reaching over Whiskey to hug me.

I spilled the entire story, telling my mother how I'd met Ivayla and came to stay at the villa, not knowing Paolo was Giovanni. I told her about Luigi and his goats, about taking hairpin twists on Ivayla's moped where I was sure I'd die. She laughed and laughed. And it felt good to hear her laughter; especially knowing I'd prompted it.

"She's coming to New York in January."

"What will happen after that? Will you carry on a long-distance relationship, flying back and forth to see each other?" she asked.

"We haven't thought that far." I melted back into the couch with a sigh. "I'm in the middle of stuff here." I told her about my initial plans to use Grams' money to buy the rental property with Toby, and Ray's opposition to it. "But all I think about is Ivayla and my art. What am I supposed to do?" I threw out a hand. "And before you say, you don't know, please, all I'm asking for is your opinion."

"I don't like to give advice. I've made too many mistakes in life. All I'll say is—" She sat up and met my eyes. "I think Ray is right about this. You're not Toby. Do your thing."

"What's my thing?" I asked.

"Oh, no." Mom shook her head. "That's for you to say."

"You're right." I nodded, convinced of my thing. "I'm an artist."

"That's why Grandma gave you the money, to go to art school. And you should go." Mom squeezed my shoulder and smiled. "Oh, I have something for you from Mike." She hopped up, rushed into the kitchen, and came back with a six-pack of bottled beer. Taped to the front of the cardboard carry case was a ragged-edged white piece of paper, a repurposed envelope, with "SORRY" penned in block print. "Mike felt bad about hitting you."

"He was protecting you. I respect that." I took the six-pack from her and set it on the coffee table. "It's good that you have someone who looks out for you. It's what a son wants for his mom."

"Mothers should want that for their sons, too." Her fingers danced on her thighs. "Which means, I also need to apologize. I should've told you about Giovanni when you were old enough to understand. I'm sorry, Eddie. Now that you met him, I can't help thinking of how different your childhood could've been. I was stupid and irresponsible. I ruined your life."

"Mom, stop. It's okay." I pulled her into a hug.

My mother gripped me hard, her body shaking.

Ivayla and Claudia and my time in Italy helped me level out

the anger I'd felt towards my mother. Mom had decided to keep her secret based on what she had and what she knew. It didn't absolve her, but it was forgivable. And, I could do that.

"It isn't, really, but thank you." She sniffled as I let go, an unsteady smile straining her face. "I want you to know, if you need money, you can have the money Grandma gave me."

"Your inheritance?" I shook my head. "No, that's yours to do what you want."

"What I want is to take care of my son," she said, reaching across to grab my hand. "If you need it, it's yours."

"Thanks, Mom." I squeezed her hand once and reached for the package I'd brought. "I have something for you."

She unwrapped Paolo's drawing of her and gasped, tears flooding her eyes.

"I remember sitting for this." Lips pressed together, she held the artwork to her chest. "You will keep in touch with him?"

"Yes," I said. "Maybe next time I go to Italy, you can come with me?"

"You know how I feel about flying," she said.

I did. It terrified her.

"Who knows? Maybe he'll come here," I said, though I suspected my efforts would be wasted trying to persuade Paolo to make the trip.

I left my mother's, got in my truck and started toward home, my body tired but mind buzzing. The conversations with my mother and brother had given me much to think about.

If I bought the rental house with Toby, it would just about empty my bank account and hold me in place for a long time. Property ownership smelled like a promise, but now that my brother reframed it, it sounded like a lie: me, lying to myself.

Again.

I realized I was good at lying. I'd done it all my life, starting when I'd allowed Tom Rudack to hold my dreams hostage. And now, I could see Ray and my mother were right. As much as I respected and admired Toby, I wasn't anything like him. And trying to mimic his life would leave me unfulfilled.

I would never again let someone's opinion keep me from what

I loved.

Italy, Ivalya, and finding my father had given me a new outlook on life. I had love, money, and opportunity, but they seemed like jigsaw pieces from different puzzles.

I passed the turn toward Toby and Claudia's house and drove south to the bay. The parking lot at the beach had only a few cars. I parked, got out of my truck and walked to the beach. An easterly wind had picked up, nudging the late October temps down. The waves moved in foamy curls, one after the other, rushing forward with a whoosh, and ending with a vibrational slap as they pounded the beach. I took a mental picture of how I would recreate it on canvas, of the colors and strokes I would use to paint it.

I opened my cell to take a photo and found a voicemail from Ivayla. I tapped the play button, my excitement to hear her voice gobbling up the sharp pang of missing her.

Hello, my love. I have cheerful news and a bit of sad news, too. The happy news — I have taken a new placement at Maria Teresa Hospital in Florence, a very agreeable position. Papà and Babbo are proud but sad that I will soon live in another city. The sad news — With this new position, it is not possible to take a holiday. I will have to delay my trip to New York until the summer months.

The rest of the message outlined her plans to move into an apartment in a neighborhood near the medical center. She sounded excited and asked me to call her later.

The message ended, and the phone slipped from my grasp, landing with a soft thud at my feet. I pulled down the hood of my Carhartt thermal sweatshirt and let the brisk air numb my ears.

Ivayla's new job felt like a seismic shift, widening the space between the two of us. It would be over six months before I would see her again. With love, being apart for a few months was painful. But half a year? Death. Any idea that we could pick up where we left off was an improbable fantasy. We'd nearly be strangers again. Even worse, with this new job, she'd meet new people, escalating her chances of meeting someone else.

I had to figure out what I was doing, too. I went home to my apartment, grabbed a notepad, and fired up my laptop. I vowed not to leave the space until I had rearranged the pieces of the jigsaw into a realistic picture of the future, one that more resembled who I was and what I wanted. What I *really* wanted.

"Ciao, ciao, Babbo!" I said with a flourish. Ending my call with Paolo, I leaned back on my apartment couch. Upstairs, I heard Lucas' newborn mew. Footsteps answered, creaking across the floor over my head, and his crying stopped. After a few hours on the computer and a lengthy phone call to Italy, I had a plan. The ball was in motion.

Now, I had to have a tough conversation with my friends.

Shoulders straight, I bounded up the stairs, passed the dining room table set with dishes for all of us, and found the family in the kitchen. Claudia tossed a salad at the kitchen island, and Toby cut slices of roasted chicken, laying them out on a serving dish. Julianne and Beatrix were coloring at the kitchen table. Lucas was watching them from his baby seat, making little tiny bubbles around his miniature lips.

"Hey, buddy." I wiggled one of his small feet.

"Uncle Weddie, look!" Beatrix held up her drawing.

"Bea, Mommy told us to call him Uncle Edward," Julianne corrected her little sister.

I leaned over to pull her pigtails. "Your drawing is amazing, Bea. And you girls can call me whatever you want."

"No, we like it," the older girl said.

"Yup, we likes it." Beatrix nodded her head in exaggeration.

"It suits you," Claudia said without looking at me. "Girls, go wash your hands. We're going to eat soon."

Beatrix and Julianne obediently slid off their chairs passing me on their way out of the kitchen. I parked myself on a stool across from Claudia, the one I always sat in when we had our talks.

"I spoke to the realtor," Toby said. "We have an appointment to sign papers tomorrow morning."

"About that," I said, wiping my damp hands on my pants. "I heard from Ivayla today. She's starting a new job in Florence. She's not coming in January."

Toby turned, lowering the knife. Claudia's hand froze mid slice.

"I'm sorry. What will you do?" she asked.

"It's a serious snafu, and I've been, um, recalculating." I glanced at Toby, my neck growing hot.

"You're leaving us, aren't you?" Claudia's eyes stayed on me, waiting for an answer. Lucas started to cry, and I jumped to my feet.

"I got him." I gently picked up the baby and cradled him in my arms. I kept my eyes on the soft little face rather than meet the intensity of Claudia or Toby's stare. "I spent the last few hours figuring out the best way to use the inheritance from my grandmother. The short answer is yes, I'm leaving. Getting to know Paolo, even before I knew he was my father, made me realize how much I love painting and drawing, being artistic. I crave it and miss it when I'm not doing it. I want to give my art an actual shot, try to make something of it." I stayed on my feet, swaying back and forth as Lucas's eyes fluttered closed before I looked up at them. "I decided to enroll in art school."

"Ha!" Claudia turned to smile at Toby. "I told you."

"Damn, bro, you could've given me a heads up." Toby shook his head. "Now I owe her a foot massage."

I laughed as I looked at Claudia. "How could you know? I never even said anything."

"I could tell." Claudia shrugged. "And it's about time."

"If you're going to try something different, you're in a perfect place to do it." Toby put the knife in the sink and washed his hands. "You don't have any pressing responsibilities."

"But you guys are my friends. You've given me a place to stay. Toby, you gave me a job, set up this house deal for us. The last thing I want to do is to be a dick and bail on you."

"I've had my eye out for a second property for a few years." He reached past Claudia and stole a cucumber from the top of her salad mix. "I was planning to buy that house with or without you. I'm not going to say it wouldn't be easier to split the cost, but I can handle it without your money. No need to fall on your sword, guy."

"There you go," Claudia said. "If that's all you're worried about, rest easy. You did as your grandmother asked. You went to Italy and earned your inheritance." Claudia put a hand on my arm. "We'll miss you, but it's time to reap the rewards. Go pursue your art."

"You guys… just wow." I said. "You're making this too easy for me."

"If you prefer, we can go down to the boxing gym and go a few rounds." Toby threw a few jabs in the air. "Cooper, the guy next door, is a boxing coach. He can set us up."

"No, no. That's alright." I grinned down at Lucas. "My God-child is going to take after me, be a lover, not a fighter."

"I'd rather you teach him how to speak Italian." Claudia took the sleeping baby from me. "With your father a natural-born citizen of Italy, it should be simple for you to get dual citizenship."

"Part of the charm of Italy is that the simple things aren't ever simple," I said. "But to see my father and Ivayla, it's worth the trouble."

"Do you remember the year before Toby and I got married?" Claudia moved to the counter next to her husband. "I broke up with him and was planning to move to Boston. But I loved him and knew we could have a chance if I focused and gave us my all. It was scary, completely out of my comfort zone and realm of experience." Cradling Lucas, she tipped her head and rested it on Toby's shoulder. "But the effort was worth it. I have the love of my life. Love is one of those things that require a leap of faith."

Toby wrapped his arms around his wife and leaned down to kiss the top of Lucas' tiny head, the three of them the idyllic family picture. "What I can say for sure is the right woman is worth chasing after."

I applied for a nine-month art program, sold my truck, bought a new suitcase and packed it. Mom, along with Ray and his fiancée, Amy, took me to the airport this time. The send-off fanfare surprised me.

"Take care little brother." Ray gave me an awkward hug and ruffled my hair like a little kid.

"I couldn't bring all of my clothes with me." I handed him a small duffle bag. "I picked some out to leave you. They'll make you feel like a new man."

"Such a girl." He smiled but took the bag.

Amy moved toward me.

"Ray will listen to you," I told her. "Make him wear the clothes."

"I will." She hugged me tightly. "If we plan the wedding for after you finish classes, you'll come back for it, right?"

"Just try to keep me away," I said and kissed her cheek.

The two of them drifted back, leaving space for my mother to step forward and say her farewell.

"Eddie," she said as her cool hand latched onto mine. "I wasn't the best mom, but you know I love you, right?"

"I know, mom." I squeezed her hand knowing I'd always be her Eddie. "You had a lot on your plate, but you were there, raising two boys on your own, doing your best."

"I did. I tried." She dug into her jacket pocket and pulled out a fast food restaurant napkin to blot her tears along with the smeared makeup from under her eyes. "You have a father, a real father, who wants to be in your life. Promise you won't forget about me?"

"Mom." I put down my suitcase and held my arms open. She emitted a muffled whimper as I hugged her. "You're my *mom. My only* mom. I love you. No distance can take that away. Not my father either."

When I went to pull back, her fingers curled into the fabric of my jacket, stilling me. "You're sure this is what you really want?"

"It is." I rubbed her back. "Definitely."

She released me, crumbled the napkin in her fist, and smiled. "Then I'm happy for you."

"Thanks, Mom." I slipped my fingers through my suitcase handle. "I know how you feel about flying, but we'll get you on a plane one way or another, to visit me while I'm at school."

"I'll ask the doctor for strong drugs." She put a hand on my cheek. "Take care of yourself, my baby."

Chapter 20

MY CELL CHIMED WITH A reminder tone I'd set—noon—lunchtime. I had plans. I flipped the cover of my sketchpad closed, corralled my graphic pencils into a bunch, and shoved the supplies into my backpack.

A few steps away, I unchained my bike from a rack and swung my backpack over my shoulders. I walked the bike past the busiest walk areas, where throngs of people were out enjoying the afternoon sunshine. Winter had passed. The sun was shining and the days warming. I lifted my face to the sun for a few seconds before I swung my leg over the bike and pumped the pedals.

The bike was old school, one I got when I arrived, for next to nothing. For the last few months, I'd been living the life of a lowly artist. No car, simple foods, a wardrobe primarily of jeans and T-shirts. I filled my days with drawing and painting classes, workshops, and seminars on art topics, mostly indoors until now.

And I loved every second.

I cruised the outside of town, head low, picking up speed, the air ruffling my hair and ballooning the shirt on my back. Cars whizzed by me as if I weren't there. It was crazy and wonderful, and I laughed at the boldness of the drivers.

I pulled up to the street-side café, popped off my bike and walked it close to the entrance, inhaling gulps of air. I twisted my arm to check the time on my great-grandfather's watch. A couple of minutes early. The watch kept perfect time, and each morning I strapped it to my wrist. I stood a little taller and smiled at myself in the mirror. I had a father who knew me and cared.

My cell phone rang with an incoming video call. I propped the bike against the café's exterior wall and answered.

Claudia appeared on the screen, her face beaming.

"We booked our flights!" she said.

"That's amazing. I can't wait to see you and Toby and show you around."

"Not as much as we can't wait to spend a week with just grownups," she said.

I chuckled. "I'm flattered that you think of me as a grownup."

"Well, maybe not *you* so much as your girlfriend," she said.

Behind me, someone called out.

"Edward!"

My heart swelled at the sound of her voice.

I turned, a smile stretching across my face as she rushed toward me. We'd been living together for months, and the sight of her still made me go weak in the knees.

"Here she is now," I told Claudia and reached out to pull Ivayla to my side.

"*Ciao, amore mio!*" Ivayla kissed my cheek and waved to Claudia "Ciao, Claudia! Edward and I are excited about your visit! Papà and Babbo insist you must stay at the villa."

"We look forward to meeting them," Claudia said.

It was the last thing I heard her say because Ivayla stole the phone from me and continued the conversation as she walked toward the restaurant.

I stood still and watched my Italian girlfriend talking about our fathers with my hometown friend.

Four months ago, scared to death, I got on a plane and flew back to Italy. I shouldn't have been scared because unlike the first time, Ivayla was there to meet me.

I moved into her small one-bedroom Florence apartment near the Ponte Vecchio. It was perfect for us. An easy commute to the medical center for her, and for me, a quick bike ride to *Piazza della Signoria* and the Uffizi Gallery, where I spent a lot of time studying the works of the masters: Botticelli, Caravaggio, da Vinci, Raphael.

Grams' little statue of Mary came too. I kept her near the door of our apartment. Whenever I went to leave, the sight of her gave me the courage to face whatever challenges the day had in store for me.

Every couple of weeks, Ivayla and I traveled to Positano to spend the weekend with our fathers. During my first few months in Italy, Paolo helped me build my portfolio. He'd been instrumental in getting me started at the *Accademia Del Giglio*. Word got around that I was the son of *Il Duco*. A local newspaper interviewed me. My instructors paid attention to what I was working on. They pushed me extra hard.

Paolo and I spent those Saturday mornings up at his hidden painting spot. Sometimes we painted. Sometimes we just sat and talked. At lunchtime, we would go down the hill to Mercedes' restaurant, where Mario and Ivayla would be at Paolo's regular table, waiting for us to join them.

I enlisted Paolo's help to work on my dual citizenship application. It was a process that would not be rushed as Italians didn't like to be hurried, but it was my birthright, and I would get it eventually and stay indefinitely.

Claudia once told me the right love empowers you to get the hard stuff done. She was right. I'd moved to Italy, not only for the art. I could have studied anywhere. I came to Italy for Ivayla. As impossible as it seemed, every time I saw her, I fell more and more in love with her. The woman had stolen my heart. I made her promise never to give it back.

I'd gone to Italy to find my father. I'd found more than I could have imagined. I'd found family. I'd found love—the true and endurable kind. I'd also found a different me. The *me* I could take pride in.

The *me* I wanted to continue exploring.

Acknowledgments

As I often say, writing is a solitary job. But it takes a village to keep an author afloat during those weeks, months, and sometimes years, that writing and publishing a novel requires. I would be mentally unstable and malnourished if it weren't for my wonderful husband, Brian, who is both a champion of my heart and of the kitchen. Our son, Scott, has taken to meal preparation much like his father. I am proud of this, and also grateful that our children mirror my husband's nature of thoughtfulness and generosity.

To my author friends Kimberly Wenzler and Deborah Garland, thank you! These ladies were there for me whenever I called out for help—sometimes daily. Their insight, editorial feedback, and wise and kind words kept me afloat throughout this process.

Many thanks to great friends, Shari Feuer, Suzanne Kelly, Carrie Logan, and Ann Marie Maud for their support, enthusiasm, and feedback on Finding Edward.

Thank you to Charlotte Rains Dixon who, in the book's early beginnings, inspired me with energetic, upbeat support to get the words on the page.

Author and writing coach Heather Demetrios provided a developmental edit showing me where and how I could provide readers with a more enjoyable story. Editor Veronica Jorden, with her much appreciated enthusiasm and gentle hand, once again helped me cross the finish line.

Thaianna Pellegrini provided guidance with the dialogue of my native Italian characters. I am beyond delighted to have met Thaianna, and now, call her friend.

I also want to thank the members of the Long Island Romance Writers critique group, a lively and astute group of novelists. Special thanks to author Lauren Rico for taking on the challenge of re-writing my book blurb.

The Cast of Characters

Finding Edward features Edward's two closest friends, happily married Toby and Claudia Faye. But Toby and Claudia's futures weren't so clear in the beginning. Before these two saw even a glimmer of a happily-ever-after, they began as a small town bad boy pining for a steadfast good girl, in an opposites-attract love saga that spans two novels.

Saving Toby, Save Me Book 1

Despite Claudia's attempt to stay away from the troubled Toby Faye, his blue-gray eyes expose a need she cannot ignore.

Loving someone through a hard fall from grace takes a lot of grit.

Keeping Claudia, Save Me Book 2

Toby has the girl he's long dreamed of finally within his reach, but one last secret hides in the dark corner of his past. The one that could undermine it all

Falling in love is easy. Staying in love is hard.

Reviews, reviews, reviews!

Lions, tigers, and bears — Oh my! There's no need to fear leaving a review. I promise, no one will show up on your doorstep to browbeat you for words, but if you enjoyed this book, please pop on over to your favorite book website and let me know. Even better, recommend it to a friend. Recommendations and reviews are greatly appreciated. Finding Edward is on Amazon.

About the Author

Suzanne McKenna Link works for a family of newspapers that cover events in and around the area she lives, on the South Shore of Long Island, New York.

An avid interest in psychology and human nature has the native Long Islander digging deep into the reasons for her characters' behaviors. As a result, her characters come to life on the pages. To find out more and to sign up for author updates, visit suzannemckennalink.com

Connect with me!
Website
www.suzannemckennalink.com
Goodreads
www.goodreads.com-Suzanne McKenna Link
FaceBook
www.facebook.com/SuzanneMckennaLink
Twitter
www.twitter.com/SuzMcKLink
Literary Love Blog
www.suzannemckennalink.blogspot.com
Email Suzanne@suzannemckennalink.com

Made in the USA
Middletown, DE
26 May 2020

95919291R00128